The Near Miss

Lily Joseph

The Near Miss

bookouture

Published by Bookouture in 2024

An imprint of Storyfire Ltd.
Carmelite House
50 Victoria Embankment
London EC4Y 0DZ

www.bookouture.com

ISBN: 978-1-83525-356-4
eBook ISBN: 978-1-83525-355-7

For CK, who was meant to be

ONE

WREN

Before Wren could take a second step from the doorway of the bookshop, she felt a rush of air from above, followed by an ear-splitting, thunderous crash. A plate-glass window fell from a great height and shattered onto the path no more than five paces in front of her. There was a spattering, like rain, over her clothes, and she looked down to see cubes of safety glass sprinkled over her jacket, balanced on the creases, along the top of her breast pocket and in the slight upturn of her shirt hem. Some had gathered on the top of her black loafers. She thought, as she stared at them, that they looked like diamante-encrusted shoes that she would never normally buy.

It took a second for a cold feeling to wash over her. The crumpled remains of the window frame lay on the path in front of her, pieces of wood criss-crossed like kindling, a sea of little blue-green glass cubes sprayed out from its edges. *Just seconds.* If she'd left Cravenwick Pages just two seconds earlier, the window would have come directly down on her head – if she hadn't paused in the doorway to check that text from Alex asking her to buy milk.

The thought made her freeze on the spot, dimly aware of a

handful of early-morning passers-by looking over with concern. Then slowly, robotically, and in more than a little shock, she brushed the glass off her jacket, kicked the fragments from her shoes and numbly walked forward around the wreckage in her path.

A man's voice came from above. 'Jesus, are you alright? I'm sorry about that.'

Wren didn't look back; she just continued walking, in a daze, until she arrived at work.

Wren sat at her desk, chewing her pen and staring into space. The office at the *Northumberland Echo* was beginning to wake – the other 'at the desk by ten' workers wandering in holding takeaway coffees, the low electronic hum of computers being switched on, murmurs of good morning. She'd arrived first to the empty office, just after half past nine, and had taken some time to settle from the shock of what had just happened.

Even after she'd picked the last cube of glass from her clothes, she still felt covered in something. Maybe it was a fog of adrenaline slowly lifting, or maybe it was the feeling that she wasn't as invincible as she thought, but she hadn't fully shaken it off. Derek and Gary eyed her shrewdly from the opposite desk then glanced at each other. The office's most experienced reporters always smelled a story in the air.

'You alright, Wren?' asked Derek, a sturdy man in his fifties who could do with going up a shirt size and had yellow fingers from years of chain-smoking.

Wren blinked, roused from plumbing the depths of her dark thoughts. 'Just having an existential crisis about fate versus chance. How about you?'

'Er, I'm alright thanks. What's that now?'

'I'm thinking... are we meant to be where we are at all

times? Or is it just random? Like we just stumble around and sometimes good things happen and sometimes bad?'

'Christ alive, Wren,' said Gary, rubbing his shaved head, his solution to early signs of baldness. 'That's a bit deep for a Monday morning. Or is this something to do with a story?'

'Maybe,' she said, deciding not to mention exactly what had happened. If she wasn't careful, Gary would be down there with his Dictaphone and a photographer, trying to expose a local dodgy workman. 'Actually, yeah, ignore me. Just thinking out loud.'

They both gave her a funny look and seemed to be about to dig a bit deeper, so she was relieved when their editor, Zara, strolled through the door, nodding and smiling at everyone as she went to her office. That stopped the conversation abruptly as the others tried to look busy with their actual job, rather than musing on the mysteries of the universe. Wren tried to do the same, but it still nagged at her like a scratchy label on a shirt.

Her desk was a mess, like always, but this morning's brush with chaos made her feel like she needed to put it in order. Haphazardly, since she lacked experience at tidying, she gathered up the half-empty takeaway coffee cups and sluiced away the greenish-brown contents into the kitchen sink. Then, after stacking some loose papers, flicking biscuit crumbs to the floor and covering a tenacious sticky mark with a pad of Post-its, she settled to work. But the words wouldn't come.

She texted Libby, who'd been phoning her frantically since she'd walked away from the bookshop, zombie-like and unresponsive to the buzzing in her pocket. As she'd slowly let the shock wear off, it had been seamlessly replaced by guilt at not checking in with her friend, since it was her bookshop after all.

How is the scene of my near miss looking?

There you are!! Wren, you can't do this to a pregnant woman. I

didn't know if you were unscathed or looking like the prom scene
from Carrie.

I'm fine. Not a scratch. Are you okay though? Is it chaos?

All is well. I made the glazier's tea with a dusty teabag I found
down the back of the microwave so we're even. You sure you're
really okay?

I'm fine.

Apart from the crushing sense of impending doom, Wren
thought.

Come for a cuppa after work. I will make your tea with a clean
teabag because you're my best friend.

Thank you.

Wren looked up to find Zara crooking a finger at her from
her office door. If it weren't for Zara being as unintimidating as
a children's TV presenter carrying a box of Labrador puppies,
she might have worried she was in trouble.

The short walk to the office door seemed to pull Wren out
of her daze – this was work, and she needed to snap out of it.

'Have a seat, darl'. How are you doing?' Zara asked, sitting
down in the moth-eaten chair behind her desk. Like the rest of
the *Echo* premises, Zara's office was tired and scruffy, in stark
contrast to the woman herself. She was dark-skinned, with
beautifully manicured nails, bouncy black curls and a perpetual
smile. She was only a few years older than Wren, at about
thirty-five, but had risen through the ranks of local journalism
like the Empire State lift – smoothly, at alarmingly breakneck
speed. Wren often felt in awe of her and thought it might only

be a matter of time before she went on to bigger and better things – especially now that the tides were turning on the need for the local paper.

'Great, thanks. You?'

She gave a wry laugh. 'Don't ask.' She looked pointedly at Wren, as if she should know exactly what she meant, and she did.

The paper had been sitting under a cloud of rumours for some time. Local papers were attracting less and less interest, with more people getting their news and information online, and the *Echo*'s own decrepit website just couldn't compete. With their funding fading away like old newsprint, there was no way they could afford the investment the site needed, and besides, their readers were of a demographic that liked something they could hold in their hand. There had been talks of merging with another local paper, meaning job cuts, or worse. Wren knew to take Zara's reply of 'don't ask' at face value too. Zara hadn't denied the rumours, but Wren knew she wasn't in any position to go into detail either.

'Have you finished that piece on the new restaurant in Hangforth? The one with the' – she clicked her fingers, trying to recall, then narrowed her eyes to guess – 'butter boards?'

Wren laughed. 'No, that was the place I went to last week in Corbridge. The one in Hangforth was the charcoal ice cream. They should both be in your inbox.'

'Right, I'll have a look this afternoon. The gentrification of Northumberland towns and villages continues to give us material. Anyway, I called you in because I've got you a new contact for your Northumberland Diamonds series.'

'Really? Thanks, Zara. I wasn't sure where to go with it next.'

Wren had been working on a story a few months ago about the North East's first full-time female firefighter. She was only in her early sixties but had no family, and early-onset

Alzheimer's, so was being looked after by home carers. She had nobody to pass her stories on to. As Wren had listened to her talk about her memories, recalling the distant past with much more clarity than she could recount what she'd had for breakfast that day, she'd been struck by how interesting the woman's life had been, and what an important person she'd been for her profession. And when her carer had told Wren that she may soon lose her longer-term memories, Wren had realised that unless they were written down and recorded for posterity, they would disappear forever. That had started her wondering how many other fascinating women were out there waiting for their stories to be heard. She knew there must be plenty, but since a lot of women just stoically went about their business without shouting it from the rooftops, she felt like she was mining for rare diamonds, hence the title of her series.

'Where did you find this one?'

Zara handed her a slip of paper, on which she'd scrawled some details in purple pen. 'Let's just say I'm well connected when it comes to women.'

'You'd better not let Petra hear you say that,' Wren said, referring to Zara's long-suffering wife, who rarely got to see her work-addicted other half.

Zara grinned. 'Her name's Edie Macmillan, founder of the Community Kitchen in Newcastle. You've probably heard of it?'

'Heard of it? I volunteered there when I was a student.'

'Even better – you'll have a good basis for an opener then. She's getting on a bit now, still lives on her own just outside of town, so you could give her a call and go and see her.'

'Right. Thanks, that's brilliant. I'll give her a call soon.'

'Smashing. Right, bugger off. I've got some crossing out to do on that copy you've sent me.'

Wren left the office and sat down at her desk, remembering the year she and a couple of uni friends had volunteered to serve turkey to the homeless at the Community Kitchen on Christmas Day. It had been one of the best Christmases she'd ever had, and she'd promised herself that she'd do it every other year. But she hadn't – life, exams and everything else had got in the way – and now felt a twinge of remorse. It would be interesting to meet the woman who'd made it all happen, she thought, resolving to call her tomorrow and arrange to go and see her.

For the rest of the day, she was absorbed enough in her work to shelve any thoughts of her earlier brush with fate. Waxing lyrical about the Cravenwick summer fete and the rise in litterbug tourists on Lindisfarne was so far removed from life-and-death situations that she was able to bury the memory like a forgotten sheet of paper on her cluttered desk. It was only when she found a single cube of glass in the upturned sleeve of her jacket as she shrugged it on to go home that she felt that icy feeling creep over her once more.

TWO

NICK

Nick knocked off at five and headed over to the Weary Traveller, the least gentrified pub in Cravenwick, which was only a few hundred yards up the street from the bookshop. The day had gone by in a fragmented way, as if he was on a long train journey, enjoying the view, yet every so often the memory of that morning would come flooding back, like the train was plunging through an unexpected dark tunnel. Despite all his efforts, flashbacks of how he'd almost killed a woman kept surprising him throughout the day.

He'd stepped back from the window with his hands in his hair and the blood draining from his face – he hadn't needed a mirror to know he was as white as a sheet; he could feel it. *Just seconds.* If he'd managed to hold on to the window frame for just a few seconds more after it started to slip, it would have landed right on top of her. Those sickening moments when he'd tried to grasp the crumbling wood and it just wouldn't stay, that feeling as fresh air rushed into his palms, and the crunching, spraying sound of glass and wood coming from below... It had been so, so close.

He'd looked down at the top of her head – he vaguely

recalled her hair being brown – and watched her walk away, seemingly in a daze, not looking up, not looking back. He'd tried as hard as he could to slow down his heart rate, but it had drummed for half an hour in a rhythm normally reserved for a nightclub playlist. She hadn't been hurt, had she? The safety glass wouldn't have been sharp, and she hadn't appeared to be anything but terribly shocked, but a wash of fear had run through him all the same. He'd bolted for the stairs.

'What the actual hell?' a voice had yelled – his client, a heavily pregnant redhead called Libby who, if he was honest, frightened him. As he'd emerged from the staircase, she'd waddled her way back into the shop from the street outside, her freckled face like thunder. 'You've just almost killed my friend, not to mention the state of the path outside,' she'd said, rustling in her pocket and producing her phone.

'God, I am so sorry,' he'd said, holding up his hands. 'Is she there? Is she okay?'

He'd gone to the open door and looked out onto the street again. Other than a few pensioners skirting the crumpled window in its halo of glass, tutting because they had to walk into the road, the street had been quiet. She must have gone around the corner. He'd been about to run out and check, but he'd seen Libby on the phone behind him, clearly trying to reach her friend. She'd flashed him a look that could turn a man to stone, so he'd decided it was better to leave her alone. He'd retrieved a broom and rubble bag from his van and set to work clearing up the mess, then spent the rest of the day making as beautiful a job as he could of the remaining windows. He would be back again in the morning to face the simmering wrath of his client, but for now he had a dinner date to attend.

The high street had quietened down now, the locals at home for the evening, the tourists back in their B&Bs and rentals. Cravenwick was the kind of place people came for tea and scones, or to buy a souvenir fridge magnet or box of fudge, maybe before a walk at the nearby coast, or after visiting one of the many Northumberland castles and stately homes. Which was why Nick rarely came here, except for work. He'd once lived not too far from Cravenwick, but... that had changed. And even when he'd lived nearby, he hadn't had much cause to pop in – as a man in his early thirties, he hadn't much use for *Live, Laugh, Love* signs made of driftwood, or artisan soaps. Now, he lived in his half-brother's spare room in Hangforth, which wasn't too far away but was worlds apart from this quaint chocolate-box place.

Hangforth was an old pit village that had once fallen on hard times but was now slowly on the up, since it was near a main road to Newcastle. It was starting to become a town of second homes, had bagged itself a Costa Coffee, and his brother had bought a three-bedroomed flat there a few years back before the prices started to skyrocket.

He walked into the Weary Traveller to find Travis himself sitting at a table for two, tapping away at the ever-present phone in his hand. The pub was busy with locals and visitors, and was the traditional type with fruit machines and a menu where every dish had triple carbs.

Travis, who wouldn't know a putty knife from a gasket roller, couldn't be further from Nick in both lifestyle and fashion choices. He had some fancy-looking trainers on instead of work boots, and his T-shirt was tucked in at the front and left artfully loose in the back, a style which Nick now knew to be a 'French tuck' after being schooled on this against his will. Travis ran a business from home, sourcing 'stylish' items, apparently very high-end, and selling them for a surprisingly healthy profit online. He used phrases such as 'capsule wardrobe' and 'statement pieces' to try and explain the value of the clothes, but Nick still felt that a hundred pounds for a T-shirt was unfathomable when you could get ten for that in the clothing aisle of Tesco.

'Here he is,' Travis said, smiling and putting his phone face down on the table. 'Tough day at the office?'

'You could say that,' Nick replied, letting out a small groan as he sat down on the banquette, the tension in his back and legs already starting to ease off. 'How about you? Sold many... bolero jackets today?' He thought bolero jackets might be a thing.

Travis physically flinched. 'Nobody has worn a bolero since 2003, Nicholas. Except for bullfighters. And maybe our mam.'

'Right. Shall we get some scran then? What do you fancy?'

'Nothing too heavy – I might be busy later.'

'Uh-huh. The Traveller's not best known for its salads, mate.'

Travis flicked a hand. 'Just get me a burger then, and I'll not eat the bun.'

Nick went to the bar and bought a lager shandy for himself, since he was driving, and a bottle of some obscure but strong Belgian beer for Travis. He ordered burgers for the pair of them and sat back down, trying to work the knots out of his neck while they waited. His thoughts drifted back to Cravenwick Pages and the day he'd rather forget.

Libby had mellowed during the day and had stopped glaring at him whenever he walked past by lunchtime. He'd apologised profusely for the window and had promised her a little discount on her bill as means of compensation, which seemed to go down well. At eleven o'clock she'd brought him a cup of tea – no biscuit; he wasn't quite forgiven enough at that point – and when he'd packed up for the day, she'd offered to let him store some of his gear in a cupboard at the back of the shop rather than loading it in the van, only to unload it again the next day. He felt like he could put the day behind him for the most part, but the close shave with that woman below still nagged at him like a stone in his shoe.

'Do you believe in fate?' he blurted.

Travis looked up and wrinkled his nose. 'Eh?'

'You know... being in the right place at the right time. Or the wrong place.' His skin prickled as he pictured the gap of only a few feet between the woman's toes and the tangled remains of the window frame.

Travis eyed him over the top of his phone. 'What are you going on about? Is this something to do with a woman? Because if it is, I'll stop threatening you with Tinder. I've got your profile built and ready to go, you know.'

'I know,' grumbled Nick, fully aware of his brother's insistence that he ought to get himself back out there. 'But no, it's got nothing to do with a woman. Not in that way anyway.' He explained what had happened that morning. 'What if she'd left the shop a few seconds earlier? She'd have been right underneath, and... well, I'd probably be in a cell right now.'

Travis grimaced. 'You really do like to catastrophise, don't you?'

'I don't. I just keep thinking about how there's only a few seconds between life going along as normal and complete disaster.'

'You think too much.'

Burgers landed in front of them, and they thanked the waitress.

Travis took a bite of his, bun and all, and groaned happily. 'See, here I am, eating this burger without even considering there might be half a mouse's head in it when I get to the middle. But what you're doing with your *window* thing is looking for the mouse. Just chill out.'

'What a lovely analogy,' said Nick dryly, putting his burger down, his appetite waning a bit. 'And that's not what I'm doing at all. I'm not saying that there are only *disasters* around every corner; I'm saying that maybe there's some kind of plan. Today you'll cheat death by two paces; tomorrow you'll have all six numbers come up on the lottery, because someone or something up there has figured it all out for you.'

Travis placed his mangled, half-finished burger on his plate and steepled his fingers beneath his chin. 'I get you. You know what you should do then?'

'What?'

'You should get that lass a lottery ticket to say sorry.'

'Very funny,' said Nick, narrowing his eyes and picking up his burger again. He'd already popped over to the florist that day and left a bunch of flowers for her at the shop, asking Libby to make sure they got to her.

Travis had paused eating and was scrolling through his phone, no doubt making arrangements with some mates who were more fun than his big brother. Although he could be doing something much worse.

'You're not seriously doing me a Tinder profile, are you?' he asked, leaning over to look at his screen. Thankfully it just looked like he was texting.

'Don't worry,' said Travis archly. 'Far be it from me to meddle in your love life. I haven't done one really. Not yet.' He smirked and continued speed-texting.

'Well, good. I've only got room for one lady in my life right now, and that's Ruby.'

Travis sighed. 'Nobody doubts your devotion to Ruby, bro.'

Nick pinched his lips between his teeth. No amount of devotion could fix his stand-off with Ruby's mother, Callie.

'But you don't need to become a monk, Nick,' Travis continued. 'You can be a dad and also get yours.'

Nick rolled his eyes. 'Trav, I'm a thirty-three-year-old single dad with a business to run. I'm not really in a great place to be hooking up with all and sundry. Unlike someone I know.' He gave Travis a meaningful look.

'Hey, I'm very discerning when it comes to men actually. Trouble is, I have wide-ranging tastes and I'm scared of commitment. You can thank our mother for that one.' He shrugged and prodded some more at his phone with one thumb while using the other hand to mash the rest of his burger into his face. 'And on that note, I'd best head off. I'm meeting someone.' He stood up and drained his bottle of beer.

'Well, be careful,' said Nick.

'Only if you'll be *less* careful...' He was walking away but turned back for a moment. 'Seriously, maybe you should listen to yourself and your hocus-pocus shite about fate. Maybe you're being set on a path to find the love of your life.'

At that, Nick simply raised his eyebrows and watched his brother head out through the throng of other drinkers. He shook his head. No, fate wasn't a thing, because if it was, the universe had it in for him. He finished his meal and went out into the street.

It was early dusk outside, cool and quiet compared to the stuffiness of the pub and the jangling, flashing lights of the fruit machine. Nick inhaled deeply, reflecting for a moment on where he was going. He seemed to be living a life in reverse. Where he'd once been an adult, a husband and father, he was now living in his little brother's spare room, rubbing along as if they were teenagers again. It was as if the last fifteen years hadn't even happened.

He thrust his hands into his pockets and headed down the road towards the van, past the chip shop, which was open, and the newsagents, which was closed, and tried not to look up at the first floor of the bookshop, where a pristine new window sat in its frame. Its presence felt vaguely judgemental.

He needed to cross the road to get to the van, so he stepped off the path, walking behind the row of cars parked in diagonal bays facing the pavement. He stopped in the road, feeling a chill as his eyes were drawn again to the scene of near disaster that morning. He thought he saw the glint of a few pieces of glass in front of the shop that he'd missed.

Then he felt a change in the air somewhere behind his back and heard the soft screech of rubber on tarmac. He turned around to find he was bathed in the red glow of brake lights. The back end of a black VW Golf was no more than an inch from his body. He seemed to forget how to breathe for a second as adrenaline pulsed through his veins.

Backing away, as if the car had repelled him, he could see the shadow of a woman in the driver's seat, hand on her chest as she craned around to look at him. He took a deep breath and signalled that he was okay, then walked away, shaking his head. It would just be typical if he'd ended up flattened under a car today. Karma for nearly crushing somebody with a window, he thought, an uneasy chuckle bubbling from inside him as he looked back just once to see the black Golf tentatively continue to reverse and then drive away.

THREE

WREN

At half past five, Wren picked up her bag and keys and took the short walk to Cravenwick Pages. She looked up at the new window above her and shivered, but then Libby waved a packet of chocolate biscuits at her through the window, luring her inside.

'Here she is, brave survivor of the Cravenwick Window Massacre.' Libby tucked the biscuits under her arm and patted Wren's arms, shoulders and cheeks. 'No obvious injuries. I won't need to contact my public liability insurer after all.'

Wren batted her away, laughing. 'You know how pregnant women don't like people touching their bumps? I feel the same way about having my face mauled by people not in the medical profession.'

'I *love* people touching my bump. Here, have a go.' She grabbed Wren's hand and pressed it to her side, where her cord dungarees rippled and pulsed. 'Ooh, I think this might be an elbow. Or maybe a knee.'

'So weird,' said Wren. 'But lovely.'

'Now have a biscuit,' said Libby, pressing a Hobnob into her other hand.

'Do you ever stop? Sit down, Lib. You're heavily pregnant, you've spent a day on your feet, not to mention having the shop and the flat upside down with workmen. Clumsy workmen at that. Shouldn't you be nesting or something?'

Libby cocked her head to one side, her strawberry blonde curls lolling from the top of her headscarf like an overgrown pot plant. 'No time for that. The window frames are literally rotten and there's damp coming in, which I'd much rather sort out now than when there's a newborn around.'

'Fair enough,' said Wren, nodding. 'You know, I think you've actually become a real grown-up, Lib.'

Libby sighed contentedly. 'I have. Finally. Who needs a boyfriend when you've got good friends and easy access to multiple editions of *What to Expect When You're Expecting*?'

'Well, I'm glad to be of service, and even more glad you're getting your parenthood advice from a book. I'd be as much use as a chocolate teapot,' said Wren, thinking how amazing it was that her friend had it all together even though her shitty 'boyfriend' had high-tailed it when he found out she was pregnant. She'd proved that she really didn't need him, even though she had one of the biggest challenges of her life coming up. It made Wren feel weird about depending on Alex so much – they'd been together so long that she didn't know what she'd do without him. Not that she wanted to do without him – he was the love of her life, obviously – but it did make her wonder.

Libby turned the sign on the door to 'Closed' and bustled off to the kitchen out back to make some drinks, waving off Wren's bid to do it for her. Libby was nearly eight months pregnant but was still running her bookshop almost single-handedly, with the help of her sole employee, a studious hipster called Jenson. Wren didn't know how she did it – it took all of Wren's energy just to look after herself, never mind gestating an infant while working a full-time job.

Wren wandered further back into the store while she

waited, meandering through the small maze of bookshelves and display tables. Libby's shop always made her feel calm, surrounded by the comfort of all those words, recorded forever between those pages. It was small but perfect, with red walls and dark wood shelves that gave the impression of a Victorian library. Empty wall spaces were dotted with artworks depicting quirky, anthropomorphic cats in top hats or monocles, quoting classic phrases from literature. A tabby wearing a buttoned-up waistcoat and bowler hat cited Oscar Wilde: *You Can Never Be Overdressed or Overeducated.* The shop was Libby in bricks-and-mortar form – practical yet unapologetically quirky.

Wren brushed her hand along the books' spines, enjoying the feel of each volume; little containers for adventure, romance and heartbreak. Tucking a lock of her dark brown hair behind her ear, she wandered from shelf to shelf, her fingers habitually rubbing at the chain she wore around her neck. It was a delicate gold chain bearing a seashell pendant, a conch with alternating stripes of gold and mother-of-pearl. It had once belonged to her mother. Wren continued to be amazed that she hadn't rubbed it into nothing, as she had a habit of reaching for it whatever her mood – stress, boredom, seeking comfort. It had been with her all her life, which was a solemn reminder that her mother hadn't been.

She slid a book from the shelf. *Life is a Rollercoaster.* She quickly pushed it back. Wren wanted nothing to do with roller-coaster-lives. All she wanted were the things that had always made her happy – Alex, her home and her job. The things that made her feel like her life was safe and predictable. Roller-coasters were for people who needed to artificially generate their thrills, people who thought spontaneity was fun, but Wren knew exactly where she was best off – with two feet planted firmly on the ground.

Libby came back, cups in hand, and they settled on the small, threadbare velvet sofa between the display cases. Libby sighed as she sat, kicking off her shoes, and put her feet up on the coffee table in front of them, nudging a stack of magazines out of the way with her stripy-socked toes. Wren took a soothing sip of the chamomile tea Libby had waiting for her and settled back too.

'So, how are things at work?' Libby asked. 'Any news? No pun intended.'

'Ha ha. And no, still no word on the downsizing. I can't tell if Zara is hiding something or if she genuinely doesn't know. But it's happening everywhere – the local paper's becoming a thing of the past. And we're probably next.'

Libby gave Wren a sympathetic look. 'But where am I going to find my ads for second-hand fish tanks and articles about the grand opening of the new leisure centre if the *Echo* closes down?' She winked and sipped her tea.

'It's not funny!' said Wren, meaning it but trying not to smile. 'I'd lose my job, you heartless cow.'

'Meh, you'd get another one.' Libby waved her hand dismissively.

'But I like my current one. And anyway, I'm trying to stay positive. Maybe the worst that will happen is job cuts.' Wren bit her lip. 'Although it might be me that gets cut.'

'Then think differently. Think bigger. You've got transferrable skills.'

'According to you, I'm only good for writing puff pieces on church bake sales,' she said, glaring over the top of her mug.

'Wren, you're a writer. You don't have to just write for the local paper.'

'But that's what I do. That's what I've always done. Straight out of uni, first job at the *Northumberland Echo*, and I'm still there.'

'And isn't that tragic? Aren't you bored? Wren, you've been there for twelve years – maybe it is actually time for a change.'

'I don't like change.'

'I know.'

Wren sighed, wishing Libby wasn't always so forthright. Her best friend reserved the right to give her opinions, but Wren wished she wouldn't do it so often – and with such razor-sharp precision.

'We can't all embrace adversity and run with it like you,' she said, fully aware of how childish she sounded.

'Yes, you can. Sometimes fate just steps in and doesn't give you a choice. It's not about being strong and capable; it's about accepting that there are things you can't change.'

'Alright, Mystic Meg. Or is that the prayer from AA meetings?'

Libby shrugged.

They sat for a while, sipping tea in silence, Libby's eyes closing every now and then, giving away how tired she really must be.

'Lib, do you really believe in fate?'

'I think I do. Are we still talking about your job?'

'No. I was thinking about what happened this morning. I mean, what if I hadn't stopped to read Alex's text before I went outside? That window would have landed right on top of me. I mean, was I meant to avoid being killed because of some bigger plan, or was I just lucky?'

Libby breathed deeply and raised her eyebrows. 'Well... There's a question. You know, I might have a book on fate and destiny somewhere...' She started to pedal her legs in front of her in an effort to get up, but Wren laid a hand on her arm.

'No, it doesn't matter. I'm just being silly.' She *was* being silly, wasn't she? It had been a lucky escape that could have gone a little differently, and she shouldn't be giving it so much significance.

'Hmm, I don't know,' Libby said. 'I actually *do* believe there's a plan for us all. A big library of books with our names written on them and a story inside.'

'Bloody hell. I didn't know pregnancy hormones could make you so poetic. Do you really think that?'

'Yeah. I think even the bad stuff that happens to us is just part of the journey to where we're meant to be.'

Wren was starting to feel like she was in the presence of a Tibetan shaman. Libby was mildly eccentric, but she'd never showed a penchant for mysticism.

'I mean, look at me and Carl,' she continued, patting her bump in reference to the baby's father. 'I was devastated when he left me. Thought my life was ruined and I'd never be happy again. But then, lo and behold, two months after he did a runner, I find out he's been done for stealing from his work, and he's been evicted from the flat he was asking us to move into.'

'So you think the universe has it in for Carl?'

'No! I think the universe saved me from *him*. If he hadn't "broken my heart" then I might have been stuck with a home-less felon. We dodged a bullet, didn't we?' she crooned at her belly, rubbing it tenderly.

'You did. You absolutely did. So... I live to see another day then. I wonder what the universe has in store for me next. Editor-in-chief of *The Telegraph*?'

Libby drained her mug and handed it to her. 'Not yet. The next twist of fate in your story is to wash these cups up for me and let me go and lie down with Netflix and a bowl of popcorn balanced on my belly. You can join me if you like?'

Wren smiled but thought of Alex waiting for her. 'No, I've got to get back. You go up and rest, and I'll switch the lights off and latch the door when I head off.' She gave Libby a one-armed hug, the cups in her other hand, and watched as her friend wearily made her way up to her flat.

'Oh, the falling-window killer left you a little present to say sorry,' shouted Libby from halfway up the staircase. 'It's in the kitchen.'

Wren went through to the little back room and washed the

cups under the hot tap with a squirt of washing-up liquid. The tap wobbled in her hand as she tightened it. Libby would probably be renovating this place forever – there always seemed to be something else on its last legs.

She looked around for a towel to dry her hands, but there was nothing in plain sight. Wondering if there might be something in the tall closet that stored all kinds of odds and ends, she pulled its door open and was greeted by a rumble and clatter as objects fell towards her. Wren drew back instinctively as a long, tall object swung forward like a headman's axe, narrowly missing her face before it hit the floor.

She looked down to see a broom, which from the angle of it looked to have been propped bristle-end up, and hanging from the edge of the brush head by a loop of cord was an electric drill, its drill bit glinting menacingly in the strip lighting. She raised a hand to her left eye protectively, realising how close that had come to her face. Her nostrils flared. For the second time today, it seemed that workman had nearly taken her out – she was sure these weren't Libby's tools.

She picked up the broom and pushed it back into the cupboard, hearing a stirring of metal against wood as she wrestled it into place. Then the nest of tools and equipment collapsed completely, and a long pole swung forward, connecting brutally with the centre of her forehead. She reeled back, stunned. From behind the broom, a metal pole with a weird suction cup had fallen onto her.

She pressed a hand to her head, squeezing her eyes shut before she dared to look at her fingers. No blood, thank God, but it ached horribly, and patting her forehead again she realised it had already started to swell. Marvellous. She was going to go to work the next day looking like a black-and-blue unicorn.

'Everything okay down there?' came Libby's voice from upstairs.

'It's fine,' she shouted back up, not wanting to bother her baby-bound friend. 'Just your workman breaking all the health and safety laws again. I'll sort it.'

'Okay,' came a quieter voice from above.

Wren heard the ping of the microwave and smelled a faint waft of popcorn.

'Thanks. Love you.' A door closed.

Wren huffed. It was bad enough that she'd had one hair-raising near miss courtesy of an incompetent glazier that morning, but this was just silly. She gathered up the bits that had spilled out of the cupboard and shoved them back inside, propping the broom up more carefully than that fool had earlier, and placing the electric drill safely on the floor.

She was about to close the door when she saw a tool she'd missed – some kind of metal scraper or spatula with a worn handle. She picked it up, wincing as her forehead throbbed. Losing the last of her patience with the workman's hazardously stored belongings, she threw it in the cupboard, where it wedged itself into a jumble of wires snaking from an extension cable, and slammed the door shut.

It was then that she saw what must be her present – a bunch of white lilies propped in a pint glass of water beside a pile of John Grisham novels on the counter. *How appropriate*, she thought. *He tries to kill me then sends me funeral flowers.* She left them where they were.

The sun was going down, and it was shadowy and cool in the car as Wren got buckled in and started the engine. Her phone pinged just as she'd put the car into gear, so she put it back in neutral and looked at the screen. It was Alex.

Where are you?

Shit. She'd forgotten the milk. The convenience store at the end of the road was closed now, but then she remembered there was another one on the way home. She'd just go there.

Popping the car in reverse, she swung back out of the parking space, seeing only at the last minute the back of a khaki jacket through her rear windscreen. With a little yelp, she slammed the brakes on, her fingertips tingling where they clutched the wheel. Where the hell had he come from?

She couldn't see anything else other than a broad chest as he turned towards the car and backed away, then his hand raised in a small wave to let her know she hadn't actually hit him. He turned and walked off, and she let out a deep sigh. Today was becoming as dangerous as a stroll through a field of landmines.

Still shaken, she carried on reversing, pausing to check the road beyond a bus that had pulled up, then started the drive home.

The drive to the house Wren and Alex owned on the outskirts of Cravenwick took only five minutes, and she'd spent those five minutes trying to shake the adrenaline rush of near disaster without much success. But when she saw Alex's car in the driveway, her tension eased a little. At least at home she knew nothing out of the ordinary would happen. She parked on the street and went inside.

'Hey, I'm home,' she said, shrugging off her jacket and throwing it over the bannister rail. She dumped her bag on the bottom stair, where it rolled to the side, spilling out a lipstick and a pen. The smell of something delicious drifted from the kitchen, and she gravitated towards it. The kitchen-diner was lit with just lamps and the light over the stove, where Alex stood stirring something in a pan.

'Mmm, that smells nice,' she said, snaking her arms around

him from behind and folding her hands over his taut stomach muscles.

'Me or the chilli?' he said. She could hear the smile in his voice.

He was tall, so she could rest her head between his shoulder blades, feeling more tension seep out of her body. 'Both. How was work?'

'Work was great. I took on two new PT clients today and got the go-ahead for the juice bar.'

'Hey,' she said softly, squeezing him. 'That's amazing. You're my hero in Lycra.'

'All the best heroes wear Lycra,' he said, turning and putting his arms around her. She laid her head on his chest. 'Superman, Spiderman...'

'Bananaman...'

'Hey, don't knock Bananaman. Bananas are an excellent source of potassium.'

'Well, you would know.'

Alex was the manager of a gym, as well as being a personal trainer and general healthy-living enthusiast. Wren had to hide her chocolate in the car.

She looked up at him, and he lifted her chin, his brow furrowing.

'What's happened to your head?'

She'd almost forgotten. It had stopped hurting, but when she touched it now, it was still tender. 'Oh, it's fine. Just a bump.'

'Wren, you need to be careful. Head injuries should be taken seriously.'

'It's *fine*. Come on! It's not like I got knocked out or anything.'

'Listen, in my line of work, injuries happen all the time. I know what I'm talking about. We should maybe get you to A&E, just to be safe.'

Wren's eyes widened. 'A&E? No way, Alex. It's a minor bump. I'm not spending eight hours in the waiting room for a bruise.'

He paused, surveying her forehead in the analytical way he usually reserved for his own biceps. 'Okay. But can you please go to the walk-in centre tomorrow? Better safe than sorry.'

'Fine,' she conceded. 'I will do that.' Anything for an easy life.

'Good. Have you got the milk?' he asked.

'Argh. No. I forgot it, sorry.' Wren sighed. She'd been so distracted by the assault from the broom cupboard and the reversing incident that she must have sailed straight past the corner shop. 'I'll go and get it now.'

Alex rolled his eyes, dropping his arms from where he'd held her. 'Wren, this is so bloody typical. I asked you to do one small thing.'

'Don't worry, I'll get it now. It's fine.'

He stood with his arms crossed in the lamplight, the kitchen feeling less cosy by the second as his mood turned. 'It's not fine though, is it? You work late all the time, even though you don't have to, or you're off babysitting your dad, and the one time I manage to hand off the evening shift and cook dinner for you, this happens.'

'It's just milk,' she said, quieter this time, readying herself to bury her irritation. She made for the door to get her bag, but he pushed past her.

'Don't bother. I'll get it. Just don't let the chilli burn. If you can manage that?' He snatched up his own car keys and stormed towards the hallway. 'Fuck's sake,' she heard him mutter, and she remembered her bag ejecting its contents onto the stairs.

Once the door slammed shut, she went and gathered everything up, hanging her bag and coat on a peg where they belonged. Then she went to the stove and picked up the wooden spoon. She stirred the food while staring at the tiles behind the cooker. Alex had a habit of blowing things out of all proportion, but she'd learned, for her own sanity, how to navigate his moods. Space, time and a tidy house seemed to be the right combination, but lately she'd found herself resenting the effort she had to make to appease him. *Should it really be this much work?* She sighed and wriggled the knots out of her shoulders. The drive to the shop would do him good. He would calm down.

Later that night, after a frosty dinner, they lay in bed in darkness. Alex had finished his night-time shower and skincare regime, and smelled faintly of biscuits. Wren suspected there was a bottle of fake tan hidden somewhere in their bathroom.

She snuggled closer to him, and he allowed her to be the big spoon. The lithe muscles of his back weren't exactly comfortable to lean against, but she wanted the contact of his skin. She kissed his shoulder.

'You saved my life today, you know,' she murmured, thinking of the text that had slowed her exit from Libby's shop.

'What?' His voice was thick with sleep.

Then she remembered that the text had been a reminder to get milk.

'Never mind,' she said and closed her eyes.

FOUR

NICK

Nick barely had time to register the spray of sparks from the cable before he was launched backwards across the small kitchen, landing with a thump against the cabinets behind him. He sat there in a daze for a moment, scarcely able to believe what had just happened, noting fuzzily that the putty chisel he'd reached for was now several feet away, having been projected from his hand by the surge of electricity. *I've just been electrocuted,* he thought, shocked in more ways than one. His heart was pounding, unsurprisingly, but felt quite regular, and his hand looked okay, no burns. The tool must have left his hand quickly enough that it hadn't had the chance to cause any real damage.

He took a deep breath and stood up, shaking himself from top to toe. Everything seemed to be in working order.

He picked up the putty chisel again, seeing that the worn handle had some exposed metal, and looked inside the cupboard. He didn't remember putting the chisel on that ratty coil of extension cable yesterday. And why would he? On closer inspection, he saw the cable had a large split in the plastic casing, copper wires glinting from inside, the perfect conductor for some sizzling electricity to pass through the chisel and into his unsuspecting body.

In fact, nothing in this cupboard was where he'd left it. He wondered if Libby had been moving things around in here, then felt a pang of guilt. What if she'd touched that chisel, being pregnant and everything? He swallowed dryly and, with care, reached down to unplug the ropey extension cable from its socket. His eyes followed the path of it to see that it had been snaked under the cupboard door and was being used to power the kettle.

Libby wandered in, mug in hand, and asked him if he'd like a brew with a look that said she didn't like the mess he'd made in here.

'Actually,' he said, 'I was just about to come and find you. You need an electrician in here pronto.' He briefly considered telling her how he'd almost become a victim of her crumbling building but thought better of it. He didn't want to add the perception of any more chaos to this job – he had a reputation to uphold. He'd already noticed that the lilies he'd bought for her friend had gone untouched, so he knew all was far from forgiven.

She flicked the switch on the kettle repeatedly. 'What's wrong with this?' she asked, seemingly so focused on her cuppa that she hadn't listened.

He picked up the ragged cable and showed her the exposed wires. 'You can't power the kettle with this.'

She sighed. 'Okay, I'll get a new extension.'

'I really don't think you should,' he said. 'It's not safe running extensions all over the place. Not with wiring this old. See?' He bent down into the cupboard and warily nudged the plug socket. It rattled around, barely fixed to the crumbling plaster behind it. 'I could put you in touch with a friend of mine. He could put you in a new socket near the counter top instead.'

Libby wrinkled her nose. 'Maybe. I'll let the dust settle after all this work, then we'll see.'

Nick went to speak again, but she'd clearly grown fed up with waiting for her hot drink and was making for the stairs instead. He thought better of chasing after her, deciding to just get on with the last bit of his job and be done with it.

After retrieving his tools, he set about replacing the little window at the back of the shop, the last of the windows in this place that had a rotten frame. He checked in from time to time to see if his heartbeat felt normal, and it did, although he did keep getting surges of adrenaline at the memory of his brush with doom. He wondered if he should get himself checked out at the doctors or whether he was overreacting.

After he'd put the finishing touches to the new window, he stood back and admired a job well done. He liked the feeling of having completed something, the satisfaction of exchanging old for new, not to mention the way his job was absorbing enough to keep him from overthinking other areas of his life. He had, in the past, been prone to long bouts of introspection, musing over and over about how he could have done things differently. Maybe he could have avoided losing Callie? He was over her now, but it didn't stop him thinking about what might have been or how they could have handled things better after the split. For Ruby especially. He really hoped Ruby had been too young to remember how little he'd been around at one point, even if it hadn't been by choice. He was trying so hard to make up for lost time now, but maybe it was too late?

He felt a throb in his chest and panicked momentarily, pausing in his efforts to pack up the tools. He pressed his hand to his heart. Had he done his cardiovascular system a number by getting himself electrocuted, or was it just that familiar ache that came from time to time? He imagined it was the latter.

He gathered up the last of his tools and took them outside to his van, then came back in to leave his invoice. There was nobody at the desk, and that hipster-looking lad was deep in conversation with a customer about Camus. He was showing no sign of stopping, and Libby was nowhere to be found, so he left the invoice on the desk, with a short note, urging Libby to reconsider about the electrician and to call him if she changed her mind. After a moment's thought, he went back out to the van, retrieved a relatively new extension cable and left it next to the note. Even if she didn't get the wiring sorted right away, at least she was safer running the kettle off this.

He was just about to leave again when he saw a small display of medical books by the door. There was a selection of biographies of celebrated physicians and some self-help books, and in the centre was a large family medical guide, the type to feed the paranoia of hypochondriacs and overcautious parents.

Looking around, almost sheepishly, he lifted the cover and thumbed through with exaggerated casualness. He alighted upon a section about accidents in the home, scanned it quickly and saw that even minor electrical shocks warranted medical advice. He let the book close with a thump.

He would pop into the walk-in centre on his way home.

Nick arrived home mid-afternoon, pleased to be done early for the day and to be finished with the Cravenwick Pages job altogether. Working at the bookshop since 'the incident' yesterday had started to feel like lingering at the scene of a crime. He felt Libby would be very glad to see the back of him, not just for his clumsiness but also for his nagging about the electrics.

He'd been given the all-clear by the doctor at the walk-in centre, who had strapped him to an ECG machine and declared his heartbeat to be 'unremarkable', which felt rather like an insult. If his heart could withstand 230 volts coursing through it, then surely it warranted a more flattering description.

He'd been glad to be out of there quickly anyway. The

waiting room had been full of odd bods, ranging from a man yelling that the lizards were coming for them all to a woman wearing a business suit accessorized with a Sea World baseball cap and large sunglasses, who was burying her face in an upside-down copy of *Homes and Gardens*. It wasn't a place he wanted to hang around.

The sound of Classic FM drifted from Travis's third-bedroom office. The 'Jupiter' movement from Holst's *The Planets*, if Nick had it right. Travis liked to work to the sound of classical music, since he'd heard that it increased a person's IQ a few points while listening, although Nick wasn't sure what the intellectual challenge of packaging T-shirts and accessories into envelopes and boxes was.

He took off his dusty boots by the door, as well as his grubbier outer clothes, as was the rule at Travis's. The flat was pristine. Clean lines, minimalist and shades of pale cream and grey, which meant that Nick's manky work clothes were verboten beyond the doormat. The doormat got hoovered approximately twice a day anyway.

He padded through to the bathroom, threw the rest of his clothes into the laundry basket, and had a shower before getting changed into joggers and poking his head into Travis's office. Where the rest of the flat was like an Instagram interiors account, the office was an explosion of colour, cardboard and chaos. As Nick entered, Travis was folding a pair of leather-look trousers to the tune of *Eine kleine Nachtmusik*.

'Alright?' he asked, leaning on the door frame.

Travis looked up. 'Afternoon, brother. Good day at work?' He said this with his lips partially pursed around a bit of parcel tape, which he then used to tamp down the packaging around the trousers.

'Not bad. Just a minor altercation with the mains electric, but other than that – okay.'

'That place sounds like a death trap. Although a little spark of electric through the system might be just what you need. Perk you up a bit. A taser to the libido.'

'Travis, you're so obsessed with my... *libido.*' The word made him want to gag. 'I'm starting to think it's you with the problem.'

'I've no problem with my libido, Nicky.'

'Quite the opposite, I'd say. Who was that I heard sneaking out this morning? Because whoever it was smelled strongly of aftershave and left what I hope were foundation marks on your towels.'

'Ugh, I know. It's come out in the wash though. And it's none of your business who it was.' He avoided Nick's eye, picked up a sheer top with sequins in the nipple area and started fussing with it.

Nick grinned. 'You don't remember his name, do you?'

'I do. I'm just not going to tell you. Besides, you don't know him.'

'Oh, I can't imagine I do. But colour me curious. What was he called?'

Travis continued fiddling with the top and surreptitiously slid his hand to his phone.

'Without checking the app!' said Nick, trying not to laugh.

Travis rolled his eyes, picked up the phone and huffed. 'Alright, I can't remember. But I won't be seeing him again anyway. My bathroom linens deserve better.' He scrolled on his phone. 'Oh, the mother ship has been in touch.'

'Oh, right. How's she doing?'

Travis scrolled through a short message, his face impassive. 'Exhausted, too old for this grafting, yada yada... Sends her love.'

Nick and Travis were used to their mother's long-distance parenting style. She was a singer and had worked the clubs when they were tiny, then as soon as she'd deemed them old enough (aged sixteen and ten), she'd largely disappeared for a life on the cruise ships, leaving them to live with their nanna. Tracey fancied herself as the Geordie Jane McDonald, and to be fair to her, although ITV had never come calling, she had carved out a long career doing what she loved. Nick had taken her absence pretty well, being older, and their nanna had been very much there for them, but Travis still seemed to feel the sting of rejection.

Dads hadn't featured heavily in their lives either. Travis's dad flitted in and out when he wasn't taking various girlfriends on holidays – whenever he'd had a lucky tip at the horse racing that made him temporarily rich – and had treated Travis a bit like a maiden aunt in a care home. He did his duty with visits, had been generous with presents, but wouldn't have entertained Travis coming to stay at his own place.

Nick had never known his own dad, and he was rarely spoken of. When he was mentioned, it was vague, with no particular identity offered up and the strong implication that he wouldn't want to know. The thing was, he kind of did want to know, but when he'd pressed his mam, she'd dodged the questions like she dodged dry land. His nanna wasn't much better – she was a proud and loyal woman, and if Tracey had asked her to keep things to herself, she certainly seemed to be sticking to her end of the bargain. She did tell Nick that his dad and his mother hadn't had a long relationship and that she herself had never met him, and Nick had read into that as any person would.

'Well, at least she's been in touch. Anyway, I'm going to head out to the coast for a walk. Do you want to come?'

Travis wrinkled his nose. 'Nah. I'm snowed under here.'

Nick regarded the small pile of items left to wrap next to the large pile already completed and smiled. 'Righto.'

He went to get his keys and wondered how long it would be before his brother started checking the messages on his dating app.

The Northumberland coast was only a short drive from Hangforth and was one of Nick's favourite places to blow off the cobwebs after busy days at work – or if something was on his mind. He parked the van and got out, looking at the sea. The tide was out and the water was a moody blue-grey, the summer weather being typically British and overcast. But it was still a view that pepped him up.

He headed down the coastal path, bouncing down the steps and breathing in the salty air, which was warm despite the clouds. After being cooped up in the dusty bookshop, this was just what he needed.

His pace slowed as he hit the sand, and he aimed for the middle of the beach where the sand was not quite wet and not quite dry, firmer underfoot and easier to walk on. A brown spaniel raced past, running after a stick, then careered into the sea, foam splashing everywhere as it zoned in on its prize. It came running back out of the water, stopping for a quick shake, but instead of running back to its owner, it raced up to Nick and stood panting in front of him, the stick still in its mouth.

'Hiya, boy,' murmured Nick, rubbing its head and deciding he was a boy despite lacking any evidence either way. 'Clever lad, fetching your stick.'

'Oy, buggerlugs!' yelled the owner, a late-middle-aged man wearing a flat cap, with shaggy brown hair hanging beneath it. 'Fetch it ower here!'

The dog's ears pricked, and he looked over at his owner.

'Sorry about him,' said the owner good-naturedly, wandering over. 'He's a nuisance, isn't he?'

'Not at all,' said Nick. 'He's a lovely dog.'

'He's a little sod. Throw him a stick, he wants a ball. Fetching back to anyone else but me. He's not normal.' The man rubbed the dog's head and produced a tennis ball from his pocket. 'You'll be wanting this instead, will you?'

The dog immediately dropped the stick and bounced up

and down until the ball was thrown, and Nick watched him tear off along the sand. The man said goodbye and wandered after him.

Nick walked along the beach, his mind drifting back to his absent father. No matter how much he'd been steered away from the subject of his paternal lineage or been led to believe that having no dad was slightly better than having a fair-weather one like Travis, he thought about his dad often. Who was he? And why had he never tried to meet his own son? Nick sighed, thinking how the lack of a father figure might have left him lacking the tools to sort out the situation with Callie and Ruby. A father adrift from his own kid, trying to swim back to her even though the waves kept pushing him back.

Then he heard laughter from nearby, out of sight. Laughter that sounded familiar. He stood up, craning his neck to see above him, where the promenade ran along the top of the beach. His heart skipped a beat.

Up on the promenade were Callie and Ruby. And *him*. They walked past, just above Nick's head, towards the car park in the distance. Ruby was between them, holding a hand either side and being swung up in the air at intervals. She was laughing and shrieking happily, her black pigtails bouncing, and the two of them were looking down at her, the picture of a perfect family. He had a cap on backwards – the twat, Nick thought with a twinge of irritation.

Nick stood there, frozen in place, watching them walk away, then decided that despite his feelings towards Justin, Callie's new boyfriend, he couldn't miss an opportunity to see Ruby.

Nick walked quickly up the ramp. By the time he reached the top, they were some distance away, so he picked up the pace, his eyes focused on his little girl.

The three of them stopped, looking in the window of the beach cafe, Ruby pointing at the sign advertising ice creams. But Callie shook her head and they walked on, Ruby's feet scuffing the sandy path, her head lowered. Nick broke into a jog, determined to catch up, making a mental note to get Ruby her ice cream when he next had her. But by the time he made it to the car park, Justin's car was pulling away onto the coast road.

Nick stood still, his happiness at seeing Ruby fading away. It wasn't the first time he'd seen Justin walk off into the distance with his family, and he couldn't face watching it again now. He turned and walked back the way he'd come.

FIVE

WREN

As Wren approached the neat red-brick bungalow, she checked her notes to make sure she was in the right place. *12, The Orchards*. This must be the one. Her journalistic instincts kicked in immediately, noting the well-maintained flower beds, devoid of weeds, and a recently painted white front door. Mrs Macmillan lived alone, according to Zara, so she must be busy all the time, keeping her house looking as smart as this, as well as still having a hand in the Community Kitchen. She pushed the doorbell and waited.

She was just about to press it again, or at least double-check she had the right date and time, when the door eventually opened to reveal a tiny woman, no more than five feet tall, with a golden-white bob and a wide smile.

'Hello, pet. You must be Wren.' She held out a hand, which Wren shook. It was as delicate as a bird, but her grip was firm and assured. Her other hand was resting on a cane Wren could swear was marked with the Louis Vuitton pattern. Her smile faltered a little as she took in Wren's appearance. 'Sea World...'

'Oh,' said Wren, snatching off the souvenir baseball cap, having forgotten she was still wearing it. Overnight, the bump on her head had spread into a magnificent purple bruise, which she'd managed to obscure with sunglasses and the only hat she owned. Now her cheeks burned red, almost as vivid as the colour of her forehead. 'Sorry about the get-up.'

The older woman gazed at the bruise, her mouth turning into a small O.

'Nothing to worry about, Mrs Macmillan. Just a little accident. Thanks again for inviting me to see you.'

She followed Mrs Macmillan into the hallway as she was beckoned, giving her host a little space to walk ahead as slowly as she needed. Perhaps she had a little help in keeping this place immaculate after all.

'I'm sorry it took me so long to answer the door,' Mrs Macmillan said over her shoulder. 'It's this bloody hip. Pardon my French.' She walked with some effort through to a tidy living room, which was immaculately decorated but had plenty of trinkets taking pride of place on the sideboard and mantelpiece – ornaments, photographs and souvenirs were placed everywhere. The figurines and commemorative plates had not one speck of dust on them, and appeared treasured and cared for.

Wren accepted the invitation to sit on the sofa, and Mrs Macmillan sat opposite. Between them, on the coffee table, was a pot of tea under a cosy, two cups and a plate of biscuits.

'Oh, Mrs Macmillan, you didn't need to go to any trouble,' said Wren, gesturing at the table as she set her notebook on her lap.

'Pfft,' Mrs Macmillan said, waving a hand dismissively. 'It's not a bother, pet. And call me Edie. I've been Mrs Macmillan a long time, but it still reminds me of my mother-in-law.'

'Oh, really?' said Wren, sensing some mischief from Edie. 'And that's not a pleasant memory?'

'You're quick off the mark with the probing questions, aren't you?' she replied with a little wink. 'But no, not pleasant memories, if I'm honest. The late Mrs Macmillan believed that women should be by their own kitchen sink, and she wasn't impressed to see her daughter-in-law "gadding about running a soup kitchen" as she charmingly put it.'

'Ah. And what about your husband? What did he think? I understand he's no longer with us.'

'No. He's not.' She smiled stoically. 'Stan passed away quite young, only fifty. But he was very proud of it all.'

'That's a long time to be doing everything on your own.' She thought again about how Edie managed to keep this place so well tended. 'Do you have children?'

'I do. I have a daughter, although she's very busy these days. She's got a life of her own. I do have the grandbairns though. They're always here, making a nuisance of themselves.' From the way her eyes lit up, Wren could see she thought nothing of the sort. 'Now, let's get the important business sorted first,' she said and started pouring the tea. 'So, your name's Wren? Interesting. Is it short for something?'

Yes, thought Wren, burying this answer as soon as it came to her. She never shared her full name with anyone. 'No,' she said. 'Just Wren.'

'Like the bird?'

'Um, yes. Like the bird. So, maybe we could start right at the beginning? The Community Kitchen began with just a trestle table and some soup, didn't it? And it went from strength to strength, now serving hundreds of hot meals a night to the homeless of Newcastle from what look to be industrial-level kitchens. You must be incredibly proud.'

'Oh, I am, although it's not me I'm proud of.' She waved her hand dismissively again, a gesture of which she seemed fond. 'We're a team. A big happy family, and if it wasn't for all of them, it still *would* be a trestle table and some soup.'

Wren smiled. 'But it was you who found the premises and converted it into the space it is now. It was your vision.'

Edie smiled back then stirred her tea distractedly, even though she hadn't put any sugar in it. Wren could sense she didn't take praise too easily and decided to change tack.

'You know, Edie, I volunteered at the Kitchen a while back. Must have been fifteen or sixteen years ago now. It was a really amazing experience – I can see how rewarding you must have found it all.'

Edie's face lit up. 'Did you now? Well, thank you for giving your time, pet.'

'I always wanted to go back and do it again but, well... I'm embarrassed to say, I never did. It was at Christmas, and it felt really good to do something for others. What's your fondest memory of a Community Kitchen Christmas, Edie?'

'Ah, there's so many,' she said, resting her cup on her lap and gazing into the middle distance. 'There was the year my daughter's partner dressed up as Santa and handed out selection boxes. And the year Sting turned up and did a turn for the diners. I kid you not,' she said as Wren's jaw dropped. 'Oh yes, Gordon's a great supporter of North East charities. That's his real name, you see – Gordon.' She gave Wren a conspiratorial look, as if she was sharing this bit of information on the down-low. 'No, I think my favourite was when my grandbairns came along for the first time. The first Christmas anyway. They left their presents behind and came to spoon out sprouts with the rest of us, and they never moaned once.'

'That's lovely. What a great memory to have. And for children to be so unselfish, that must be in the genes.' Wren smiled, hoping a little flattery would help open Edie up some more. But she looked bashful and distracted again.

'So...' Wren said, steering away from Edie being the focus again and wondering how on earth she was going to take it when she found out the piece was specifically about inspiring women. Edie didn't seem to have a self-promoting bone in her body. 'Why don't you tell me about some of the people who you — who *the team* have helped over the years?'

This went down much better, and Wren spent the following half hour scribbling copious notes to go along with the recording she made on her phone. There were stories that were sad, funny, uplifting, heartbreaking. It was going to make for a very interesting article.

'Edie, I can't thank you enough for telling me all of this,' Wren said, folding her notebook closed and sliding it into her bag. 'I was just wondering if it would be possible to come to the Kitchen itself? Meet a few volunteers, take a few pictures?'

'Of course you can, pet. In fact I'm going there myself on Thursday to do my shift. The hip doesn't allow me to be there full-time nowadays. Silly bloody thing, pardon my French. How about you come along?'

'That would be great. Would you like me to come and pick you up?' Wren hadn't seen a car outside and suspected Edie's hip might preclude her from driving.

'No, no, pet. The grandbairns are taking me down. No need. Now, have we finished for today?'

'Yes, thank you,' said Wren, standing up. 'Don't get up – I can see myself out.'

'Thank you. I'll stay put. Oh...' A thought seemed to flash over Edie's face, but she did her signature hand wave.

'What is it?' asked Wren.

'Oh, it doesn't matter. I'm forgetting myself. I'm thinking you're one of the grandbairns and I was about to ask you a favour.'

'That's no problem. What do you need?'

Edie hesitated, wincing. 'I don't like to ask, since you're here in a professional capacity. Oh, and with your sore head as well... But I've got a box of books in the spare bedroom – I went a bit overboard at the car boot sale – and I can't reach to put them up on the bookshelf. Would you mind?'

'Not at all!' said Wren, putting her bag down and heading over to the door Edie was pointing towards.

The bedroom was as clean and neat as the rest of the bunga-low, with the exception of two overstuffed bookcases. *Libby and Edie would get on,* thought Wren. On the bed was a box of books, hardbacks and paperbacks – there must have been nearly twenty of them.

Wren regarded the bookcases, seeing that one was completely full, and the other had only the top shelf free. She could see how Edie would have no chance of reaching it. It begged the question of how she would reach a book she wanted to read, but Wren decided it was best to just do as she'd been asked. She transferred the dusty books from box to shelf, until the top shelf was completely full. There were still quite a few books left once she'd filled it, so in the absence of a better option, she loaded the remainder onto the top surface of the bookcase itself. Not ideal, but at least the box was now empty. She left it on the bed and returned to the living room.

'All done. I've just left the box on the bed – is that okay?'

'Yes, yes, of course. Thank you so much, pet. Now, I'll see you Thursday, shall I?'

'You will,' said Wren, finding herself smiling warmly at Edie, still sitting in her chair. As she left, carefully replacing her dark glasses, she realised she was looking forward to seeing her again.

The early evening sun made the coastline glow like embers. It reminded Wren of weekend nights from years ago, when she was a teen, lighting campfires on the beach with her friends and drinking contraband beers. Teenage Wren would never have considered that she'd one day be driving along this sandy road in her own car with a boyfriend (that she *lived with*) sitting in the passenger seat. She'd felt so grown-up back then that it would have been hard to comprehend being any more so, let alone cohabiting and driving a sensible Volkswagen. A sensible Volkswagen that she'd hastily cleared of coffee cups and bits of paper before Alex had the chance to grumble.

As if he'd read her mind, he asked, 'Did you remember to put the dishwasher on?'

'Yep,' she replied. Then, feeling like this conversation could take an overly domestic turn, she gave him a sideways look and a smirk. 'But I think, when we get home, unloading it can wait until the morning?'

Alex groaned. 'I don't see why. It gets all clammy in there if it's—' Then he caught her meaningful glance. 'Ohhh. Right. Well, maybe it can wait. I've got the late shift at work tomorrow after all.' He grinned and settled back in the passenger seat, his man-spread legs spreading that little bit wider.

Wren had found herself doing this more often lately – trying to season their relationship with a little spice that it had been lacking. If sex kept him distracted from the household to-do list and the occasional lapse of her involvement in it, then all the better.

She drove down the narrow driveway to the seafront cottage, where her dad, Alan, was already waiting for them. The cottage was shrouded in dusk's shadows but exuded cosiness, from the white-painted porch and dormer windows to the overgrown climbing plants around the door. It was ramshackle but pretty and always gave Wren a little rush of nostalgia.

'Hello, pet. Come in. How do, Alex?' Alan said from the doorway, backlit by the light from the kitchen beyond. He gave Wren a bear hug and Alex a firm handshake.

'What's happened here then?' Alan asked, gesturing at Wren's forehead.

'Oh, it's nothing...'

'Wren had a close encounter with a window fitter's tools,' said Alex, shaking his head.

Alan paled. 'Oof. That's not young 'uns' speak for something else, is it?'

'No, Dad,' Wren interjected, cringing. 'I literally got knocked on the head with some glazing equipment, and I'm absolutely fine.'

'Right. Well, I'll take your word for it. Oh, here comes buggerlugs as well,' he added as a brown spaniel skittered across the kitchen tiles and swam around Wren's legs like a hairy shoal of fish. Alex stood back. He wasn't overkeen on pets as a rule, and she was never sure whether it was his feelings about the dog or her dad that meant she mostly came here alone. A few times a week in fact, since she always felt guilty about her dad's solitary existence out at the coast. He would never be drawn away from the sea, though; even his job at St Nicholas Lighthouse visitors' centre ensured he always had the waves in sight.

Wren bent down. 'Hello, Johnny boy,' she said, rubbing the dog's sides and ruffling his pendulous ears. He gave her a sly lick on the cheek and rushed off again, probably in search of some toy he wanted her to throw.

She put her handbag on the one remaining space on the kitchen counter that wasn't covered in unwashed plates or piles of papers and magazines and tensed. She could sense Alex flinching at the sight of the mess, but he was doing his best to cover it up, exchanging manly pleasantries with her dad about an upcoming football match.

Wren didn't normally give the grubby chaos of her dad's cottage a second thought – after all, they'd lived together like this for the first eighteen years of her life. But because of Alex the counters would need clearing, the plates and cups washed, and the kitchen table would need a good scrub to remove the crumbs and dried egg.

'Dad, you should really get a cleaner,' she said with a light laugh, giving Alex a hasty glance. Wouldn't hurt to try and show him some solidarity.

'It's lovely to see you too,' he sniffed. 'And I don't need a cleaner when it's only me here. I'm not bothering anyone.'

'You'd be bothering the health inspectors if they popped round,' said Alex, aiming for a jokey tone, although Wren could see through it. 'And the RSPCA.'

'John loves it,' said Alan. 'He gets to lick the plates, don't you, boy?'

John had returned, a grey-stained soft toy in his mouth, and Alan rubbed the top of his head.

Wren braced herself for Alex's horrified reaction, but he just said, 'How about we drive out for a takeaway, Alan? Save you cooking?' Alex frowned then raised his eyebrows at Wren as he ushered Alan out of his own front door, giving the waste-land of the kitchen a despairing last look.

Wren took the hint. She found some bin bags and threw out the orange-stained polystyrene and foil containers, junk mail and anything else she couldn't wash. Then she filled the sink with hot water and detergent and started the lengthy process of washing-up.

There was an incredible view out of the kitchen window over the beach. Wren's parents had inherited this cottage from her mother's family when they were newlyweds, in the days before Northumberland sea views commanded eye-watering house prices. Her dad was probably sitting on a rat-infested goldmine. She had spent many, many hours looking at this view as a teenager while scrubbing pots. Once she was old enough, she'd reluctantly taken control of the basic elements of domestic hygiene. Not that Alan had asked her to, but because if she didn't, they would simply run out of cups and plates. She'd known as she made the drive that she'd end up elbow deep in soap suds, mainly to appease Alex. Her natural, genetic tendency towards messiness had been curbed over the years as she'd tried to avoid him complaining.

She finished the washing-up and then went to tackle the living room.

On the dusty mantelpiece were her mother's ashes. She stood in front of them, in their jade-green urn, and said a silent hello. She could only remember small details about her mam. Black curly hair that tickled her cheek when she was carried on her shoulder. Being in a playpen and seeing her mother's face chequered through the gauze walls. Her mother lying down a lot, her dad saying that she was tired. And then one day, she wasn't there anymore. Caron Rowbottom had died, and instead of seeing her through the tiny holes of the playpen, she was now inside a jar above the fireplace.

Her mother had called her Serenity – that was her given name, the name on her birth certificate. She thought she could remember being called that when she was very small, and it must have been her mam who'd used it, because her dad had always shortened it to 'Ren'. Wren added the 'W' later, when she wanted to have a name that sounded complete... But deep down she knew that she kept the name Serenity to herself because it was a link to her mam, a special word that was meant only for her, and only from her mother's mouth. She touched the urn once, lightly, then the seashell necklace at her throat, and went to the bathroom to tidy some more.

'You love your chow mein, don't you, Johnny boy?' said Alan, dangling strings of noodles over the dog, who lapped at them like bait on a hook. Her dad had declined a plate and was eating out of the boxes from the Chinese takeaway they'd brought in, along with some beers – alcohol-free for Alex, who was driving them home, and full-belt alcohol for Alan. Wren sipped her second large glass of Merlot.

'It's not long 'til you're off on your holidays now, is it?' said Alan.

'Yeah, we can't wait,' Alex replied, putting down the remains of his stir-fried vegetables. 'Sorrento has some amazing hiking paths apparently – I was researching on the InterTrails app. I've saved some ready for our trip.' He grinned.

Wren smiled less enthusiastically. 'Not forgetting the amazing wine, desserts, pizza, pasta...'

'All the more reason we'll need those hikes. Burn off all those carbs drenched in olive oil.'

'Is it a holiday you're going on, son, or boot camp?' Alan asked with a wink and a swig of beer.

Alex's eyes flickered with poorly disguised annoyance. 'Oh, I think there's a lot to be said for a healthy balance.' He looked down at his glass, which was only a quarter full. 'I'll go and get a top-up. Anyone want anything?'

'No, I'm good,' said Wren, who'd already polished off the best part of half a bottle of wine, and Alan shook his head. Alex disappeared off to the kitchen.

'So, have you dusted off your hiking boots and compass then?' whispered Alan with a cheeky grin.

'Shh, Dad. It's his holiday too, so if he wants to go on a few walks, then that's what we'll do.'

'Aye, well make sure you get a bit of time to relax an' all. That's what a holiday's for. In my opinion, if you don't come back half a stone heavier...'

'It's a holiday wasted,' she finished, grinning. 'Anyway, will you be alright while I'm away? I'll ring to say hello.'

'Get away with you. I'm alright,' he said, waving a hand and giving her a stiff smile.

Wren knew her dad felt guilty for depending on her for company, and she knew that her couple of visits a week were something he looked forward to. But she didn't mind at all, although Alex openly begrudged it. Alan had spent her whole childhood being a single father, taking care of her, and other than his one friend from work, he hadn't managed to build a thriving social life. She often wondered if he was lonelier than he let on.

'Alan,' interrupted Alex from the doorway. He was holding a full pack of non-alcoholic beers still encased in their card-board sheath. 'Why are there still six of these?'

'We haven't started on them yet, son. I was finishing up the other pack first.'

'For God's—' Alex's lips pursed. 'I got these for me. They're non-alcoholic. I'm driving, or at least I was. I thought I was just feeling a bit tired, not half-drunk!'

'You'll be alreet,' said Alan. 'You've only had a couple.'

'Dad, no, he won't be alright. And don't be so cavalier about drink-driving. I've had too much as well, so we're both over the limit.'

Alex's nostrils flared. 'Well, what are we going to do now? A taxi's going to cost a fortune.' He barely tried to conceal a glare towards Alan, who was sitting there looking like butter wouldn't melt.

'I'm sorry, son; I didn't really think. And you don't need a taxi – you can just stop here and go home in the morning.'

'Makes sense,' agreed Wren. 'You don't start work until the afternoon, and if we're up early, I can drop you home before I go to work for ten?'

Alex's jaw clenched, and Wren could sense he was trying and failing to find a problem with this. 'Fine,' he said through gritted teeth, sitting down. He opened a bottle of non-alcoholic beer and poured it into his glass. 'I'll stick to this though. I'll be fine to drive in the morning, but I don't want to be hung-over for work.'

Wren nodded sympathetically, discreetly topped up her own glass of Merlot and steered the conversation back to the shores of Sorrento.

SIX

NICK

'I can't wait to see you too, darlin'. Have you decided where you want to go?'

'Ermmm, can we get ice cream? From that place at the beach?'

Nick's jaw tightened at the mention of the beach, remembering his disappointment the other day. But then he smiled, knowing he'd now get to treat her to the ice cream she'd missed out on. He gripped the phone between shoulder and ear, signalling to Travis to go ahead of him into Nanna's house. Travis hopped out of the van and disappeared up the garden path.

'Of course we can. But this time you'd better not eat all of my sprinkles.'

Ruby giggled down the phone. 'I might. They're the best bit.'

Nick smiled easily this time, the sound of her laugh making his whole body flood with endorphins, as if he'd just listened to his favourite song.

'Right, well, extra sprinkles for Ruby then,' he said. 'Anything for my baby girl.'

'I'm not a baby!'

'You'll always be my baby. Okay, I'd better go now, darlin'. I'll see you at the weekend. Can you do the Daddy squeeze?'

'I'll do it when Mammy takes the phone. I need both arms.'

'Well, make sure it's a tight one. I miss you.'

'Miss you too, Daddy.'

And she disappeared. Nick imagined Callie hovering near his daughter, snatching up the phone, spiriting Ruby away to do something else, something that wasn't anything to do with Nick. Then he imagined Ruby wrapping her arms around herself and pretending it was him, just like he'd taught her to do when all this began, and he felt a potent mix of contentment and sadness. He was about to hang up when Callie spoke.

'Nick?'

'Um, yeah?'

'I'm going to ask Laura to drop Ruby off with you.'

'Right. Though I can always come and pick her up from yours. Save Laura the bother.'

Laura was Callie's best friend. She'd once been *their* friend, but she'd understandably stuck with Callie since the split. Laura being involved with passing Ruby from hand to hand was becoming a more frequent occurrence.

'No, it's not convenient.'

Nick tried to suppress a sigh. 'Listen, Callie. I... I don't mind. If he's there.'

Callie made a soft noise that could have been a laugh if it hadn't sounded so weary. 'Nick. We've been there before, haven't we? Let's not pretend...'

Nick grimaced as he remembered a handful of frosty exchanges with Justin at the front door, which had once bordered on a toe-to-toe row.

'That was ages ago. I don't see why—'

'No. Nick, no. It's easier if Laura comes to you. She'll be there at ten on Saturday.'

And the line went dead. Nick sat for a moment, looking at the black screen, contemplating. Then he took a deep, steady breath, put the phone in his pocket and got out of the van.

Inside the bungalow, he could hear hoots of laughter from the living room.

'Oh, Travis, you daft bugger! Pardon my French,' came the voice of his nanna, and as he rounded the doorway, he saw what all the fuss was about. His octogenarian nanna was standing in the middle of the room wearing a T-shirt with a wild cat on the front and the slogan: *Cougar on the Prowl*. It was embellished with glitter, rhinestones and all manner of bejewelment, making Nick wonder if it might weigh more than the woman herself.

'Travis, man, you can't be giving her that,' he said, shaking his head and suppressing a smile.

Nanna laughed and did a little twirl for them. It wasn't the first time Travis had brought her a little gift from his online emporium – she had all kinds of bling, from her designer walking stick to a Mulberry clutch that she never dared take out of its wrapping.

Travis stood back with his balled fist under his chin, like a fashion designer critiquing his latest work on a model. 'I think it needs a scarf,' he said, reaching into the bag he'd brought with him and producing a filmy leopard-print scarf that he draped artfully around her neck. He gave his creation a chef's kiss.

'Ooh, I'll have to put a bit of lippy on for this afternoon, if I'm wearing this get-up,' said Nanna, plucking at the scarf and looking in the mirror above the fireplace.

'You're going to wear this at the Kitchen?' said Nick, raising an eyebrow.

'Why not?' said Nanna. 'It's snazzy.'

'Yeah, Nick. It's snazzy,' agreed Travis with a sly nod.

Nick pinched the bridge of his nose. 'Nanna, do you even know what a *cougar* is?'

She looked down at the top. 'Well, it's a big cat. Like a leopard. Lovely-looking animal.'

Travis looked at Nick with wide, innocent eyes. 'Yes, Nick. I don't know what you're suggesting about this *majestic creature.*'

Nick gave him a withering look and was about to explain to his nanna that she was a walking advert for gentleman callers when she gave them both a knowing wink, a mischievous smile playing across her lips.

'I'm not as green as I'm cabbage-looking, you two. Now, Nicky, before I forget – I promised I'd bring *Wolf Hall* for Deirdre to borrow. Would you fetch it from the bookcase in the spare room for me, pet, while I get my shoes on?'

Nick decided he could address the sartorial issue again in the van and left Nanna with Travis, coaxing her feet into her slip-on suede boots in the hallway, ready for her lift into the Community Kitchen.

He went into the spare bedroom and looked at the heaving bookcases. He scanned through the one nearer the door, but he couldn't see the title he needed. The second bookcase was stacked to the rafters, books even on top of the bookcase itself. He took one look at it and was glad he'd fitted those furniture straps to the back a few years ago – Nanna's favourite thing to hoard was books, and these bookcases would weigh a ton.

He looked down the rows, spotted the hefty tome in a lower shelf and bent to get it. It was jammed tight between two other books, unsurprisingly, so he ragged a little at the cover to pull it free.

As the book came loose and the neighbouring volumes flopped together, there was an ominous twang from behind the bookcase. He barely had time to stand up and put his arms out before the bookcase creaked and fell forward, books cascading onto his head before the bookcase itself landed on him with a crash.

There was a flurry of noise from the doorway as Travis ran in.

'Oh my God! Are you dead?'

Nick felt the weight of the bookcase lift off him – a not inconsiderable weight, but after the books had tumbled out, not enough to cause internal organ damage at least. He sat up, shaking his head in shock and giving silent thanks that his nanna had chosen to buy her bookcases from IKEA and not from an antique shop specialising in hardwood furniture.

'Seriously, are you alright?' said Travis, his face pale, as he dusted books off him. By this time, Nanna had appeared in the doorway.

'I'm fine,' Nick said, standing up and wriggling his arms and legs to make sure he was, actually, fine. Nothing felt broken or too sore. 'Bloody strap broke, with all the books stacked on it.'

Travis fingered a hole in the plaster – the strap hadn't broken but had come entirely out of the wall. Nick felt a pang of guilt at his own workmanship. He did most of the odd jobs around the bungalow and he'd screwed that in himself. But then again, he'd never expected the bookcase to be stacked like it was going for a Guinness World Record.

'Well,' he sighed, looking at the mess. 'We'd better get this cleared up. Nanna, go and sit down – we'll sort it out.'

'I will,' she said. 'And mind you put the books back where they were. I've got a system.' She disappeared.

'*System?*' said Nick, helping Travis fully upright the bookcase and put it back against the wall. 'It was stacked like feckin' Jenga.'

'Pardon *your* French. Well, let's see if we can get it tidied for now.'

They gathered up the books, putting them back into the shelves wherever they would fit, finding they had a massive excess at the end, which they stacked neatly by the wall.

'She'll not be happy about that,' said Travis.

'Well, she's just nearly killed her own grandson, so she'll have to lump it.'

Back in the living room, Nanna was standing at the mirror, carefully blotting her freshly applied lipstick with a tissue, which she then folded and slipped into her handbag.

'It's sorted,' said Nick. 'But what possessed you to cram that many books into the case? It was an accident waiting to happen. God forbid it had landed on you, Nanna. You'd have been squashed flat!'

'It has nothing to do with me. I had a lassie over this week, from the paper. She was interviewing me for an article. She helped put the books away.'

'Well, "help" isn't the word I'd be using,' said Nick, rubbing his ribs, which were now starting to feel a little sore. 'They were halfway to the ceiling on the top of the bookcase. And what do you mean *interview*?'

'She was a *journalist*. She's after doing a story about the Community Kitchen. She's coming along this afternoon actually. You'll meet her.'

'I'll be glad to,' said Nick, more than a little grumpily. 'I'd like to give her a lesson in safe weight distribution.'

'You'll do no such thing.'

Nick sighed. 'Fine. I'll come back later to fix the wall, but in the meantime, is there anything else she's made into a safety hazard before we go?'

'Not that I know of.'

'Good,' said Nick. 'Come on – let's get to the Kitchen for your shift.'

Nanna stood up and rearranged her scarf again, heading for the front door. 'Yes, let's get ourselves away. This cougar wants releasing into the wild.'

As she ambled down the path, she gave a little shimmy, as best she could while leaning on her cane, and Nick and Travis exchanged a look.

'What have I done?' whispered Travis.

They entered the Community Kitchen to the usual fanfare of Edie's arrival. Her visits were almost ceremonial these days, since she couldn't do as much as she used to due to her hip, and she was treated like a guest of honour each time she came. She always batted away the attention, but Nick noticed a little glow of happiness about her from just being in the building.

They'd managed to find a space in the small car park and had walked the short distance to the red-brick building, criss-crossed with dark beams, sporting a large brass sign bearing the Community Kitchen's name. Once inside, Edie was greeted with hugs and handshakes from staff and diners alike, and once she'd received everyone, she piped up, 'Right! Where's me pinny?'

Nick breathed a sigh of relief as she strapped the apron over her lewd T-shirt, and watched her slide comfortably into her role behind the serving counter. It was mid-afternoon, but the Kitchen served all day. The day of a homeless person didn't always run to conventional mealtimes, so Edie had insisted since the start that hot food would be available all day. She smiled up at a tall man wearing a thin tracksuit jacket and a flat cap, greeted him by name – one of many regulars to the Kitchen – and dished him up some pasta.

There was a tap on Nick's shoulder, and he turned around to see Cath, one of Nanna's longest-serving volunteers. She was about sixty, with dark brown skin and short-clipped black hair, and missing teeth at the sides of her broad smile.

'Now then, young man,' she said, pulling him in for a cuddle. 'I haven't seen you in here for a while.'

'Hiya, Cath,' he said, giving her a squeeze. 'I know, I know. I've been snowed under.'

'Jobs coming out of your ears? Well, that's never a bad thing.'

'Yeah, something like that.' He smiled and scratched his head. 'How's the family?'

'Well, last week I became a great-grandma. I don't look old enough, do I?' she said with a wink.

'You must have been a teenage bride, Cath,' he said, and she batted his arm.

'And your Ruby, how old will she be now?'

'About to turn six.'

'Ah, that's a lovely age. Make the most of it, Nick – you'll never get these years back.' She patted him on the arm. 'Anyway, I need to go and help your nanna. Lovely to see you, pet.'

She walked off, and Nick held his smile until she'd gone a few paces. It collapsed like a punctured soufflé as he allowed himself to think about the time he wasn't ever going to get back with Ruby. The days she spent with a family that now didn't include him. But then he straightened himself up and decided to do what he usually did when he felt these thoughts creep in. He looked for a job to do.

Nanna, in between cheerfully loading plates with food from the huge serving dishes under the heat lamp, tasked him with seeing to the handle on the walk-in freezer, which was getting a bit stiff. After retrieving some tools from the van, he set to work taking the handle apart and seeing what he could do – a glazier he might be, but he was pretty handy with most things. He'd only just oiled the components and put it all back together when he heard a commotion coming from out front.

He went through to see Travis helping a lad, who was maybe in his mid-twenties, into a seat in the dining area. He had light brown skin and close-cropped black hair, and was bleeding from both nostrils. He had the beginnings of a purple swelling under his eye. As he wilted into the seat, the entire staff swarmed towards him, including Nanna, leaning on her stick.

Cath sucked in an audible breath and outpaced everyone. 'Liam, what happened?' She held his cheeks and looked at his bloodied face.

'I'm fine, Grandma. It's nothing.'

'I found him outside,' said Travis, a little out of breath. 'There were some wrong'uns chasing him. I scared them off.'

Liam looked up at him briefly. 'Cheers, mate,' he said quietly then winced in pain.

'Never mind *I'm fine*,' clucked Cath, giving Edie a look that spoke from one grandma to another. 'What have you been getting into now?' she asked. Her tone was mostly sympathetic but Nick noted weariness too.

Liam rolled his eyes, but then seeing Cath's assertive stare, his cheeks coloured. 'I was just minding my own business.'

Cath's nostrils flared, and Edie touched her arm.

'Well, I think you'll live,' Edie said, 'but we best get you checked over at the hospital. Nicky, could you take him?'

'Yeah, no bother.'

Liam looked up at him with a cowed expression and hunched shoulders. 'Cheers,' he said again, barely audible.

The other staff started to disperse now that the situation appeared to be under control, and the gawking diners returned to their meals. Nick went over to help him up.

'How's about we get you cleaned up first, eh?' said Nanna. 'Pop him through the back and we'll see to this bleeding.'

'Okay,' said Travis, stepping forward eagerly. He always revelled in a crisis. 'We'll sort it, Nanna; you get back to what you were doing.'

Edie nodded and went back behind the counter, to murmurs of 'What lovely lads she's got'.

Cath rubbed Liam's head and patted his cheek gently. 'I'd best phone your mother.'

Liam groaned. 'Grandma, I'm twenty-four. I don't need to be treated like a bairn.'

'I'll be the judge of that,' she replied, reaching for her mobile phone.

Nick and Travis helped him through to the staff bathroom out back, where he sat on the toilet lid. Travis went to get the first aid kit, while Nick dampened some paper towels and passed them to the patient.

'If your mam's anything like your grandma, you might have a bit of explaining to do.'

Liam's mouth set in a grim line and he nodded.

'Do you make a habit of this then?' Nick asked.

'Trouble seems to find me,' Liam said, shrugging and pressing the paper towel to his eye.

Nick seemed to remember overhearing snatches of conversation between Cath and other kitchen staff, when she'd grumbled about one of her grandsons being a bit of a handful. He'd heard later that he was a little more than a 'handful' and had been occasionally in trouble with the law for stealing.

'You know, there's a bit of this drama that I'd love to know a bit more about,' Nick said.

Liam looked at him and waited.

'I'd like to know how the hell my little brother managed to frighten off a gang of rat boys?'

Liam's face broke into a grin, which immediately made him wince in pain. 'He ran at them, screaming.' He shook his head. 'They didn't know what to do so they just scattered.'

Travis, by now, had come back in holding the first aid box and rolled his eyes. 'It's actually a recognised technique for self-defence,' he said archly. 'Making so much noise that it draws attention.'

Nick raised an eyebrow. 'Well, that was a bit of a gamble. What would you have done if they *hadn't* run away?'

'Kick to the nuts?'

'Fair enough. Right, let's have a look in here.' Nick rifled through the first aid kit and found some cotton pads. 'Here, hold these under your nose,' he said, giving them to Liam.

Travis plucked a tube of antiseptic cream from the box, unscrewed the lid and started dabbing it on the grazes on Liam's forehead.

'Ah, man, I'm alright,' snapped Liam, batting Travis's hand away, his face breaking into a scowl. The tube of antiseptic cream went flying. 'Listen, I've got stuff to do. Just let me out the back door and tell me grandma I've got a taxi or something.'

Nick shook his head. 'Sorry, mate, but I'm not incurring the wrath of both Cath and my nanna. Or I'll end up looking worse than you.'

Travis stood back with his arms folded, looking offended that his attempts at nursing had been rebuffed, but he joined Nick in taking Liam by the arms and encouraging him to stand up.

'Ha'way,' said Nick gently. 'Or none of us will hear the end of it.'

Liam sighed and nodded, allowing himself to be led from the bathroom. On the way out, Nick felt the squish of the antiseptic tube under his foot as he accidentally stepped on it, and he kicked it out of the way.

They shepherded Liam out of the back exit, to save him being put on show again – much to the relief of Cath, who, after giving Liam a gentle hug had pretty much barred the door back into the dining room – then loaded him into the van. As Nick reversed, he noticed a black Golf parked next to him that hadn't been there before. It looked vaguely familiar, he thought fleetingly, but then his attention was drawn to his reluctant passenger, the blood oozing through the gauze pads, and the traffic between them and the Royal Victoria Infirmary.

SEVEN

WREN

Wren parked up between a battered old Fiesta and a workman's van and brushed herself down before heading into the Community Kitchen. She was wearing her standard-issue journalist outfit of a trouser suit and modest heels which, with the addition of some red lipstick and some bigger earrings, would double as an outfit for Libby's book launch event that evening, which she'd promised to attend despite it being a bit of a rush. The bruise on her forehead had faded just enough to be disguised with make-up, so thankfully she'd been able to ditch the embarrassing hat.

She took a few pictures of the outside of the building then went inside. The dining area, with it being mid-afternoon, was sparsely filled, and there were a few volunteers milling around the tables, chatting to the diners. One young member of staff was scrubbing at the floor beside a table. Was that... blood?

She scanned the room for Edie. The place was both familiar and unfamiliar – she remembered the general layout from when she volunteered years ago, but the tables themselves looked new, the decor had changed, and there were artworks and photography framed on the walls. It looked fresh and invigorated – this place was most definitely a thriving concern.

She spied Edie behind the counter, chatting to another member of staff while they checked over the trays of warm food, shifting chips and pasta around under the heat lamps.

'Oh, Wren, pet! Here you are,' said Edie, beaming.

She noticed Wren glancing at the bloodied floor. 'Don't you worry about that. Not an unusual thing to happen here, as you can imagine. Now, would you like a cuppa before I show you around?'

'Oh. Yes please,' said Wren. 'Actually, can I just pop to the loo before we get started?'

'Of course, pet – oh, hang on. Cath, are the boys still in the staff toilets?'

A woman standing by the 'Staff Only' door shook her head. 'No, they've headed off to the hospital now.'

Wren's eyebrows twitched upwards.

'Like I said, nothing to worry about,' said Edie breezily. 'It sounds like the facilities are all yours. I'll put the kettle on.'

Wren nodded and headed for the door she was directed to, which led to a staff area and a loo marked with the male and female stick figures of a unisex bathroom. She went inside, had a hasty wee and washed her hands, noticing an open first aid kit on the vanity unit and a few rolls of bandage strewn about. 'The boys' clearly hadn't tidied up after whatever kind of first aid had been administered here.

She took a step back from the mirror, smoothing her hair, and looked down to see a puddle of white cream on the floor, and a squashed tube of antiseptic nearby.

'Well, that would be ironic,' she murmured as she bundled up some paper towels and bent down to clean it up. Slipping and breaking your neck on something that was designed to improve your health would be very unfortunate indeed. She bundled up the paper towels and put them in the bin, then turned on her heel towards the door.

She put one heeled shoe on an unrolled strip of crêpe bandage, and the next thing she knew she was flat on her back with a searing pain in the back of her head. She'd clipped the edge of the toilet seat as she'd gone down.

Edging up onto her elbows, she winced at the pain in her skull and also the mortifying feeling of lying flat on her back on a public toilet floor. Nearby, she could see a pair of slim metal tuff cut scissors from the first aid kit that must have been under the sodding bandage. Her face glowed with shame at landing flat on her arse, even though there was nobody to witness it, and she got up.

The mirror revealed a rush of blood to the cheeks but thankfully none exiting the body. She tapped the back of her head gingerly. Another lump to replace the one that had only just disappeared at the front. She thought back to Alex insisting she should get head injuries checked out. *Not another visit to the walk-in centre*, she thought, giving herself a shake. *I am not falling to pieces; I'm just having some bad luck. It is perfectly normal for a human being to suffer mild injury from time to time. Isn't it?*

Pushing her shoulders back, she took a deep breath, gathered up the bandages and scissors into the first aid kit, and headed back to the dining room.

Edie was waiting for her, having taken her apron off and emerged from behind the counter, and she was wearing quite a suggestive T-shirt. It was enough to take Wren's mind off her tender skull, and her eyebrows rose for the second time that afternoon.

Edie gave an impish smile and handed her a mug of tea. 'Excuse the T-shirt, pet. I like to indulge my grandsons' sense of humour. Even if they don't realise it.'

'Ah.'

She brushed at the rhinestones. 'Besides, I like the jazzy bits, and as long as my pinny's covering the *message* most of the time, then none of these fellas will get the wrong idea.'

A bearded man in a beanie hat looked up from his plate of pasta and winked.

Edie narrowed her eyes and pointed a finger at him. 'It's fellas like you I'm talking about, Lenny,' she said with a twinkle in her eye. 'Come on, Wren – I'll give you the tour.'

Wren sipped her tea as she followed Edie around, listening as Edie described the updates they'd made, the donors who'd bequeathed them money for renovations, and the volunteers who'd given their time to clean, paint and decorate. Not once did she pat herself on the back for any of it – it was always down to the efforts of someone else.

They passed by a wall decorated with a collage of photos, protected and framed by a rectangle of Perspex. There were pictures of various vintages, smiling faces, young and old. Wren's eyes rested upon a picture of Edie looking younger, with an even younger woman beside her and two little boys in front. The slightly older child was dressed as Buzz Lightyear and grinning with his eyes shut, and the littler one had his arms crossed in a pose reminiscent of boy bands from the nineties. She touched it with her finger. 'Are these your grandsons?'

Edie beamed. 'That's right. And that's my daughter, Tracey. You might meet the boys if they come back later. But Tracey's out somewhere in the Caribbean right now. She's been doing the cruise ships for nearly twenty years now. I'm very proud.'

Wren did some quick maths. 'Your grandsons must have still been very young while she was away.'

'That's right, pet. They lived with me.'

'Wow. So you were running this place, bringing up two... teenagers, would they have been?'

She nodded. 'That's right. But I wasn't doing it alone. Now

come on, *Wrenata*, and you can meet some of the people who *really* keep this place afloat.'

Wren laughed. 'I told you, it's just Wren.'

'Well, I suppose that isn't out of the question. Being named after a bird isn't that unusual – our milkman's called Robin.'

Wren smiled and shook her head. She went to change the subject but paused. Maybe it was Edie's natural warmth or her years of caring and counselling, but Wren felt she was one of the rare people to whom she could give an honest answer. 'Okay. Full disclosure, and I'm only telling you this because I like you. My full name is Serenity. But nobody calls me that anymore.'

'Serenity!' Edie clapped her hands together. 'See, I knew it must be something. Do you know, I'm sure I met someone once whose daughter was called Serenity. You don't hear it much. I'm sure it was here, in the Kitchen.' Her eyes went a little hazy as she seemed to search her memory.

Wren looked at her in surprise. No, you *didn't* hear it much. At all. In fact, she'd never met anyone else who shared her name.

'When was that?'

'Oh, it was years ago, pet.' Edie still seemed to be filtering through her recollections, and her expression was briefly troubled. Then it cleared like a break in the clouds, and she smiled. 'I might be mistaken, of course. In fact, maybe it was Felicity – or Serena.' She chuckled and avoided Wren's eye.

Wren's journalistic senses piqued, fuelled by a sudden curiosity that was much more personal than professional.

'It's an unusual name, isn't it?' she said carefully. 'My family's lived around here our whole lives. Can I show you something?' She reached into her handbag, retrieving one of the few photos she had of her family – her mam, dad and herself as a baby.

'Do you recognise anyone? Not the baby obviously – that's me. But my mam or dad?'

Edie scrutinised the picture, narrowing her eyes and lips. She seemed to think for a long time.

'You know, I think I *might* remember. I think I recognise your dad's face. Yes, I see it now. I could have met him anywhere, of course.'

'But you said before, you thought it was at the Kitchen. Do you think that might be it?'

'It might well be. Why don't you ask your dad, pet? I'm so sorry I can't remember more.' She smiled over-brightly. 'Now, come with me, I've saved the best bit 'til last.'

Wren followed Edie, slotting the photo back into her bag. She would definitely ask her dad about this – it would be such a strange coincidence if he'd been here too, and odd that he hadn't mentioned it when she'd volunteered here herself.

'We added this on a few years back,' said Edie, ushering Wren through a door. 'Sometimes people need more than just hot dinners.'

It was a spacious room with various zones – comfy seating areas with colourful cushions, a desk with a display of leaflets and resources for help with accommodation and financial assistance, and two computers. There was a station for making your own tea and coffee, and an area that had information about jobs and opportunities. The room had a few visitors, all women, other than an older man at one of the computers, and the atmosphere was both peaceful and studious.

'We found that some folk, especially people newly home-less, would know how to find us but didn't have a clue where to go next. So we put all this together. An education suite, if you like.'

'I get it. So this can point people in the right direction to start getting back on their feet.'

'That's right. Some people have got enough on their bloody

plate – pardon my French, and the pun – without having to do the circuit of municipal buildings trying to figure out where they can get help. So at least we can give them a starting point.'

Wren nodded.

On the sofa were two women, talking quietly but intensely. Other than their state of dress – one slightly shabby, the other smarter – they mirrored one another in their body language, and they looked like they knew each other well. The conversation seemed to come to an end, and they stood up and hugged, then the more down-at-heel woman pulled a rucksack over her shoulder and said goodbye to Edie too as she passed.

'Ta-ra, pet,' she said then turned to Wren. 'Come and meet Ailsa.'

Ailsa, the smarter woman, sat back down on the sofa. Her hair was cropped short, and she was wearing leggings and a black jumper.

'Ailsa, this is Wren. She's writing a piece on the Community Kitchen for the paper.'

Wren shook Ailsa's hand. 'Lovely to meet you. Edie's being modest – the piece is about her really.'

Edie waved her hand. 'Nonsense. Like I said, none of this is just down to me.'

Ailsa rolled her eyes good-naturedly. 'Wren, you'll never get her to admit otherwise. Many have tried and failed.'

'*Anyway*,' said Edie loudly, 'I'm introducing you to Ailsa because she's one of the regular counsellors we have coming to the Kitchen to talk to people if they want it. We try to have someone on hand most of the time.'

'I see,' said Wren, taking out her notepad. 'So, do you find you're quite busy, Ailsa?'

Edie and Ailsa exchanged a wry smile. 'I'd say. In fact, I'll have to make my excuses, I'm afraid.' She gestured to the doorway, where a member of staff had ushered in a young woman, dressed in a stained puffa jacket and with eyes like a frightened animal.

'It's a very short journey,' Ailsa said to Wren. 'When you're struggling, life gets very small. The bad things that happen feel much worse, and the good things feel much more significant. So when you're treated kindly it leaves more of a mark.'

Ailsa got up and touched the girl's arm gently, leading her towards another seating area. She looked no more than a teenager and shied away a little as the woman who'd brought her through handed her a mug of hot tea. Wren could see Ailsa talking gently to her, radiating warmth.

'This is amazing, Edie,' said Wren. 'It's a safe haven already, and to have professionals on site too...'

'Do you want to know what's really amazing?' said Edie, giving her a sideways look. 'Ailsa used to come here when *she* was homeless.'

Wren blinked. She looked at Ailsa, well put together, self-assured, a professional counsellor. Helping others, when she'd once come here for help herself.

'She wanted to give something back, and to help others in her situation. And she's not the only one. We have Farida who was coming here for a while for help – now she has a job and a flat, and comes here a few times a week to run a book club. Some of the serving staff used to be diners here too.'

Wren looked around. So many of these volunteers were women and girls. Maybe she didn't need to worry about casting her net so wide and finding hidden gems all over the North East for her series. It seemed like she'd found a treasure chest right under her nose.

'Edie? Do you think it would be okay if I came back a few more times? I think it might be good if I could speak to a few other people too.'

'I thought you'd never ask. As it goes, we're having a little do at the Kitchen this Friday. It's our fortieth anniversary. So you can get your glad rags on and do a bit of mingling at the same time.'

'Amazing, I'd love that.'

Edie smiled, her eyes twinkling. 'And I'd like you to meet my grandson, too. He's a smashing lad, and I don't see a ring on your finger.'

'Oh! I'm taken,' Wren said, her face warming up. 'Although I'm sure he's lovely.'

'Well, that's a shame.'

Wren opened her mouth, almost ready to say, 'It is,' and then snapped it shut again. Where had that come from?

Wren half ran up to the bookshop where Alex was waiting outside, leaning up against the window and scrolling on his phone. She'd only just had time to run into the coffee shop next to the Community Kitchen to grab a sandwich before heading over. She'd been too starving to skip dinner, and the book launch would only have a handful of cupcakes and bowls of crisps to soak up the wine, so she'd run in, bought a sandwich, thrown a pound in the direction of the tip jar to thank them for assembling it so quickly and hoofed it out of there, cramming it into her mouth.

'Have I got mayonnaise on my face?' she asked Alex by way of greeting.

'Nice to see you too,' he said, tilting his head to one side.

'Sorry. I've just had a mad rush to get here.' She pecked him on the cheek.

'No mayonnaise that I can see,' he said. 'Listen, can we make this quick? An in-and-out job? I'm knackered.'

Wren's face fell. 'We're here for Libby. I don't want her to think we don't care.'

'I know, but it's a bit boring, isn't it? At least we'll show our faces.'

Wren tried to keep her expression passive. It wouldn't bode well to get into a fight before they'd even arrived. Maybe he would get into it once they were inside.

'Okay, well, let's just see how we go?' She pasted on a bright smile and led the way inside.

The shop was bustling with more guests than available chairs, and Jenson, Libby's assistant bookseller, was being dispatched to the off-licence for some more bottles of white wine. Libby saw Wren through the throng and waved excitedly over the top of a sea of heads. Wren could just make out the author holding up his book for people to take photos.

Alex shoved his hands into his pockets and declined the offer of wine from a passing helper with a tray of glasses, and Wren considered taking two.

'We're supporting Libby most of all,' she said. 'She's our friend. And the book looks really interesting, to be fair.'

Alex snorted and picked up a copy from a nearby table. '*In Pursuit of Boyhood*,' he said disdainfully, reading the title of Max Pearson's debut novel, then flipped it over to read the blurb. 'Blah blah, discovery of a childhood secret, blah blah, semi-autobiographical. Sounds like self-indulgent shite.' He tossed the book back onto the table, and Wren snatched it up, feeling heat in her face as she glanced to check nobody had seen.

'Don't be so rude,' she whispered. 'I'd better buy this copy, since you've dog-eared it, throwing it about.'

He rolled his eyes and retrieved his phone from his pocket, as if he had better things to be doing. 'It's just a book, Wren. Don't be so precious.'

Wren's nostrils flared. 'Just because you don't like something doesn't mean it isn't important to other people.' She was about to add that he wouldn't take too kindly to someone slagging off the selection of protein shakes at the gym but noted the twitch in his jaw muscle and let it go. Before he had a chance to reply, there was a parting of the crowd, and Libby emerged, looking gorgeous in a boldly patterned maternity wrap dress, her red curls like an explosion on her head.

'Guys! Thanks so much for coming. I can't believe how busy it is.' She looked shiny-eyed with excitement, and Wren felt a swell of happiness for her friend. She deserved all of this and more.

'It's amazing, Lib,' she said, hugging her and kissing her cheek.

'Yeah, well done,' said Alex, sounding, to Wren's relief, reasonably sincere. Alex, for all his misgivings about literature and 'self-indulgent' writers, was fond of Libby.

'You have to come and meet Max. He's just lovely, and he really deserves all this attention. The book is... *mwah*.' She mimed a chef's kiss and dragged Wren through the crowd, Alex loping along behind.

He hovered impatiently while Wren was introduced as a fellow writer, and she asked a few questions for a small piece that she'd write for the paper. She took a few photos of him with her phone, posing with his book and with Libby, then asked him to sign the copy she was about to buy.

Max signed it happily, and they stood for a while chatting about the concept of the book and his experience of writing it. Alex continued to hover nearby, oozing irritability. Eventually, at a polite juncture, Wren wrapped up the conversation and turned to Jenson, who was taking payment for Max's books. He was wearing a tweed jacket and a bow tie, and had waxed the tips of his little moustache for the occasion.

She fished around in her purse for some cash and noticed something was missing. A souvenir penny from her dad's lighthouse; the kind you put through a penny press to emboss the tourist attraction's logo on. She'd had it for years. After a moment's thought, she realised she must have thrown it in the tip jar at the cafe. She felt a pang of guilt, not just for the poor barista who would go without a tip but for her dad, who had given the penny to her. It was too late to get it back now, but, on the upside, she thought the penny might at least bring in a new visitor to the lighthouse.

'All done?' Alex asked, face stony as he bore her away from the book-signing table.

Wren nodded, tucking her purse away, and took another sip of wine. 'At least for work purposes anyway.'

'Let's go then.'

'We've only been here for half an hour, Alex.'

'Yes, and you've got what you came for, so let's go.'

'But we're here for Libby too. We can't leave yet – she'll be offended.'

'Libby won't mind. We've shown our faces, so we've done our bit.' He took her hand and started to lead her towards the door, but she pulled back.

'Alex, she's our friend.'

At that moment, Jenson appeared at her side. 'Wren, are you off? I just wanted to ask if you're taking those flowers or if you want me to throw them out. They're looking a bit tired.'

'What flowers?' said Alex.

'From the glazier?' said Jenson. 'After the *incident*.' He had a habit of saying most things in an arch way, and in this context, the word sounded vaguely lascivious.

'You mean the bump to the head? You didn't say he'd bought you flowers.' Alex's voice was light, but his smile was tense.

Wren could sense where this was going. It wouldn't be the first time he'd questioned her intentions where other men were concerned. When they'd first got together, she'd thought of it as protectiveness – a sign that she meant so much to him. A little part of her had liked it. But as time went on, she'd begun to suspect that he wasn't putting her on a pedestal anymore. Instead, it felt like he was trying to put a cage around her.

'Um, thanks, but you can throw them away,' she said, and Jenson shrugged and walked off. She pinched the bridge of her nose, took a deep breath and turned her attention to Alex. 'I didn't *not* tell you about the flowers. I just didn't remember.'

He said nothing for a moment. 'Right. And you forgot to bring them home too.'

'Alex, I wasn't trying to *hide* them,' she said, her voice becoming reedy with frustration. 'I didn't bloody want them.'

'Mm-hmm.' He looked pointedly at his watch. 'Anyway. It's getting late. And I've got work in the morning.'

Wren faltered. She considered all the times she'd gone to awful events at the gym – 'parties' full of hard-bodied health freaks, ignoring the buffet and droning on about macros and spirulina. She'd stood there for hours at a time, pretending to be interested in the latest generation of kettlebells. Why couldn't Alex just give her one night in return?

'No,' she said. 'I think I'll stay.'

Alex's face was neutral. He looked over at the crowd hovering around Max and waited a beat before saying, 'Fine. I'll see you at home.' Then he turned without kissing her and left.

Trying to ignore the leaden feeling in her stomach, Wren downed the remainder of her wine, picked up another glass and headed back into the party.

Some time later, Wren's phone vibrated in her bag. She didn't notice it as she was having such a nice time circulating and talking to people. But she would read the message later.

If you think I didn't see the way you looked at that 'writer' twat, then you're wrong. I'll know if you've slept with him.

EIGHT

NICK

The guy with the spaniel was on the beach again, throwing a ball for the lolloping animal. Its paws splashed wet sand all over the place as it dashed in and out of the shallows, salty water dripping from its mouth as it retrieved the ball. Nick pushed his hands into his pockets and watched him for a while, at the same time as keeping half an eye on Ruby. She was prodding around in a rock pool with her toy lobster under her arm. He'd won it for her at a funfair a few months back and she'd decided to call him Ian.

'I saw them here the other day,' he said to Laura, realising as he did that he wasn't referring to the man and his dog. Laura was bending down and stretching her hamstrings, clad in Lycra as usual. 'Callie and Ruby. And Justin.'

'Ah. And how did that go?' she asked, looking up at him. She'd asked if she could come along in the van when she dropped Ruby off at the flat, saying she was going to run on the beach then go to a hot yoga class while she waited, and she was just limbering up before she left them.

'It didn't. I, um... I didn't want to interrupt,' he lied, remembering how he'd raced along the promenade only to watch them drive away. He smiled tightly. 'Anyway. It is what it is.'

Laura grinned. 'As they say on *Love Island*.'

'Ha. The irony,' he replied, scuffing his foot on the sand.

The man with the spaniel was in the distance now, and Ruby was kneeling in the sand digging a hole with a plastic spade Nick had bought for her.

'You met anyone nice?' she asked with an attempt at nonchalance.

Nick doubted she was asking on behalf of Callie – Laura was just naturally nosy. She had her hands on her hips, rotating her torso from side to side.

'Nah. There's only one girl for me.' He nodded to Ruby. 'How about you?'

She smiled an enigmatic smile. 'There might be someone...'

Nick raised an eyebrow. 'Go on then – tell me more.'

'It's early days, but... who knows?'

'Ah well, be mysterious then. But I'm happy for you, whoever they are.'

She pulled her foot up behind her then did the same with the other one, looking off up the beach with the beginnings of determination. 'Cheers. Anyway, I'm ready for the off. I'll be back at about two. That okay?'

'Yeah, two o'clock's good. See you later.' She was running before he'd even finished talking, her blonde ponytail bobbing up and down.

'Alright, kiddo?' he said, scuffing down the sand towards his daughter. She got up off her knees and slid a sandy palm into his.

'I love the beach, Daddy. It's my best place, I think.'

'Is that right? What do you love most about it then?'

'The ice creams,' she said, laughing.

'Ah, you can get ice creams anywhere! That's not the reason.'

She looked up at him with big eyes, and he knew he'd be making a trip to the cafe for two cones before the next half hour was out. Knowing the effect those eyes had on him, he'd be out for an extra scoop for Ian the Lobster too.

'Okay then, seashells.'

'Seashells? I see. Shall we find you some to take back to your mam's then?'

'Yes! Let's go and see. Justin likes purple – there might be some purple ones.'

Nick's jaw tensed reflexively, and he made a conscious effort to smile, forcing a softness into his eyes that was pure pretence. 'Brilliant! Let's see what we can find then.'

They trawled back and forth along the beach, scouring the sand, holding up bits they found and discarding anything that didn't make the grade. Every time Ruby found a good shell she squealed with excitement and rushed up to Nick to show him her spoils. Nick found her a tiny white curly shell, which she was mesmerised by, and also the shell of a razor clam. Soon, her pockets were stuffed with the vacated homes of sea creatures.

Nick saw a decent-sized shell and bent down to pick it up. He blew the sand out of its curved interior, revealing a deep lilac colour, and paused for a moment, looking back and forth from the shell to his daughter, bent over a pile of stones she was picking through. He hesitated then crouched down next to her.

'Here you go,' he said, handing her the shell. 'A purple one.'

She took it and her face lit up. 'You found one! I was looking everywhere. Justin will be happy.'

I know, darlin'. And so will you.

Two o'clock came too soon, and after driving Laura and Ruby back to Laura's car, he found himself getting back in the van and driving into Newcastle, not wanting to just sit in the flat with the vacuum left by his daughter. He parked in the

Community Kitchen car park (feeling a twinge of guilt, but parking in town was expensive and hard to find) and wandered into the city centre.

He bought a doll for Ruby, one of those that drinks water and pees, already looking forward to giving it to her at his next visit. As he worked his way through the department store, he found himself standing over a bedding set in baby blue, Ruby's favourite colour, and wished he could buy that too. But he had no reason to. Callie had refused to let Ruby come and stay with him, even if he gave up his bed and slept on the sofa. Which was fair enough, he supposed. It wasn't ideal.

On reflection, 'less than ideal' was an understatement. He thought about how the split had unfolded. It had begun with his glazing business taking a turn for the worse – through bad luck or bad judgement, jobs had dried up and money had grown tight. He and Callie had been at each other's throats with the stress of it all. And then she'd met Justin. It had taken a while for Nick to find out, and by that time, she'd hardened her heart to Nick and they were over. She'd gone off with Justin, taking Ruby with her, and the very reason they'd fallen apart – his lack of financial security – became the reason Ruby had slipped further and further away. Now that Nick had no home of his own, Callie had an excuse to limit his time with his daughter, and there was little he could do about it other than keep grafting until he could make it right.

He stood there for a while, picturing the flat he might one day afford, then forced himself to stop.

'Pack it in,' he murmured under his breath and headed for the escalators.

As he came out of the department store, he saw a familiar face in the bistro opposite. Laura was there, her elbows on the table, glass of wine in her hands. She was staring deep into the eyes of a handsome, chiselled-looking guy who was looking back at her like the world had melted away around them. *Good for you*, he thought, smiling. Nick may have been sworn off love, but he liked to be reminded that it still existed.

He wandered back to the Kitchen, paper bag in hand, and was just about to walk into the car park when he spied another familiar face in the cafe next door. Two familiar faces in fact. He pushed open the door and went inside.

Travis and Liam were sitting opposite each other at a table, Travis leaning his chin on his hand and laughing coquettishly. Liam was more smartly dressed this time and looked significantly more composed.

'Alright?' said Nick, looking at Travis askance. He'd assumed that they'd left Liam safely at the hospital and that their good deed was done. But here he was, his face now turning shades of purple and yellow, sharing a drink with his little brother.

Travis looked up at him, clearly surprised, and flashed a glance at Liam, who also appeared a bit spooked by Nick's sudden appearance. He half stood, as if he was going to bolt, then wavered and sat back down again. Nick could sense an atmosphere.

'What are you doing here?' asked Travis.

'I was going to get a coffee. But I'll not, if I'm interrupting you?'

Travis shook his head. 'No, not at all. We just bumped into each other in town. We were having a chat.'

'You feeling better now, Liam?' asked Nick, remembering his manners.

'Yeah. I'm alreet. Cheers for sorting me out.'

'I take it your mam didn't finish the job then?' Nick gestured to Liam's healing face.

'Nah,' said Liam. 'She's used to it really. Anyway, back in a minute.' He stood up and made for the customer toilets.

Once he'd gone, Nick turned to Travis. 'New pal?'

Travis rolled his eyes. 'I'm just checking in on him. His

mam's chucked him out, you know. He's staying with Cath for now.'

Nick raised his eyebrows. 'That's a bit harsh.'

'Tell me about it.' Travis paused. 'I think there might be more to it. Liam's gay, and his stepdad is... a fucking Neanderthal. All muscle and no brains, not to mention one of the dying breed of homophobes.'

'Christ,' breathed Nick. 'Poor lad. Saying that though, and no judgement, but he's in his twenties. Can he not get a place of his own?'

Travis shrugged. 'It's not easy nowadays. He says he can't get a job.'

Nick said nothing for a moment. He felt uneasy hearing about Liam's situation, a tale he'd heard from many people at the Kitchen – the last few steps before they found themselves at his nanna's door. Even though he couldn't see Cath letting her grandson down, the warning signs were still there.

'Be careful,' said Nick, after a while.

'I don't know what you mean. I'm just having a chat with the lad.'

Nick sighed. Another thing that didn't need saying was Travis's tendency to flirt outrageously and often with intent.

'He's obviously got a lot going on.' Nick tried to be diplomatic.

'You mean he's trouble.' Travis folded his arms across his chest.

'I mean he's... *troubled*.' Part of Nick wondered if being around Liam could bring Travis grief. He pictured Travis being chased down the street and thumped too, and shuddered.

Travis rolled his eyes but seemed to be taking this in. There was a flicker of uncertainty across his face, which made Nick feel a twinge of guilt for lecturing him.

'Give me a minute,' said Nick, needing time to think what to say next. 'I'm going to get a drink.'

He waited while the barista took a cup from a stack on the counter and performatively filled it at the coffee machine. Nick paid and took it back to the table, where Travis still sat alone.

They said nothing for a moment then Travis sat forward abruptly. His face flamed. 'Look, I might have a bit of a reputation for... playing the field. But just because I'm socialising with him doesn't mean anything.'

'Good. Because the lad needs help. Not complications.'

They sat there sipping their coffee for a while, Liam still in the bathroom. Nick started to worry he'd slipped out of the bathroom window. Eventually, Nick decided he'd better go check on him and stood up, swigging the last third of his coffee.

A hard lump slid from the cup, and before he could react, he felt it lodge in his throat. He panicked and dropped the mug, hearing it shatter on the floor as he clutched at his throat. Travis got up with a screech of chair legs against the floor and rushed to him.

Something was stuck in his throat, and he couldn't even muster the breath to cough. Adrenaline coursed through him, fight and flight chasing each other in circles, the hands at his throat tingling. Travis slapped him roughly on the back. He was dimly aware of a commotion around him, people getting up from nearby tables, murmurs of concern. Then suddenly, a pair of arms wrapped around him from behind and yanked sharply under his breastbone. He jerked forward and felt a rush of air as the object flew out of his mouth, a dull clink as it landed on the floor. Nick sucked in precious air, wheezing as he did, bent over and panting with his hands on his thighs.

He turned around to find Liam standing right behind him, breathless, and Travis giving Liam a look of pure admiration. Liam had just saved his life.

'Thanks,' he croaked, a word which hardly seemed enough but was all he could manage.

'Nee bother,' Liam said, then he gave a nod to Travis and sloped out of the cafe.

Travis helped Nick to his seat, and the barista brought him a glass of water.

Nick saw a coin sitting in a puddle of his own saliva. He bent down to pick it up, turning it between his fingers. A coin. But not a normal coin – it had been flattened out in one of those penny-press machines. He coughed and took a sip of water, turning the coin over in his hand. It was stamped with the logo of St Nicholas Lighthouse.

The barista's face was etched with worry, presumably in case Nick might make a complaint. He pointed to the counter where the tip jar sat next to stacks of empty cups. 'It must have fallen in. I'm really sorry. Can I offer you a complimentary biscotti?'

Nick waved him away. The very idea of eating something dry and crumbly was as unpalatable as the coin in his hand had been. He looked at it again – he seemed to remember going on a school trip to that lighthouse years ago. He slipped it into his pocket.

'I think we should get you home,' said Travis, seeming calmer now his brother wasn't facing imminent death. He craned his neck at the window, watching Liam make his way down the street.

'Come on then. The van's in the car park.'

'I'll drive,' said Travis.

'No, you won't,' Nick replied, retrieving his keys from his pocket and heading for the cafe door. The last thing he needed was to have nothing to concentrate on but his latest brush with death, so he wanted to focus on the road. He shivered as he wondered if someone up there had it in for him – and also, what kind of person left a souvenir penny as a tip?

Before they went home, they took a detour to Edie's so that Travis could drop off the dress he'd picked out for her for the Community Kitchen party. As Nick watched Travis unzip the clothing bag, he held his breath. Some of the options he'd shown Nick had been composed of Lycra, or had sheer panels that wouldn't have looked out of place on Strictly Come Dancing. With enormous relief, Travis revealed a navy blue dress with a few sequins here and there.

Edie gasped, and Nick suspected that was with relief too. 'Ooh, it's lovely,' she said, running her hands over the fabric.

'It's a showstopper, just like you, Nanna,' said Travis, with a wink.

'Behave. Now, I know you'll be gussied up to the nines,' she said to Travis. 'But have you got yourself a nice outfit, Nicky? And what about Ruby?'

Nick's stomach twisted. 'She can't come. Callie's taking her to Center Parcs. But don't worry, I'll dig out my old suit.'

'That's a shame,' said Nanna diplomatically, but she looked disappointed.

It was a shame indeed. Nick had tried to talk to Callie again about having Ruby to stay over from time to time but she'd swerved and prevaricated as normal, and now he would miss out on his weekend time with her too.

Edie patted his hand. She could always see when he was putting on a brave face.

'Right, well I'll put the kettle on. Will you pop my new dress on the spare bed, pet?'

Nick did as he was asked, but as he was about to go back to the living room something caught his eye. Underneath the bed, on the carpet, was a book, splayed open face down on the floor. He looked warily at the bookcase that had not long ago pincered him to the floor and realised he must have missed it.

Crouching down, he foraged underneath the bed frame until he put his hand on it, and as he stood up, a folded piece of

A4 paper fell from between the pages. Curious, he unfolded it and saw it was a printout of an email. For some unknown reason, his nanna was obsessed with having hard copies of everything and routinely printed out her emails, usually storing them in a folder, but this must have slipped through the net. He skimmed it, expecting it to be from a utility company or something similar, then froze.

The missive was short. But what it said knocked the wind out of Nick, and he sat down on the bed with a thump, adding yet more creases to the sequinned dress.

Dear Edie,

I hope that this reaches you. I saw a documentary about the Community Kitchen, and when I recognised Tracey I couldn't believe it. She might have told you about me, from back in the day – I'm Nicholas's dad. I hope he grew up to be a fine young man. I know this is out of the blue, but I'd like to get in touch with him. Please reply and we can discuss.

Yours, Richard

Richard. His father's name was Richard. The sender's email address was *info@ristorantegiorgio.it*. Was that Italy? His nanna had known that his dad was looking for him, and the date on the email was over a year ago.

NINE

WREN

'Hello, pet. To what do I owe the pleasure of this call?'

Wren could hear the smile in her dad's voice down the phone.

'Oh, just checking in,' she said, tapping her foot. She was sitting on the stairs, wearing an emerald-green dress she'd resurrected from the depths of her wardrobe. At the bottom of the stairs sat a pair of heels and her handbag, ready for the Community Kitchen party that night. 'And, I wanted to ask you something. Did you ever volunteer at the Community Kitchen? I've been there quite a bit for work, and Edie, the lady who runs it, thinks she might have met you. She remembered someone with a daughter called Serenity anyway.'

There was silence from the other end of the phone. It lasted long enough for Wren to take the phone away from her ear to check the screen and see if they were still connected.

'Dad?'

'I'm here. Um, you know I think I *might* have met her. Edie you say?' He went quiet again. 'Uh-huh. That's it. I met her at a function. Back in the nineties.'

'A function? That sounds fancy. What kind of function?'

Her dad had worked at the lighthouse visitors' centre for as long as she could remember. He'd hardly been in the line of work for hobnobbing.

'Might have been a wedding actually. Something in a hotel. Hang on a sec...' There was a clatter of commotion, muffled sounds of a phone being fumbled. 'I've got to go, pet. John's got into the bread bin. There's crusts everywhere.' And he rang off.

Wren looked at the black screen of her phone for a while. Was he being evasive, or was it just his usual forgetfulness and scattiness? He'd had to think for a while before coming up with an answer, but Wren supposed that he may have just been plumbing the depths of his memory. She decided to redouble her efforts and ask Edie later if a wedding rang any bells.

She was snapped from her thoughts by the front door opening. Alex came in, the atmosphere immediately awkward. She'd stayed at Libby's the night of that text, not even bothering to reply to it. He'd sent a slew of messages that night and the next morning, veering from placatory to apologetic to self-righteous.

Then, when she'd eventually come home, he'd broken down in a surprisingly repentant manner. He explained that he'd been thrown by the flowers she'd received; it had sparked a flash of jealousy that came from his deep fear of, one day, losing her. He had looked so devastated that she'd agreed to try and forget about it and move on. But since then, they'd skirted around each other. Alex acted like he was walking on thin ice, and Wren felt like the blast of chill that had frozen it. She had still not thawed.

'You look nice,' he said. 'I thought you said it was a work thing.'

'It is,' she said, dabbing on some lipstick in the hallway mirror at the same time as poking her feet into her shoes. 'But it's a formal do, so I need to look the part.' She patted her up-do, a chignon with loose strands at the front that had taken a surprising amount of time to do considering how effortless it looked.

Alex watched her in silence for a bit.

'So what time will you be back?' he asked, and she could hear the effort of lightness in his tone.

She bristled. He was doing it again. Suspecting her, even though he thought he was covering it. Still trying to be on his best behaviour, but the distrust was seeping through. She took a steadying breath before replying. 'I don't know. I might only be a couple of hours. Unless there are lots of people to talk to.'

'Okay,' he said stiffly. 'I'll see you when you get back then.' He kissed her on the cheek and went into the kitchen.

On the hallway table was the brochure and paperwork for their Italian holiday. They were due to go next week. She flicked the brochure open to the well-thumbed page featuring the hotel they'd booked. Her throat felt hot and thick as she looked at the squat, whitewashed building, drenched in sun and bougainvillea. What kind of holiday would it be now? She tried to imagine relaxing on the sun terrace, drinking wine with Alex, and even though the vision was bathed in Mediterranean sun, in her mind they were sitting in shadows.

The Kitchen was buzzing with a party atmosphere when she arrived. There was an eclectic mix of guests, with local dignitaries and friends of the Kitchen mingling happily with the homeless diners. Edie was standing in the midst of the throng, holding court with some guests and wearing a lovely navy dress that sparkled under the lights.

The place was decorated with streamers, bunting, and balloons sporting the number forty, and several tables had been pushed together to house a huge buffet. Wren's stomach rumbled, reminding her she hadn't eaten any dinner, but she needed to get some work done before she could relax and join the party.

She greeted Edie and Cath and some of the other volunteers she'd already spoken to and left a gift-wrapped present for Edie alongside some others that had been brought along. It was an old photograph of the Kitchen from the *Echo* archives, which she'd had framed. She then dived into the crowd, striking up conversations with anyone she could find who didn't have a mouth full of vol-au-vents or sausage roll.

She spent a productive hour mingling and collecting quotes and stories from the guests, until there was the tinkling sound of a knife against a champagne flute. The room quietened down and turned expectantly to a small, raised platform. Wren wondered if Edie was about to make a speech, but instead a well-built man, who looked to be in his fifties, stepped up, hands clasped in front of his broad chest. Next to the platform stood a woman of a similar age, who appeared to be his wife and had her arm around a waifish girl of about eighteen with thin mousey-brown hair and a pale complexion. They both looked up at him, waiting for him to speak. The man cleared his throat.

'Hello, everyone,' he started, a little hesitant. He raised his voice as he spoke again. 'I'd like to say a few words, if I may. I know everyone here has a special place for the Community Kitchen in their hearts – that's why we're here after all.'

There was a smattering of applause.

'My family, like many others here, and countless more who couldn't be here tonight, has a lot to thank the Kitchen for. It's hard to believe that just two years ago, we were being torn apart. And it's thanks to this place, to the staff and most of all to Edie Macmillan that we made it through.' He smiled at his family, and his daughter's eyes welled up as her mother rubbed her arm soothingly.

'Addiction is a terrible disease. No family thinks it's going to affect them, especially one like ours. Nice house, nice car, holiday once a year in Majorca. Your kid goes to a good school, you work five days a week. You would never imagine that you'd find yourself owing everything to a "soup kitchen". But here we are. Together again.'

The daughter's mouth was a thin line, but it twitched upwards at the edges, a little sparkle beginning to appear in her dewy eyes. Wren's heart throbbed.

He raised a glass, which Wren could now see was filled with orange juice. 'I want to thank everyone here from the bottom of my heart. Two years ago, I was an alcoholic, having drank away our home and our lives. I left behind my beautiful wife and daughter, living with family, while I scratched around looking for my next drink. I disappeared, and for that I will always be sorry. But Edie didn't rest until I'd sorted myself out and been reunited with my ever-forgiving family. Because that's what the Kitchen is all about. It's a family itself, and the people here believe that you deserve to be with people who love you.'

His voice wavered and he paused for a second, composing himself.

'To my lovely wife, Kendra. Thank you for taking me back. And my daughter, Katherine... Sorry, *Katie*. She'll kill me for using the full name.'

The crowd chuckled, and Katie narrowed her eyes playfully.

'Thank you, Katie, for forgiving me. I'll never let you down again. And thank you to Edie and all the staff here. You gave me back my life. To the Community Kitchen.' He raised his glass to thunderous applause.

Wren joined in, but a thought tugged at her. *Katie*. The man had corrected himself after calling his daughter by her full name. Just like her dad would. He never called her Serenity, only Wren, and had done her whole life. If he'd met Edie years ago, he would never have said he had a daughter called Serenity. She stood there, a smile fixed on her face, clapping her hands, as her stomach twisted. Her dad had told her on the phone that he'd been the one who'd told Edie her name. But now she realised that made no sense.

Wren found herself back at the photo wall, sipping a glass of elderflower cordial and scrutinising the faces in the pictures even more intensely. The sinking feeling of knowing her dad might have hidden something from her had boiled itself down until it had condensed into rabid curiosity again. But nobody in the pictures looked even vaguely familiar – there was nobody who looked like her mother, father, or anyone else she knew.

She had no extended family to ask either.

What could be the reason for being so evasive? Had something happened that involved Edie, since the mention of her name had seemed to throw her dad for a loop? Or had something gone on at the Kitchen that he didn't want dredged up. An affair? It didn't make sense.

'That's me,' came a voice as an arm reached past her, pressing a finger against the photograph of Edie's grandsons. She turned to see a man smiling at her.

'Which one?' she asked. 'The Buzz Lightyear fan, or the miniature fashion model?'

The man stood back and gestured to himself with both hands, up and down his frame. He was wearing a very snug-fitting suit without socks, loafers and a conspicuously absent shirt. 'I think this speaks for itself. I'm Travis, the miniature fashionista. The Buzz Lightyear fan will be along in a bit. Anyway, I know who *you* are. Our nanna has mentioned her journalist friend more than once. I think she's hoping you might hit it off with my brother.'

'Oh,' said Wren, blinking. 'Um, well, that's lovely. But I've got a boyfriend...' She almost added the word *unfortunately*.

'So I hear...' he said with a little smile.

If there was ever a subject that needed changing, this was it. 'So! I was thinking of hitting the buffet. I'm starving.'

'Me too,' he said, trotting along beside her. He then started to talk about his online shopping business, and if he hadn't been so charming, she might have been annoyed at his attempts to hijack his nanna's event to get coverage of his own business. But then, an impeccably dressed woman came over and sidelined Travis for a chat.

There was the usual selection of finger foods: quiche, sandwiches, stuff in pastry. Wren absent-mindedly gathered some bits onto a paper plate, thinking with surprising satisfaction how Alex would be appalled at the calorie content. She added another sandwich, almost out of spite. But when she looked at it, she saw that it contained prawns. Wren bit her lip. She didn't mind prawns but couldn't stand them smothered in that pink Marie Rose sauce, so after a brief hesitation, she put it back. She felt a bit grubby doing it, but it was marginally better than wasting food in an establishment like this. Then she realised she'd put it back on a plate of chicken sandwiches by mistake, but as she reached to pick it up again and move it, the Mayor of Newcastle looked over disapprovingly. She smiled, diverted her hand to pick up an unwanted chicken sandwich and crammed it into her mouth as she wandered back into the crowd.

Some broccoli quiche and one small slice of corned beef pie later, she found that she'd exhausted any new people to talk to in the room, or at least anyone who hadn't had one too many glasses of Prosecco. She saw Edie from a distance and considered going to talk to her, but she was deep in conversation with Cath and Travis, so she hung back. It was nearly nine o'clock now, so she decided to call it a night and think about how to approach the subject of her mam on another day.

She dropped her paper plate into a bin, walked outside and searched her bag for her car keys. It was starting to get dark and the street lights were dim, so she strained to see, rifling through old receipts and lipsticks.

There was a noise through the darkness, a shuffling of feet. Somebody was out there, in the shadows. Wren saw movement and realised that it was just beyond her car. Her throat went dry. It could be nobody, she thought, to calm herself down. Just someone getting something out of their car. But being alone in the dark, in an otherwise deserted car park, made her skin tingle.

She approached the car, keeping one hand in her bag, wrapped around a small canister within. She and Libby had attended a self-defence class last year, and they'd been flogging something called 'personal defence spray' – intended to look like pepper spray but instead it covered the assailant with a horrible odour and an invisible UV dye. She'd never had cause to use it, until now.

As she reached the car, a man emerged from the shadows. Blind panic bloomed in her chest, and she raised the spray and let loose.

TEN

NICK

Nick was just about to head inside the Community Kitchen, pulling at the tight collar and tie at his neck as he did so, when he heard a commotion from the car park. He hesitated, wondering whether it was any of his business, but then heard a woman's voice. Peering around the edge of the building, through the semi-darkness he saw the back of a woman in a green dress with her hair in a dishevelled topknot. Standing opposite her was a man who, through the shadows, looked to have his fists ground into his eyes. Was he... crying? Nick chewed his lip. Was he walking in on a private argument?

'Alex, I'm so sorry...' he heard the woman say.

'For fuck's sake!' said the man in a muted scream, his hands still covering his face. 'What did you do that for?'

'I panicked. Oh God, are you okay?' She went towards him, arms outstretched, but he turned away. They both went quiet for a moment. 'Hang on,' she said, so softly that Nick could barely hear. 'Why are you even here? Were you... *following me?*'

The man didn't reply, his face turned away, breathing heavily. What was going on here?

She took a step back, still facing away from Nick, and put her hands in her already chaotic hair. Her voice was fire and ice. 'I can't believe this. You were checking up on me...'

She was about to turn around, so Nick whipped back around the corner of the building, feeling a twinge of guilt for listening in. It definitely seemed to be a couple's disagreement that he had no business getting involved in, so, satisfied that the woman was in no danger, he slipped away and went into the Kitchen.

Never a dull moment at the Community Kitchen.

He scanned the crowd to see if he could see Edie. The email he'd found was tucked away in his sock drawer at home, but it might as well have been on fire in his hand, burning his fingertips, for all the good it did to try and forget it. He hadn't stopped thinking about it, not even when he'd pretended to Travis and his nanna that nothing was amiss.

'Oh, here he is!' exclaimed Nanna as he approached. 'Come and give me a cuddle, sunshine.' She pulled him down to her for a hug, and he squeezed her gently, feeling a confusing mix of comfort and resentment.

'You missed my reporter friend,' she said. 'The one I wanted you to meet last time she was here. Cath said she just saw her go.'

'Not to worry, all's forgiven for the bookcase,' he said, gritting his teeth. If it hadn't been for the books going flying, he'd never have seen the email, and right now he half wished that he hadn't.

'Come on then, let's get you some buffet. I think the vol-au-vents are all gone though.'

She was right, the vol-au-vents had all gone, but there were a few sandwiches and slices of quiche left. Nick picked up a piece of cheese-and-tomato quiche and crammed it into his mouth in one bite. His nanna was right on one count – he could do with feeding. He was hungrier than he'd realised.

'Nicholas! Manners,' she said, handing him a paper plate and a napkin.

In a fit of, admittedly childish, rebellion against her molly-coddling – and probably more than just that, if he was honest – he grabbed a sandwich from the platter marked 'Chicken' and stuffed the whole triangle in his mouth in one go too. He chewed quickly, reaching for another, but recoiled at the taste. It didn't taste like chicken. It didn't taste like chicken at all. He looked at the label on the platter again.

'Nanna,' he said, feeling his throat start to itch. 'There aren't any prawn sandwiches here, are there?'

'There were, but they all got eaten. What are you after those for anyway? You're allergic. That's why I told Cath to label the plates.'

Nick swallowed, feeling a thickness at the back of his mouth that hadn't been there before. The skin on his neck began to feel hot and itchy, his lips tingling.

'Nicky?' said Nanna. 'What's the matter?'

Nick loosened his tie and tried to breathe deeply. 'Prawns.'

Nanna shot a sharp look at the plates. 'Oh hell. Nicky, where's your EpiPen?'

In the flat. His breathing grew threadier, and the room started to sway. *In the flat... twenty minutes drive away.* His throat felt like it was almost completely closed.

Then the lights started to fade, and the floor rushed up to meet him.

What followed next was like a series of blurry snapshots. Panicked darkness punctured, literally, with the sting of an injection to his thigh. Relief, blessed air, a thumping headache. Then wooziness, feeling like he was drifting in and out of sleep as he jostled around in the back of an ambulance. Travis sitting with his chin on steepled fingers nearby. Then a hospital bed, with his nanna beside it, her mouth a grim line.

'Eeh, pet, what are we going to do with you?' she said, sounding weary.

Nick blinked into the harsh light of the A&E cubicle and winced. His head still throbbed from the adrenaline, and he felt like he might be sick.

'What have I told you about leaving your EpiPen at home?' she chided.

He closed his eyes again. What the hell was wrong with him? It was like something up there was determined to see him maimed or worse. Either that, or he needed to stop being so distracted by things and watch what he was doing a bit more. His mind cast back to nearly swallowing that coin, getting electrocuted, being flattened by a bookcase. *That bloody bookcase.* 'Nanna, I found the email from my dad.'

It had escaped from him almost against his will. Whether it was the drugs or the quiet, or just being unable to contain it anymore, he didn't know.

Her hand tightened on his arm, almost imperceptibly. 'I see,' she said. 'And where did you find that?' Her tone was light, but her voice had lost its usual composure.

'I... didn't go snooping, if that's what you think. It was under the spare bed, in a book that must have fallen out of the bookcase when that journo—' He sighed. 'That's not really the point. I didn't realise what it was until I'd opened it.'

'But you opened it.'

Nick paused, feeling at once guilty and indignant. 'I did. And I'm sorry, but I had no idea. I thought it might be an old bill or something.'

'Nicholas, you had no right...' she began, but her voice cracked, and he realised that she was on the verge of tears.

He sat up quickly, full of concern, but a blinding pain in his head stopped him from fully getting up. He pressed his palms against his throbbing eyes.

'Nanna, I'm sorry. I really am,' he whispered through clenched teeth. 'But I've seen it now, so I know he's out there. Why didn't you tell me? Why didn't you give me the choice?'

She pursed her lips, which were now trembling, and her eyes were bright with tears. 'Oh, I don't know, pet. You were going through all that with Callie. It just didn't seem the right time.'

'So were you ever going to tell me?'

'I thought about it.'

'But you didn't.'

She shook her head and finally looked him in the eye. 'Nicky, I agonised over it. I really did. But that man showed no bloody interest this whole time, and then all of a sudden, he shows up out of nowhere. I... I wasn't sure what his intentions might be.'

'His *intentions*? What does that even mean?' As Nick's voice raised so did the tenor of his headache, but the pain only frustrated him more. 'Nanna, you should have told me!'

'I needed to *protect* you,' she said, her voice reedy.

'From what? I'm a grown man.'

'Oh, Nicky. You and your brother are my whole world. Your mam, though I love my daughter to high heaven, has put herself first when she should have been there for you two. And I've always tried to make sure that the two of you had as normal a life as possible. So some fella writing to me out of the blue from *Capri*, of all places, grubbing about for information... I just didn't trust it.'

'But it's not up to you...'

'That's as may be. But I did what I thought was right.'

'So is that all you've heard from him? That email?'

She folded her hands into her lap and looked down at them.

'Nanna?'

She sighed. 'There was another one. An address. He said he'd forgot to put it in the original email.'

'So you know where he lives?'

She nodded stiffly.

'Can I have it please?'

Just then, Travis came through the curtain holding two plastic cups filled with tea. Nick and Edie both flinched.

'What's going on?' he asked.

'Travis?' Nick asked, not breaking eye contact with his nanna. 'Have you got anyone who could cover your orders for a few days?'

'Eh? Maybe... What are you talking about?'

'Pack your Italian phrasebook. We're going on a little holiday.'

ELEVEN

WREN

The hotel was a two-storey whitewashed villa with a covered veranda on the roof, immaculately kept – the white paint was so fresh and bright it was almost hard to look at in the sunshine. It had climbing greenery across the walls and plants on the veranda above that spilled their leaves over the top, so that the building looked enveloped in nature. The garden was mature with shrubs and lemon trees, and smelled divine.

As Wren walked up the uneven footpath, trundling her small suitcase behind her, she was glad she'd come. Even if she would be sleeping alone.

The smiling man at the small reception building by the entrance had given her a chunky brass key with the number three inscribed on the fob. She hoisted her case up a short flight of stairs and let herself in.

The room was lovely; a double bedroom decorated with pale creams and beige, with features that leaned more towards North African, such as the intricate headboard, which was carved with a swirling cut-out pattern, and the co-ordinating Moorish-style bedside tables. There was a small, neat kitchenette and an en-suite bathroom, tastefully decorated with teal herringbone tiles and a huge white bath which she longed to sink into as soon as she could. A door was open to a first-floor courtyard terrace that looked out over the Bay of Naples. The place was like something out of a dream.

A dream she should have been sharing with Alex, she thought, blinking away the sting of tears as she put her suitcase on the bed and started to unpack. The tears felt acidic, laced as they were with anger as fresh and raw as their break-up.

He'd followed her to the Community Kitchen to check up on her, to make sure she really was where she said she was. The thought of it still made her pulse quicken with rage. He'd still refused to admit that was why he'd been there, and instead he'd just been incandescent with fury at being covered with the defence spray. Any guilt Wren felt from accidentally coating him in the stuff, which stank to high heaven, was assuaged by the realisation that their relationship couldn't continue. She'd known it right then, standing in the dark car park. It had been almost like turning off a lightbulb – Alex's face, twisted with anger at the spray and the accusations, had become unpleasant to her, almost repulsive, and her heart had hardened with a speed that had shocked her.

In the following hours, after sleeping in the spare room, she'd emotionlessly planned her next steps. And the next day she'd executed them, packing some bags, heading to Libby's, where she'd started making lists of things she needed to do to disentangle herself from him. House, bills and so on. And then she'd cried for hours. Regardless of how he'd treated her, dismantling her financial ties to him was going to be infinitely easier than letting go of the emotional ones. The happier times, before he'd grown more and more hard to please, were the memories that seemed to push their way to the front, making her grieve for a relationship that she now knew had been lost long ago. And it was this realisation that reassured her that, in spite of her heartache, she'd done the right thing.

That night, she'd texted Alex, asking him if he was planning on going to Sorrento on his own, to which he'd responded with a long, rambling message about how she'd shattered his dreams and how dare she even suggest... So she'd taken the opportunity, while he was on his evening shift, to go home, grab her suitcase and passport and, after a moment's consideration, offer Alex's place on the plane to someone else.

'Knock knock,' came a voice from the doorway. 'Eeh, this is posh,' said Alan, looking around the tasteful room. 'Is that a coffee machine? Very swish.'

He made a beeline for the Nespresso machine on the kitchenette counter and started tinkering with it, opening the water dispenser and peering inside. He picked up a little espresso cup and mimed holding it to his lips, pinky finger extended, then fumbled the cup, catching it at the last minute before it shattered on the tiles.

'Reflexes of a cat,' he said with a wink, then proceeded to knock the stack of coffee pods all over the floor, upending the full water dispenser as his hands flailed to catch them.

'How's your room, Dad?' asked Wren, gathering up the pods as he swabbed the floor with one of the expensive-looking hand towels from the bathroom.

'Oh, it's smashing, pet. It's spot on.'

Wren had booked her dad the only available room in the complex – a small single with a 'garden view' that might possibly be overlooking a small patch of grass and a whitewashed wall. She hoped Alan wasn't trying to make her feel better about the stark comparison with her own room, which he'd refused to take instead of her. She'd decided that Alex's plane ticket shouldn't be a complete waste. It had been years since her dad had been on holiday, and he didn't really have anyone to go with, so she'd invited him along. Despite his ability to wreck a Nespresso machine, she knew he would also be good company.

Alan caught sight of the open terrace door and rushed outside. 'Well, it's almost as nice as the view from the cottage,' he said with a grin. 'Hey, kidda, who'd have thought we'd be standing in a spot like this, eh?'

Wren smiled, but immediately Alan winced.

'Sorry, pet. I know you'd rather not be here with your dad.'

Wren breathed deeply. 'I would actually.' And she realised this was true. 'To be honest, when I think about standing here with Alex, all I can imagine is that bloody itinerary he made up. I'd have had three seconds to look at this view, then he'd be dragging me off to get fitted with abseiling equipment.'

Alan grimaced. 'Would you mind if we don't make use of all the bookings. I'm not that fond of heights, and abseiling always looks a bit constraining on the knackers.'

'Lovely,' she groaned, although her lip twitched at the corner. 'But I'm in full agreement. Let's make this holiday as lazy as possible. I want to go home half a stone heavier, with pasta poisoning and stripes imprinted on my back from a sun lounger.'

'Count me in. Now, how's about that first dose of pasta then?' Alan bobbed on his heels, visibly enthused.

'No time like the present,' agreed Wren.

She scanned the room once more. It really was beautiful. But it needed just one thing to make it feel like hers. She opened her suitcase, tipped it over and poured all of her clothes, toiletries and accessories over the bed. The suitcase made a gratifying clunk as it dropped onto the tiles. A ripple of satisfaction went through her. Alex would have had a fit. But Alex wasn't here.

Taking a deep breath, she turned away from the comforting chaos and followed Alan out the door.

They walked down to the bay, weaving through the narrow streets between tall buildings painted yellow, orange and warm cream. Above, there were red-brick clock towers, patches of sky that were beginning to turn from blue to amber and barely a cloud. The compact streets should have felt oppressive, but to Wren they were the opposite – the burnished tones of the walls around her made it seem almost cosy. There were hanging baskets of bright flowers, and shops with colourful awnings, one selling rows and rows of sandals, hung from the wall by ribbons of every shade in the rainbow. Fruit stalls and coffee shops were bursting with colour and aroma, so that just walking down the streets was a treat for the senses.

'Looka!' said Alan, twirling a postcard stand. 'I should send this one to Johnny Boy.'

He plucked out a postcard bearing a cartoon picture of a dog slurping up spaghetti, a close-enough approximation to a certain classic film that Disney would raise an eyebrow.

'Aw, Dad, do you think he's missing you?'

'Not at all,' he said, chuckling and putting the postcard back. 'Cliff sent me a photo of him eating his own little roast dinner, stuffing, the lot. He's having the time of his life.'

Alan's friend – his only friend – had taken John in while they were away. Cliff worked with her dad at the lighthouse visitors' centre, and his name, considering his place of work, still made Wren smile.

Near the postcards was a shelf with various leaflets for tourist attractions. One in particular caught Wren's eye.

'On the subject of lighthouses...' she said, presenting one to her dad.

'Oh, now that's a beauty,' he said, holding the leaflet at arm's length to admire it. 'Punta Carena lighthouse. It's on Capri, it says.'

'Just over the bay. Do you want to go and see it?'

'Well, aye. If we've got time.'

'We've scrapped the itinerary, remember? We've got all the time in the world.'

Alan grinned and tucked the leaflet into his pocket. 'Talk about a busman's holiday. Wait 'til I tell Cliff.'

Wren shook her head. To be fair, if there was one person in the world who would be chomping at the bit to hear tales of Italian lighthouses, it would be Cliff. She, on the other hand, would suffer a visit to make her dad happy.

'Come on,' she said. 'Let's get some food, and we can see about Capri tomorrow.'

They walked towards the coast and emerged onto the Marina Grande, a pretty harbour. It was, confusingly, smaller than its sister, Marina Piccola, according to her basic research on Sorrento, and was bustling with tourists and Italians.

There were signs being erected here and there, advertising the Festa di Sant'Anna. A quick word with a friendly local revealed that this was an annual festival, celebrating Saint Anne, the patron saint of pregnant women. Wren looked up at the lights being strung up around the church and along the harbour railings, and took a photo for Libby.

She texted it to her and received an immediate reply:

Patron saint of pregnancy, my arse. I'm going to worship the gods of the epidural.

Wren and Alan took a table at a seafront restaurant, ordered glasses of wine and the catch of the day, which turned out to be sea bass.

It was a strange feeling, being there, eating freshly caught fish and drinking Pinot Grigio with her dad as the sun went down over the Bay of Naples. She watched him destroying the pile of chips he'd ordered as a side, and her mind wandered back to the Community Kitchen and her realisation that he might not have been telling her the whole truth. The sun was dipping lower, and the day had grown cooler, but she couldn't be sure if that was the only reason for the goosebumps that now prickled down her arms. She opened her mouth to say something but was interrupted.

A man wearing a pale, crumpled linen suit appeared beside them and started playing a tune on his violin, smiling at each of them in turn. Wren stared up at him, and he winked. The song was in Italian, but she distinctly heard the word *amore* on more than one occasion. Her smile had already frozen on her face when he paused playing and reached into a knapsack at his side, producing an imitation red rose wrapped in heart-patterned cellophane and nudging it towards her dad.

Alan's face went instantly puce. 'Nah, nah, son. She's not—'

'I'm his daughter,' yelped Wren so loudly that other tables looked over. The violinist looked confused so she said again, lowering her voice. 'Me and him... not *together*. Um, father and daughter?'

The violinist frowned and pushed the rose towards Alan more insistently, the language barrier not helping at all, and her dad pressed it back with his hand.

'*Bella signora...*' he said, gesturing at Wren, slightly pityingly. 'Beautiful, no?'

'Yes, yes, very beautiful,' said Alan through gritted teeth. 'But she's not my wife. *Not. Wife.*' He pointed to his ring finger, where the wedding ring he'd received from Wren's mam many moons ago still sat, and then at Wren's bare ring finger.

The man's eyebrows rose then waggled. 'Ah! *Naughty, naughty...*' He made a tutting noise while grinning. Wren buried her face in her hands.

'Not that either,' growled Alan.

When Wren looked up, she saw her dad pushing a five-euro note into the violinist's hand, face like thunder. 'Now bugger off.'

This the violinist seemed to understand, so he tossed the rose onto the table and walked off with his nose in the air.

Wren finally met her dad's eye, then they both looked down at the rose and exploded with laughter.

'Oh my God,' whispered Wren. 'What just happened?'

'Talk about lost in translation,' Alan said, chuckling as he wedged another handful of chips into his mouth and shook his head.

'Well, thank you for the rose,' she said, thinking that if Alex had been sat opposite, he probably wouldn't have bought her one even though they *were* together.

Their waiter bounded over to top up their wine. He was young, maybe early twenties, and had previously been polite and efficient, but now he looked positively fizzing with attentiveness.

'Apologies for our musician. Anyone can see you're father and daughter.'

He held Wren's eye and gave her a smile as he poured. 'Very beautiful,' he said.

Wren flushed. Was he... hitting on her? In front of her dad?

'The Isle of Capri,' the waiter quickly added, nodding to the island in the distance, now bathed in the glow of the sun as it set behind it. 'It's very beautiful – you must go.'

'Oh! Right. The island.' Wren cringed. Of course he was talking about the view. She was extremely deskilled at interpreting advances, clearly. Years of being in a committed relationship would do that to a person.

'Of course,' he said with a smirk. 'It is a magical place. You've heard of the sirens?'

'Um...'

'The sirens were beautiful ghost women on Capri – they lured fishermen to their deaths with their singing. And the Blue Grotto... you have heard of that, of course?'

Wren nodded. She'd heard of the grottoes on Capri, caves filled with sea water that glowed an eerie blue and green.

'Well, inside there, legends say there were mermaids and witches. It's an isle of beautiful, dangerous women.' He held her gaze more intensely this time, and Wren realised she wasn't actually mistaken about his intentions. She bit her lip, trying not to laugh. He was trying this in front of her *dad*. 'Actually, my uncle has a boat. How about tomorrow—?'

'I'm busy!' she chirped, trying to quell the bubble of amusement that threatened to burst. She had to give him credit for the myths-and-legends spiel, but he was far too young, and she shuddered to think how many women he'd tried this on before. '*We're* busy,' she reiterated, nodding towards Alan. 'But thanks for the recommendation – we'll be sure to take a look before we go home.'

He pursed his lips and nodded, beating a hasty retreat before she could even say thank you for the refill.

Alan slurped his wine and raised his eyebrows at her over the top of the glass.

'Don't even...' she warned.

He put his glass down and ran his pinched fingers over his lips, a smile quivering at their edges.

They looked out across the bay for a while in contented silence. Capri sat in the middle distance, its twin hills backlit by the setting sun. The silence made space for Wren's thoughts to work back to a less cheerful place. Before she could stop herself, she turned to her dad.

'Did you ever go on holiday with my mam?' she asked, circling her finger around the top of her wine glass and trying to keep her tone light.

'Once or twice. Nowhere as snazzy as this though. Shame, she would have loved it here.'

'Would she?' asked Wren carefully. 'I feel like I know so

little about her. What with never meeting my grandparents. And we don't really talk about her that much.'

Alan shifted in his seat and took a drink. Playing for time. This happened often when the subject of Caron was raised.

'I know.' His voice was quiet, the mood plummeting. 'I've said before, it's difficult.'

Wren didn't say anything for a moment, daring herself to ask him the question. Why had he clammed up when he'd said he'd met Edie and talked about his daughter Serenity? A name he never used. She chewed her lip and tried to build up the nerve to ask.

But then the waiter returned to take away their plates and the moment was lost. She gratefully received the dessert menu and was surprised to feel relieved when Alan started enthusiastically and inaccurately trying to pronounce *delizie al limone* when making his order. She ordered a panna cotta and decided that a sweet distraction was probably for the best – for now.

TWELVE

NICK

Travis stood at the hotel window, hands on his hips. If it weren't for his snappy attire, it seemed to Nick he would have looked like he was pricing up a glazing job. Travis had dressed his best in an effort to get an upgrade to business class on the plane, but since he'd had no luck, he'd had to suffer economy wearing an extremely close-fitting tan-coloured suit with co-ordinating maroon tie and pocket square. He'd exited the plane with sweat patches oozing through the unforgiving material and a look of outrage on his face – an expression which had yet to change.

He turned around and folded his arms. 'Well, this isn't the elegant Italian holiday I was promised.'

Beyond, through the window, the hotel overlooked a yard full of storage containers and scaffolding. Municipal buildings formed the backdrop to this, but at least, above them, the sun was shining and the sky was blue. Naples had turned out to be the cheapest place to stay for visiting Capri, not to mention the one with the most availability. But this part of the city wasn't exactly the Italian idyll, or even the tourist mecca holiday brochures boasted of. Even to Nick, who generally erred on the practical side, this area seemed to be the Italian equivalent of an industrial park.

'I never said it would be elegant. Come to think of it, I was kind of playing fast and loose with the word *holiday* as well.'

Travis ran a finger along the bedspread of one of the twin beds and wrinkled his nose. 'Well, fine. But you could have at least booked somewhere that knew the meaning of "thread count". I think these would barely pass fire regulations.'

'We're on a budget,' said Nick tersely, flinging some clothes from his suitcase into a drawer. His jaw tensed as he reflected on how this little flight of fancy wasn't helping his financial situation. He'd almost been ashamed to accept the small loan from his nanna to cover the cost – and a loan it would be. She'd tried to insist on paying for the whole thing, saying she felt she owed it to him for keeping her secret. But pride, and also a sense of his own regret for reading her private correspondence, had made him insist he would be paying it straight back. He'd just need to figure out how.

This trip felt both wildly out of character for him but also strangely inevitable. He'd been living his odd half life for too long now, waiting for some kind of change, and this felt like it might be it. A step out of the routine, and an answer to some of his biggest questions. He felt like he was finally taking some control.

Travis was now perched awkwardly on the bed, as if he didn't want to come in too close contact with it, and was scrolling through his phone.

'Business or pleasure?' asked Nick, stacking some deodorant and aftershave bottles on his chipped and peeling bedside table.

'Both,' murmured Travis absent-mindedly.

'Eh?'

Travis's shoulders straightened. 'Business, I mean. Just checking in on the website.'

'All okay? You got a mate to pack your orders, didn't you?'

'Yep,' said Travis, standing up and putting the phone in his pocket. 'It's all in hand.'

'Who did you ask? The girl with the Lego-man haircut, or the lad that wears pantaloons?'

Travis cocked his head to one side. 'Ha ha. They're harem pants actually. Very big this season. No. I asked Liam.'

'*Liam* Liam? As in Cath's Liam?' Nick's jaw dropped. 'Trav, you barely know him.' His thoughts shifted uneasily to Liam's chaotic lifestyle and his history of getting into trouble with the law, and he bit his lip.

'What?' said Travis.

'Nothing. Just...' He didn't want to, but he had to say it. 'Didn't Cath say he'd been in bother for stealing stuff?'

Travis sighed. 'Nick, that was ages ago. And, if you must know, it was one of the many times his arsehole stepdad threw him out. It doesn't make it right, but he had no money and he was desperate.'

Nick looked at the floor.

'I trust him,' Travis said quietly. 'Now, I'm getting out of here. The static from this bedcover is starting to make me itch. There has to be somewhere nice to go around here.' He looked hopeful – no, desperate.

'Well, go and do a recce, would you?' asked Nick, trying to bury the nagging worry that Liam was currently in just as dire circumstances as he'd been in the past. He knew he was being overprotective of his brother, but he just hoped Travis knew what he was doing. 'I'll finish unpacking then catch up with you.'

Travis shoved on his sunglasses and went out, stabbing at his phone for local bar recommendations and frowning. Nick shook his head and watched him go.

It was only a short walk down to the seafront where, instead of golden beaches, there was a busy, not very pretty port, where Nick paused on his way to find Travis. The first thing that caught his eye was a vast sandstone building with tall windows and columns that looked to be the main ferry terminal. Alongside it were vast swathes of concrete, with car parks and rectangular brick buildings that featured the logos of various ferry companies. He spied the one he'd had the foresight to book for the following day, after learning tickets could sell out fast.

Beyond the scrappy coastal area of Naples, across the azure sea, was the outline of the island of Capri. In the distance, it sat solidly, its broad shape baked against the horizon, one half of the island taller than the other. Tomorrow he would visit the Ristorante Giorgio – Nanna had given him the second email that had a street address on the island, as well as his father's full name, Richard Keyes.

The location had been a surprise; he'd always thought that Capri was quite fancy, and for some reason he'd never imagined his dad to come from somewhere so highbrow. Did he own the restaurant? It seemed possible if he'd given it as his address. Did he live there with a wife? Other children? Nick had considered what felt like every possible outcome. A Google search of the restaurant hadn't been helpful – there was only an 'under-construction' domain and a smattering of positive Tripadvisor reviews describing it as 'cosy' and 'traditional'. It seemed to be a place that flew under the internet radar.

He wondered if he would recognise his father straight away. Maybe that was where he got his sandy-coloured hair from, or his feet that looked almost wider than they were long across the toe area. Maybe he would be completely unrecognisable, some kind of anomaly that had sprung Nick forth from his loins, as much a stranger in the genes as he was in real life. The anticipation was intense and terrifying.

He looked back at the Bay of Naples behind him, buildings, large and small, stacked up the hill, interspersed with patches of greenery. It was prettier in that direction, but only just.

His phone buzzed and he saw he had a text from Travis.

I'm round the corner on via Travertino – it's called Beer Bar but they do Aperol Spritz!

Nick wasn't quite sure what an Aperol Spritz was, but the name of the bar was reassuring. He slipped his phone into his pocket and headed for the town.

The next morning they were up bright and early, and had a lacklustre continental breakfast in the hotel restaurant, which seemed to be an optimistic term for a small room with bistro tables and a selection of dry pastries and coffee. They boarded the ferry at half past nine, and Nick was pleased they'd booked. Even on a Tuesday morning, this crossing was heavily in demand and was full of tourists snapping pictures of the ever-closer island.

Nick had called it a day after two beers, but Travis had gone a bit overboard on the Aperol Spritzes so was sporting dark sunglasses and a slightly hangdog expression. Nick reached into his rucksack and retrieved a bottle of water, handing it to Travis as they disembarked.

'Thanks, Mam,' said Travis, sipping it gingerly. 'You wouldn't happen to have a few paracetamol in your bag of tricks, would you?'

'I'm afraid not.' The rucksack he'd brought was full of useful items – water, sun cream, even a towel in case they decided to dip their toes off the shore of Capri, but he hadn't thought to bring painkillers. 'Look, there's a pharmacy,' he said, pointing to a building with the telltale green cross on the sign.

Travis sloped off to get his medicine, and Nick took a moment to breathe. They'd arrived at the marina amongst clusters of other boats, large and small. Despite passenger ferries arriving here, it had the air of a fishing village, with rows of cream and pastel-painted buildings across the shore, beyond which were the hills of Capri. He'd looked at a map to see where the Ristorante Giorgio was and found that it was in Capri town on top of the smaller of the two main peaks on the island. He stared up at it and chewed his lip. A short walk up the hill and he could change his life forever. His stomach churned as if he'd had more than just two beers the night before.

Travis came out of the shop, slugging down tablets. He'd bought himself a straw fedora while he'd been gone, and if it wasn't for his pale skin and rainbow hi-tops, he might have passed for a local.

'You ready?'

Nick crossed his arms and looked up at Capri town again. 'I don't think I am actually.'

'Right.' Travis looked at his watch. 'Well, we've got approximately eight hours to kill until we get back on the ferry. Do you think you can get hotel rooms by the hour, just for a lie-down?'

'I wouldn't like to ask,' murmured Nick, still gazing up at the hills. 'Listen, can we go for a walk first? Just to get my head straight.' He eyed the taller of the two peaks and liked the way it looked separate from the one that housed Ristorante Giorgio.

Travis went slightly green but stood up a little straighter. He had a brotherly duty to gird his loins after all. They set off in the direction of Anacapri.

They walked until they came to the foot of the hill and came upon a large whitewashed building. Its sign read *Seggiovia Monte Solaro*, which they quickly ascertained was the chairlift to the top of the peak. A slow smile spread over Travis's face.

'No chance,' said Nick. 'I said a walk, not a granny lift.'

'But—'

'Nah. Let's get some exercise.'

Travis scowled but followed along.

Nick eyed the building with faint suspicion as they walked past. He never really talked about it but, despite his job, he wasn't very keen on heights, and he'd read enough cable-car and chairlift horror stories to make his hair stand on end. But the other reason was that sitting still in a chair would give him too much time to think, and what he really needed now was some distraction to calm him down. So he put one foot in front of the other, climbing steadily up the foothills of Monte Solaro, happy that the burn in his shins and thighs was the main thing he could focus on.

It took longer than he'd envisioned to climb it – about an hour at a good pace – and when they reached the top, Travis's red face and thin lips said all he needed to say. But then, as they crossed the viewing terrace at the top, it felt more worth the bother. Below was the crystal-blue sea and a cluster of huge rocks jutting from the water, one of which had a tunnel underneath it. They watched as a boat chugged through it.

'Canny view, eh?' said Nick, hands on his hips, feeling his breathing return to normal.

'Not if it's the last view I ever see,' Travis puffed. 'Are you trying to kill me?'

'Get away with you,' said Nick. 'It's only a little hill. Maybe you need a bit more exercise. Wrapping clothes in brown paper isn't exactly getting your heart rate up.'

'That's what you think. I managed to score some knock-down Prada purses the other week, and I thought I was going to faint.'

Nick grinned. His brother and he might be very different, but Travis always knew how to make him smile.

'Did you manage to get hold of Mam?' asked Travis, mopping his brow and upper lip with a silk handkerchief.

'No. I left a message on her mobile, but I just said I needed a chat.'

'Has she still not managed to figure out the Wi-Fi on the ship?'

'I'd imagine not, since she hasn't replied. And if I've got her schedule right, she's somewhere off the coast of Florida right now. I suppose she'll get the message when she docks.'

Travis rolled his eyes. 'For a woman who likes to think she could give "young 'uns" like Taylor Swift a run for their money on stage, she sure is old-fashioned when it comes to technology.'

'Yeah. Although, I was dreading asking her about it anyway.'

'Why? I've always thought it was weird that he's just never mentioned.'

'Exactly. If she's never wanted to talk about him before, then I doubt she'll be happy being ambushed about him now. But maybe she'd have given me a heads-up on what he's like before I meet him.'

'Well, maybe it's just better to find out for yourself. It might have taken him a while to get in touch, but he's going to be pleased to see you when you find him.'

Nick's stomach squirmed, with nerves or excitement – he couldn't be sure. 'I hope so.'

'So, do you think you're ready now?'

'No. But I didn't come all this way just for the views. Ha'way, let's go back down.'

'Okay. But I'm just going to pop to the loos in the chairlift station before we go,' said Travis, patting Nick on the back as he left.

Nick stood for a while, looking down at the sea and taking some deep breaths. Maybe he should have tried ringing the restaurant. Or writing to Richard instead. Resting his hands on the low wall, he thought of all the ways he could have done this differently. Was there a right or wrong way to meet your estranged father? Well, he was about to find out.

'Yoo-hoo!' came a yell from behind him. He turned around to see Travis comfortably descending the slope in a chairlift, grinning smugly back at him as he waved.

'Travis, what the...?' Nick shouted back.

Travis made a gesture pretending he couldn't hear him then turned away to enjoy his trip.

Nick groaned and looked at the sky. It would take him an hour to get back down if he walked, and Travis would give him grief about it. Grimacing, he marched over to the station and bought himself a ticket. A smiling Italian man in his sixties led him to a very flimsy-looking chair made from slats of wood, with what seemed to be a very insecure lap bar that did not lock into place.

The chair scooped him up without stopping, and he yanked the lap bar down as far as it would go. The ground drifted away from his feet, and he tried not to look down. He could kill Travis for this.

His rucksack was rocking about on the seat next to him, so he took one of the carabiners that he had dangling from the straps and clipped it to one of the metal rods supporting the wooden slats. Right. At least he was fairly secure, he thought, as treetops passed below him.

He barely moved a muscle as he made his descent, wary of rocking the chair any more than he needed to, and when he reached the bottom, he ragged at the carabiner to free his bag, conscious that he would only have a few moments to step safely off the contraption. He felt his feet touch the ground, and a flood of relief coursed through him. Then, as he slung his bag over his shoulder, he noticed that the carabiner was gone. Looking back, he saw it glint in the sunshine, still attached to the chairlift as it made its ascent back up the hill. Well, he was never going to see that again.

Travis was waiting in the courtyard, smirking gleefully as Nick joined him.

'Why, Nick, you look a bit pale.'

'Do I? I feel fine.'

Travis tutted. 'Hmm, I'm pretty sure I saw you coming down the hill with your eyes shut.'

'Don't know what you're on about,' said Nick.

'Well, you can thank me later,' said Travis. 'After facing your fear of heights, meeting your dad will be a walk in the park.' He paused, peering at Nick. 'Seriously though, you do look a bit green around the gills.'

Nick didn't want to admit it, but he did indeed feel a bit queasy.

Travis frowned. 'Let's get you a drink.'

Nick allowed himself to be led by the arm to the chairlift visitors' centre, where he sat on a bench while Travis procured him a bottle of water. He felt better just for sitting down on a surface that wasn't swaying in the breeze.

'Kayak tours! Available today! Sir, can I interest you in a kayak tour?'

Nick looked blearily up at a lithe, bronzed man wearing a baseball cap and a wide grin. He was waving some leaflets very close to Nick's face.

'Sir, you look like just the kind of person who enjoys water sports.' Nick blinked. 'And today is your lucky day. We have a few spaces available on our kayak tour of the famous grottoes. Can I interest you in a ticket?'

'Um... actually, I'm busy...'

The tout's smile didn't waver a millimetre. 'No problem! Please take a leaflet in case you change your mind.' He stuffed the flyer into Nick's hand and wandered off, yelling about kayak tours once more.

Travis returned and gave Nick his water, which he drank gratefully. He stood up, folding the leaflet into his pocket. 'Come on then. I'm ready.'

He paused at the corner of the street. This was it – when he walked around the side of this handbag shop, he would see it – *Ristorante Giorgio*. Years of wondering, and a frantic week of discovery, planning and travelling, and the moment was upon him. He prepared himself and walked on, Travis hovering at his shoulder.

They rounded the corner – his heart sank, but his feet kept moving. Within moments he was standing at the neat railings of an empty terrace, no tables or chairs to be seen, and the wooden shutters drawn. He looked up to double-check the name, but it stayed mutinously unchanged. This place had shut up shop, and it looked like it was for good. In this bustling area of clinking glasses, laughter and fragrant seafood, the Ristorante Giorgio was desolate. He felt Travis's hand on his shoulder.

'Well, at least I tried,' he said, sighing deeply.

'I'm sorry, bro. Listen, it might not be the end. We can—'

'Go for another ride on the chair lift?' Nick turned and tried a smile for his brother, but it felt weak, as if the corners of his lips were anaesthetised.

'I was going to say we can keep trying.' Travis's expression was almost as hopeless. 'Capri isn't a very big place.'

Nick gripped the railings more firmly, feeling the warm metal bite into his tendons.

'You're right. It's not a very big place. But I'm not sure I'm in the mood to play detective right now, Trav. Can we just get a bit of lunch or something?'

'Yeah, no bother.' He looked up at the empty restaurant. 'Let's go somewhere a bit livelier, eh?'

They had lunch at a little pizza place, where Nick only managed a slice before he'd had enough. He had the appetite of a person who'd braved a chairlift and suffered a crushing disappointment all in one day. Travis tried, tentatively, to suggest things they could do to find out where Richard Keyes might have moved on to, but Nick could only half-heartedly nod and mumble assent. Whatever happened next, he would need to sleep on it, and hopefully tomorrow he would be in a better frame of mind. Right now, all he could think of was the thousand and a half miles he was from home, from Ruby, who he should be prioritising. Maybe he shouldn't be on this wild goose chase after all.

They finished their drinks and paid the bill, and wandered out of town towards the sea. They still had hours to kill until the return ferry, so they took their time, looking out at the view and conspicuously avoiding the subject of Nick's father. Travis was pretty good at sensing the mood and jabbered on about how lovely the shops were, and how he maybe needed to branch into Italy for his next wholesale purchase.

Travis went into a sunglasses shop and spent an inordinate amount of time trying on various styles of shades, while Nick looked on from the doorway, thinking it seemed a lot of trouble to go to just to keep the sun out of your eyes. And expense. Then he heard someone call, 'Richard!'

He whipped round, scanning the street to see where the voice had come from, and saw a woman of about his age waving across the road. Hurrying towards her was a man of no more than forty, American he would guess, or otherwise an enthusiastic fan of the NFL, judging by his attire. Definitely not old enough to be his dad. His heart sank, and he felt at once stupid and frustrated.

Travis came out of the shop wearing his new purchase.

'Trav, listen,' said Nick. 'Do you mind if I go off for a bit? I just need a bit of thinking time.' He was going to go mad if he kept roaming aimlessly, hoping to see his father around the next street corner.

'Of course not,' said Travis, his brow knitted with concern. 'You are alright though? I'm not going to have to come and pick you up from the police station for drunk and disorderly later, am I?'

'Nah. I'm just going to go and clear my head.'

'Okay. I'm going to hit the shops a bit harder then,' said Travis. 'I was holding back for your sake. I'll see you at the ferry terminal later?'

'Yep. I'll be there.'

They said goodbye, and Travis zoomed off with ill-disguised enthusiasm, the lunch and the promise of spending money seemingly putting paid to his hangover.

Nick started walking with purpose, even though he had no idea where he wanted to go. Whatever he did that afternoon, he needed to keep his mind busy. Never mind licking gelato and gazing into the horizon – he needed some meaningful activity.

He looked down at the coastline and saw a busy beach below, sunbathers and surfers and volleyball players zipping around like ants. Then, as he was heading for the steps, he saw a sign in the distance, next to a beach hut. Brightly coloured flags fluttered at its corners.

KAYAK TOURS OF CAPRI. VISIT THE FARAGLIONI ROCKS, THE WORLD-FAMOUS GROTTOES, AND MORE! EQUIPMENT HIRE INCLUDED.

He narrowed his eyes at the hut, then withdrew the leaflet from his pocket. It was the same company. An athletic, tanned woman with a clipboard was hovering outside the beach hut, and a crop of people in wetsuits gathered nearby, manhandling kayaks and oars. He wandered over.

'Er, one for the kayaking please?' he said, suddenly feeling foolish under her steely gaze.

'You have reservation?' she asked with a strong Italian accent.

'Um, no. I'm just a walk-in. I have this,' he said, waving the leaflet and losing confidence by the second. 'Sorry, I'll just...' He backed off – so much for the advertised availability.

The woman held up a hand in the manner of a strict teacher. 'I have one place left. Cancellation. Do you mind partnering with someone else?'

'No. No, that's fine,' he blustered.

'You wait here,' she commanded and thumbed towards the hut. 'Your partner is getting changed in there. What size are you? Large?'

Nick unconsciously put his hand on his stomach. 'Um, medium?' Medium, some pizza and last night's beers. And then he stood there, waiting for this slightly scary lady to fetch him a rented wetsuit, realising that even if he'd changed his mind about the kayaking, he wouldn't dare back out now. But if spending an afternoon kayaking submissively behind her was what it took to distract his mind, then it would be worth every euro.

THIRTEEN
WREN

Wren thought of the sirens of Capri as they made the crossing over the water and came to the solid conclusion that a myth was indeed a myth. How anyone could imagine that a place as beautiful as this could be shrouded in horror stories was beyond her, although she supposed that would be exactly what the sirens would want her to think.

'I can't see the lighthouse,' said Alan, sounding faintly worried.

'It's on the other side of the island, Dad. See that taller hill? It's behind there.'

'Oh, right. Smashing.' He rubbed his hands together and smiled. 'So, what else do you fancy doing? I won't bore you with the lighthouse all day long, I promise.'

Wren shrugged. 'Well, there are lots of shops and cafes. Some museums, I think. The beaches if you fancy a bit of sun worshipping?' Wren had put her bikini on under her clothes just in case the day took that kind of a turn.

'Oh, I'm not sure the Italian sands are ready for my pasty flesh, Wren. Besides, I'd only be thinking of beach walks with Johnny Boy. I hope he's doing alright.' Alan's shaggy brown hair blew around in the sea breeze as he put his elbows on the rail and looked out over the water.

'He'll be fine,' Wren reassured him, confident that John would be getting thoroughly spoiled at Cliff's. But the thought of home reminded her of last night's aborted conversation about her mam, and how, before they'd left for the airport, she'd put a letter through Edie's door.

She felt a little regretful about that now. She'd written the short note in the heat of the moment, when she was in the midst of the break-up and not thinking straight. Despite being a professional writer, she suspected the content might have come across as slightly unhinged. Explaining her suspicions that her dad wasn't the connection to the Community Kitchen after all, she'd asked again if it could be her mam and said she'd pop in again when she was home. And now she worried that she'd been too heavy-handed and the older woman was sitting at home fretting about some kind of showdown. She would have to apologise and thought she might find a nice gift to take too.

Contrary to the legends, the ferry docked safely in the marina, and they disembarked with the rest of that morning's tourists. It was ten o'clock on a Tuesday morning, but Wren guessed that Capri wasn't the kind of place to have a quiet spell; it was thronging with people, so they shouldered their way out of the crowd and made their way uphill, away from the water's edge.

This place was gorgeous, she thought, as they walked along street after street of colourful buildings. The shops all looked eye-wateringly expensive – jewellers, clothes, perfumes – so they mainly window-gazed and soaked up the atmosphere of an island that was its own little high-class world.

Alan looked in the window of a gift shop selling poster prints, throw blankets and ornaments.

'You could get that in Home Bargains for a quarter of the price,' he said, turning up his nose at a set of wood wick candles, which were admittedly the cost of a decent pair of shoes. But then they happened upon a crop of slightly more affordable shops where Wren bought a cute little baby outfit for Libby, and Alan snapped up a dog toy in the shape of a piece of farfalle pasta. Then, in the last shop, Wren found a snow globe with a tiny model of the island of Capri inside, the lighthouse and the famous grottoes sitting in a sea of blue plastic. Remembering how Edie had a penchant for trinkets, she bought that too, hoping it would go some way to make up for pestering her.

They then stopped at a pretty cafe on the edge of town, with a canopy of lemon trees shading the outdoor seating area, and had strong coffee and *sfogliatelle*, delicious shell-shaped Neapolitan pastries filled with ricotta and candied fruit.

'We're going to have to walk this off, Dad,' she said, patting her tummy.

'Aye,' he agreed. 'Let's have a wander. Maybe in the direction of the lighthouse?' he added hopefully.

Wren smiled. 'Come on then.'

They walked towards Anacapri and found themselves at the foot of Monte Solaro, the peak they'd seen from the ferry. The name rang a bell. She checked the holiday itinerary Alex had emailed her several weeks ago, so she was fully briefed and ready. Sure enough, a hike up Monte Solaro had been pencilled in. She also remembered that he'd shown her photos of the view from the top, which she had to admit had looked incredible. And then she saw a chairlift.

'What do you think?' she asked Alan, nodding towards the chairs, a satisfyingly lazy way to get to the top. 'Then we'll go to the lighthouse after?'

'Why not?' he agreed, and they went to pay for tickets.

As they made their ascent, she imagined Alex stomping his way up the rough path below and settled smugly into the rickety wooden seat.

The journey up was breathtaking, with the scrubby ground

and trees below, and the vastness of the sea to look out on to the side. She looked back to see her dad grinning happily as he also took in the scenery. When they reached the top, the views were even more impressive. This was the highest point in Capri, and according to other people's chatter as they wandered by, one of the most stunning views on the island. She couldn't disagree as she stared out at the unending blue sea below, hazy in the midday sun. Rugged outcrops curved into the bay below, and a series of tall rocks, like sentries, jutted from the water. One had a tunnel underneath it, and she watched tiny boats scoot underneath. She was glad they'd come, and equally pleased she could enjoy it without being sweaty and out of breath from a strenuous hike.

They spent a while roaming to all corners of the viewing terrace, taking photos and enjoying the breeze. Then they reboarded the chairlift, Wren nestling her beach bag beside her, safely away from the edge of the chair.

When the chair reached the bottom and Alan got off ahead of her, Wren looped the straps of her straw bag over her shoulder, ready to dismount, but as her feet reached for the ground, she felt a jolt. Her bag was stuck. It wasn't coming with her, and her shoulder was still tethered under the strap. Her heart spiked as she realised she'd missed the dismount point and the chair was starting to make its way around the corner to ascend the slope again. She tugged at the bag – no joy, the straw loops were stuck on something. The Italian chairlift operators shouted and waved their arms.

In a panic, she realised that the ground was slipping further away from her, so she pulled at the bag even harder, slipping in the seat as she thrashed back and forth. The chair gave a sickening swing, and below, she saw tanned faces goggling up at her and the whiter-than-usual face of her dad, mouth hanging open. Then, with a final, panicked tug at her bag, it suddenly came loose, and she lurched backwards, slipping from the polished slats. With a shriek, she slithered off the edge, just able to grab the armrest before plunging to her death, legs swinging in the air like a ragdoll. Shouts and screams came from below, and from the other passengers suspended around her. Everything came in terrifying snapshots.

The chair juddered to a halt, and the squawk of an alarm bell emanated from the control box. Wren dangled there for what seemed like a long time but was probably only half a minute. A weird thought popped into her head. *Alex would be amazed at my upper body strength.* Then the chairs dropped slowly into reverse and she was delivered back to safety, her toes shakily touching the ground.

Officials ran over, barking at her in Italian, gesturing wildly at the chairlift, at her, at her bag. She kept saying sorry, over and over, her face burning at her captive audience, all staring at her from their chairs or in the queue. As much as she'd been praying to live a minute ago, she now wished she could simply die and be buried exactly where she stood.

One of the staff wrangled with the chair she'd been sat on and produced something, holding it up to her face, as if it were damning evidence. It was a carabiner – her bag must have got snagged on it.

'It's not mine,' Wren said, shaking her head, but the official pressed it into her hand, tutting. Not having the wherewithal to argue, she shoved it in her bag.

Alan pushed through the small crowd, his white face now sporting crimson patches across his cheeks. 'Bloody hell, Wren, what happened there?'

'I think I've just shown my bikini bottoms to half of Capri,' she blurted then started laughing, slightly maniacally.

Alan rubbed his hand through his hair, not enjoying the joke, then another official wearing the chairlift uniform marched over to them.

'Come with me,' the official said, unsmiling, taking Wren by the arm. He led her towards the visitors' centre at a brisk pace, Alan trotting behind.

'Now wait here a minute, sunshine,' he said. 'She's done nothing wrong. It's your safety measures that need looking at.'

Wren glanced nervously at the official as he took her inside. 'Am I in trouble?' she asked, her voice meek from shock.

'Sit here,' he directed, and she obediently took a seat on a bench. It was a tourist centre with a gift shop and information leaflets rather than an intimidating office.

The man strode off, and Alan, after checking Wren was okay, followed behind, continuing to give him an earful.

Wren leaned back and rested her head against the wall, closing her eyes. What if she'd fallen? She imagined tumbling to her death in front of her dad and felt sick.

'Kayak tours! Available today! Can I interest you in a kayak tour, madam?'

She opened her eyes exhaustedly and saw a leaflet six inches from her face, and beyond that its bearer, a cheerful man in a baseball cap.

'Madam, you look like just the kind of person who enjoys water sports. And today is your lucky day. We have a few spaces available on our kayak tour of the famous grottoes. Can I interest you in a ticket?'

She robotically accepted the leaflet, squinting at it. The picture showed some smiling people in dayglo lifejackets posing in front of the mouth of a cave. Her eyelids fluttered, and she felt a little faint. When she looked up again, the tout was being hustled out of the centre by the man who'd brought her in here, who returned to press a cool bottle of water into her hand.

'Drink this – you'll feel better.'

She did as she was told, and she did indeed feel better. Satisfied she wasn't going to create even more drama by passing out, the man left her be. At the other side of the visitors' centre, Alan was having an animated conversation with a woman, with lots of hand gestures involved. Wren sighed and got up unsteadily. She was fine – he didn't have to make a fuss.

'Dad, I'm okay,' she said, plucking at his sleeve. 'Let's just go.'

He looked around almost in surprise and unexpectedly buoyant. 'You'll never guess who this is,' he said with a broad smile.

Wren looked at the woman, who was as tall as her dad, strong-looking, with black hair in a rough topknot. Her lightly lined skin was a little ruddy, as if she spent a lot of time outdoors. On reflection, she wasn't wearing a chairlift uniform, so maybe Alan wasn't lodging a formal complaint after all.

'This is Lina,' said Alan, his voice tinged with excitement. 'She works at the lighthouse!'

'Oh! Hello,' Wren said, holding out her hand for Lina to shake, realising only after she did that her palm was clammy from shock. Lina, however, didn't flicker or wipe her palm, much to her credit.

'It's lovely to meet you – and your father,' she said in excellent English.

'Oh, we're honoured to meet *you*,' interjected Alan, almost standing on his toes. 'Wren, did you know that Punta Carena has the second-brightest light in the whole of Italy?'

'Second only to the Lanterna in Genoa,' said Lina with an air of pride.

'Um, that's great,' said Wren, nodding and smiling. Wren had lost any enthusiasm for lighthouses in her early teens, when any parent's job becomes very dull to a kid.

'Lina's going to take us up for a look! It's not manned anymore, but since she volunteers there, we can get inside!'

'Amazing!' Wren was slowly shaking off the adrenaline of her near-death experience but was still too befuddled to do anything but agree. So she found herself following along as Lina led Alan out of the building and in the direction of the coast.

He checked cursorily to see if Wren was truly alright then walked beside Lina, talking feverishly about geographic range and Fresnel lenses. They may as well have been talking Italian. However, Wren wasn't too put out at being excluded. Her dad looked absolutely thrilled to be talking to a fellow lighthouse enthusiast, and it was nice to see him socialising – a rare event. Plus, it gave her time to continue regaining her composure, and as they approached the sea, she found herself looking at the waves and feeling a greater sense of calm.

They came to a split in the path, and Alan and Lina paused to let Wren catch up. Lina pointed up the path to the right, where Wren could see the lighthouse in the distance. Then Wren looked back at the sea. If it had been a plate of food, her mouth would have watered. After the drama of the morning, she felt hot, sweaty and rattled, and the thought of sitting on the beach and cooling off in the sea felt incredibly appealing.

As she approached, Alan was jabbering again, something about focal planes and arcs of visibility. She realised by the look on his face that he'd clocked her hesitation.

He paused. 'Are you sure you want to come, pet?'

'Yeah!' she said as brightly as she could muster, but her eyes were drawn back to the coastline.

Alan frowned. 'Ah, well it's only going to be shop talk. How's about you go and have a rest? I'll meet you when I'm done.'

She hesitated, hoping he wasn't covering any disappointment, but then he gave her a little wink. Feeling more relieved than she'd anticipated, she agreed and they parted ways.

Wren strolled down to the south side of the island via numerous stone stairways to reach the Marina Piccola, where she could see the same rock formations she'd looked down upon from Monte Solaro.

Walking along the top of the beach, she found it was busier than she'd imagined. Rows and rows of towels and sun loungers scored the strip of sand, and the shoreline was chaotic with families splashing in the shallows. She wondered if it would be as refreshing as she thought to stand in the breakers with a beach ball being bounced off her head. Maybe not. Then, in the distance, she saw a row of large beach huts with signs outside. A group of people were hovering nearby, and some men and women were dragging kayaks from the huts onto the sand. She remembered the flyer the tout had thrust upon her and retrieved it from her bag. It was the same company, and what was more, it sounded familiar. A quick check of her phone confirmed she was right – it was the kayak company Alex had booked, and the reservation time was only twenty minutes away.

She looked out at the sea again. Away from the shore, which looked like a boiling pot of water with all the activity going on, it looked so peaceful. It took her only a few seconds to make her decision and head over to the huts to show the online booking on her phone.

A tanned, athletic and bossy Italian woman was clearly in charge and directed Wren to a nearby hut to get changed into the provided wetsuit and rubber shoes. She followed Wren to the door and said, tapping her sports watch, 'You be quick now – we're leaving very soon. Put your bag with the others; it will be waiting for you on the other side of the island when we're done.'

Wren nodded and resisted the urge to salute, then quickly got changed, slapping some factor 30 onto the bits of her arms and legs that the short wetsuit left exposed, and clipping herself into a lifejacket. By the time she got outside, the others were bobbing in the shallows, all except for one kayak and a man standing beside it.

'Sbrigati! You go with this one here,' the wiry little woman shouted from the shore, waving her hands impatiently at the remaining boat and shooing the man into the hut from where

Wren had just come. She tapped her wrist again, and Wren grimaced, rushing forward.

A few minutes later, she felt the back of the kayak bob down as the man climbed in. She turned around and smiled politely. He was about her age, with a mop of sandy hair and an honest, smiling face, pink from the sun.

'I'm Wren, by the way,' she said over her shoulder as he settled himself into his seat.

'Nice to meet you,' he replied, handing her a paddle. 'I'm Nick.'

They pushed off into the water and let the waves draw them forward.

FOURTEEN

NICK

Nick and Wren spent half an hour just a little off the shore being talked through the basics of sea kayaking, how to paddle, how to steer and what to do if the kayak capsized. Nick jiggled in his seat. It was hard to imagine this thing rolling over – it was surprisingly stable even on the bobbing waves – but he listened anyway.

'If you capsize, *do not* let go of your paddle,' barked the instructor, Paola. 'And if you do let go of it, which you should *not*, then you must get it back right away. They will float, but they will also float far away from you – and quickly. Your kayak is no use without the paddle. It will be hopeless.'

'Ha,' murmured Wren over her shoulder. 'I think I'm going to be hopeless at this with or without a paddle. Sorry in advance.'

It was the first time since their brief hello that she'd spoken and Nick realised she had a North East accent. It sounded both out of place and nicely familiar while bobbing on the Mediterranean sea. Her dark brown hair was scooped up into a messy ponytail, and she was wearing little gold earrings and a thin gold chain clasped at the back of her neck. Despite her misgivings, he thought she looked strong enough with the paddle.

'I think you'll do fine,' he said. 'In spite of having to lug me around behind you. I feel like a kid in the back seat of the car.'

She laughed. 'As long as you don't keep asking me if we're there yet.'

'I'll try not to drop crisps everywhere too.'

She laughed again and turned to smile at him, and he felt instantly gratified – a warm feeling spread in his stomach. But before he could try for a comedy hat-trick, Paola's voice cracked like a whip and they were off.

The going was quite tough in the breakers, but once they were further out, it became smoother, and they coursed along amongst the other kayakers. Everyone exchanged happy, living-their-best-life smiles as they glided along like a crowd of baby swans behind Paola.

'Okay, guys!' she shouted. 'Off we go. We go first to *i Faraglioni.*' She pointed to the crop of rocks Nick had seen from the hilltop, and they paddled off towards them.

'So, you're from the North East then?' he asked as they glided along.

'I am. I'm detecting an accent from you as well.'

'*Why aye,*' he said, instantly regretting using such a stereo-typical term and squeezing his eyes shut. 'I'm, er, from Northumberland.'

'Oh right? Me too. Well, it's nice to meet a fellow Northumbrian. I would say it's funny we never crossed paths, but it's a bloody big county.'

'It is.'

They paddled steadily for a little longer, until they arrived at the rocks, which seemed to loom above like skyscrapers. They weren't the only kayak group hovering to get a closer look, but after a while, the boats dispersed enough for them to steer their vessel through the magical-looking arch beneath one of the stones. Nick felt unexpectedly excited as they passed through the narrow cavity, felt the cool of the shadows underneath, and emerged from the other side. Wren laughed in delight, looking up at the sun, and Nick felt a rush of happiness and gave an uncharacteristic whoop.

'Enjoyed that?' she asked.

'Best thing I've done all day.' The dour feeling of disappointment he'd felt that morning had lifted. His main reason for being here in Italy would rear its head again, and soon, but right at that moment, he was able to just enjoy being out in the waves. It was like riding a very gentle rollercoaster – he could focus on little else, and the endorphins were flowing.

On they went, following the curve of the island, until they reached a cave on the coast of the island itself.

'Here is *la Grotta Verde*, the green grotto,' shouted Paola, signalling to the cave mouth. 'This *grotta*, we can go inside, to see the beautiful green colour in the water. It is like nothing you've seen before. We were hoping to go inside the Blue Grotto on the other side of the island later, but the sea conditions are no good.'

There was a collective sigh and muttering from some of the group.

Paola held her hands up. 'It is forbidden when the sea is rougher, and dangerous. So we look inside *la Grotta Verde* now, and then we wave hello to *la Grotta Azzurra* on the way past later. The sea is the boss, not me.' She shrugged and ignored the mild mutiny around her, waving people on to the cave opening.

'Lots of people not very happy,' murmured Wren.

'Yeah, it's a shame,' said Nick. 'It's what most people come for, the Blue Grotto, I think.'

'Some waiter in Sorrento told me it's haunted by mermaids and witches,' said Wren with a chuckle. 'Maybe we're best off out of it.'

'Maybe. I think the currents bashing us off the rocks inside makes me more nervous though,' said Nick.

'Just like the sirens.'

'The what now?'

'Another of that waiter's old stories. The sirens were mythical women, luring sailors onto the rocks to their deaths.'

'Well, that sounds cheerful,' he said. 'Hopefully the green one is a bit more friendly.'

They followed the group and ducked slightly as they passed below the roof of the cave entrance.

Wren gasped, and Nick's eyes widened as he registered what she was seeing. Below them was an eerie but beautiful green glow from the crystalline waters.

'Oh my God,' she breathed. 'This is amazing.'

'It really is,' murmured Nick.

The water looked at once transparent and sparkly but also seemed to glow from within. The green shades changed like a kaleidoscope, from turquoise to emerald to aquamarine, depending on the way the light hit the water. He couldn't take his eyes from it. Around them, people were taking out phones from their wetsuits and snapping pictures.

'Damn. I left my phone in my bag,' he said, realising his mistake.

'Me too,' said Wren. 'I feel like an idiot now.'

'I guess we'll just have to remember it the old-fashioned way.'

They looked around, trailing hands in the water. Nick watched the ripples change colour as Wren's hand passed through it, and as she reached back to do it again, her little finger grazed Nick's as he did the same. The tiny, momentary contact of skin on skin under the water made him catch his breath. Maybe it was the thrill of being in such a beautiful, unusual place, or maybe it was being in the sun too long, but it was a strange sensation, like static electricity combined with déjà vu.

She pulled her hand back as if scalded and gripped the paddle. Nick yawned and stretched performatively. The easy conversation seemed to have stopped.

The next part of the excursion had been described as the most strenuous part – Paola had warned in advance that they would be powering up and around the east coast of the island, heading towards the north without stopping to look at anything else until the Blue Grotto. Nick's arm muscles were aching, and he hoped they would at least take a break when they got there, even though they weren't going to be able to go inside.

They'd fallen to the back end of the group, and the gap between them and the next kayak was steadily growing wider. Maybe he was more tired than he'd realised following his hike up Monte Solaro and the fruitless circuit around Capri town.

'You okay up there?' he asked Wren, whose shoulders flexed and pulsed with activity.

'Bit tired,' she said, sounding a little out of puff. 'I've had a bit of a day, to be honest. I think I've had the stuffing knocked out of me.'

'We'll catch up though,' he said. 'And we only need to stick to the coastline.'

'Yeah, I imagine Paola will stop to regroup in a bit.'

She sounded uncertain, and Nick didn't blame her. Looking ahead, he could see Paola in the distance, castigating some guy who was trying to stand up on his kayak to take photographs.

They ploughed on, Nick using all the strength he could muster, but before long, the rest of the group was further ahead than ever and disappeared around the coastline as it turned to the north side of the island.

'It's fine,' Nick said. 'They'll stop at the grotto and we'll catch up then.'

Wren gave a determined nod and kept going. Then, as they skirted the north coast and he saw the grotto in the distance, there was no group of kayakers bobbing nearby. Instead, he could see them much further ahead, presumably making their way to the end point at the marina. A pang of anxiety hit him. What was the worst that could happen though? They would arrive at the marina half an hour late, and Paola could tear strips off them before they went home and never saw her again. They were grown adults and could follow the coastline without a problem, surely.

'At least we can still see them. It's fine,' said Nick, although he subconsciously put some extra power into his next few strokes.

Just ahead and to their right, notched into a rocky coastal wall, was the small mouth of the fabled Blue Grotto. It was late in the day, but there was a smattering of solo kayakers hovering nearby to take a look, and at a further distance, the tour boats holding other disappointed visitors who'd hoped to get inside. Near to the cave opening was a small jetty with narrow boats that usually transported tourists from the larger boats inside the tiny opening, but they were all tied up and bobbing energetically in the choppy waters. A white foamy spray lapped at the rocks in small crashes, filling the mouth of the cave with water then emptying again. It was easy to see why it wasn't possible to sail inside right now.

Despite their aim to catch up with the group, they'd both slowed to a halt. Wren seemed to be transfixed by the cave, staring at the wild opening, and was panting with exertion. Nick, if he was honest, was glad of a rest, so they sat there for a moment, catching their breath in silence. Within a minute, the cave mouth looked a bit larger, and the rock face looked a little clearer, and he realised they'd drifted towards the rocks in the swells.

'Um, Nick,' said Wren, reaching for her paddle, which in her exhaustion she'd just rested across the front of her instead of securing it to the kayak. 'I think we'd better...' Her hand fumbled for the paddle, and before she could get a proper grip of it, it rolled off the kayak and into the water.

'Shit!' she said, trying to stand up to reach for it. Since she'd dropped it, it had already floated a metre or two from the kayak.

'Whoa there!' shouted Nick as the kayak lurched violently to the right. 'Wren, don't! Just leave it.'

'But Paola said...' Her face was stricken.

The paddle shot away from the kayak, taken by the current, and was enveloped by the foam. All of his attention had been held by Wren's panic, and they'd drifted even closer to the rock face, but her only concern right then seemed to be getting that paddle back. His heart raced, and common sense slipped away. He pushed his weight over the side, hands grabbing at the water in search of the pole, but nothing was there.

He handed her his own paddle, questioning his own sanity with even that simple exchange.

'Just sit down and hold tight,' he said, kneeling up on the kayak and reaching further into the water. His fingers were just shy of the paddle. If he could just reach a bit further...

Wren gasped from beside him as the kayak gave in to his thrashing, and it very nearly tipped over. He gritted his teeth and reached for the paddle one more time, stretching with a ferocity that was strongly linked to a desire to impress, and fell into the water with a splash. The spray had cooled him nicely while inside the kayak, but the shock of the cold now took his breath away, and he was tossed around by the currents. Above him, he heard Wren yell something, although it was garbled in the chaos of the waves.

Although he was a strong swimmer and wearing a lifejacket,

he couldn't overcome the strength of the coursing water, and his head went under. Coughing out sea water, his eyes stinging with it, he could just make out the end of his own paddle being prodded at him from above. He took it and yanked, trying to pull himself closer, but then felt the weightlessness of a paddle that had nobody on the other end.

Blinking through the spray, he could see Wren with her hands in her hair, and the paddle he'd yanked free floating uselessly nearby. And then he felt the rocks at his back, scraping at his arms and legs, and a heavy, pulling sensation as he was dragged along the wall. There was a brief moment when the sun still shone upon him, before he felt like he'd been sucked into a vacuum and everything went black.

FIFTEEN

WREN

I am going to die saving this complete stranger.

The thought reeled through Wren's head on a loop as she plunged through the cave opening, mostly because her brain couldn't compute any other logical thought. In any case, all logical thought seemed to have stopped the moment Nick had been swept into the cave mouth, because she'd leaped in after him without a moment's hesitation. The last thing she could remember was the raised voices of the onlookers – shouts of alarm and disbelief.

She could understand what they meant now she was in the tunnel, being buffeted against the walls, only a foot or so of air space above her to breathe. It was dark and chaotic – she could hardly tell what was up and down, but it was also a mercifully quick journey, thanks to the sucking tide of water pulling her inwards. She emerged, thrashing, into the cave, which, despite its reputation for being magical and breathtaking, was shadowy and dim.

She trod water, her heart racing as she looked around, dreading seeing a floating form in the water. But what she saw instead was Nick, looking pitifully like Tom Hanks in that castaway film, dripping wet and perched on a small platform of rock at the side of the cave. His wetsuit was ripped from neck to stomach, revealing his heaving chest as he caught his breath. He gestured her over and she was propelled, mostly by the surging water, partly by a frantic doggy paddle, to the outcrop of rock. His strong arms helped to hoist her as she scrambled up.

At first, she just stared at him, panting, as he did the same. Then, bizarrely, they both started to laugh, Wren covering her mouth with her hand, wide-eyed with shock. The noise reverberated off the walls and they stopped, blinking into the gloom.

'Okay, I'll start,' said Nick, still breathing heavily. 'What the fuck just happened there?'

Wren shook her head. 'I think we just made a terrible mistake.'

'Well, *you* did,' he said, grimacing. 'What possessed you to dive in after me? If that's what happened... Or did you fall in as well?'

'No, I'm your knight in shining armour apparently. Well, until now. I suppose we're both in trouble.'

Nick winced. 'I'm so sorry. I can't believe I'm in here in the first place, but you didn't need to be. Are you okay?' He assessed her anxiously, looking for injuries.

Wren patted herself down. 'I'm fine. It's fine. A split-second decision. One I think I'm now regretting. But you... are you alright?'

Without thinking, she reached out and touched his bare chest, which was exposed by the huge tear in his wetsuit. As soon as her fingers made contact with his wet skin, she whipped her hand away and looked down at the water. Her cheeks warmed, despite the chill in the cave.

'I'm fine,' he said with a wry smile, rubbing the place she'd just touched. 'Just a few grazes, a dented ego and a strong suspicion I'm not getting my deposit back on this wetsuit.'

'No. I don't think you are. Listen, I'm sorry. You wouldn't

have fallen in at all if you hadn't been trying to get the paddle back. I'm such an idiot.'

'Nah, you're alright,' he said.

'I mean, it's just a paddle. You could have died.'

'And you. Jumping in to save me. We both could have.'

Wren shivered, and it wasn't just because the temperature in here was comparatively glacial without the warmth of the sun. She'd felt she had no option at all but to plunge into the water, as if she hadn't been in control of her own actions.

'The sirens...' she said. 'Maybe those old stories have something to them.' She immediately felt stupid, but he didn't laugh.

'Well, something made me temporarily lose my mind,' he agreed. But then he shook his head. 'To be fair, I was probably more scared of us facing Paola with one less paddle than facing the spooky stuff in this cave.'

Wren laughed but still felt uneasy. The sea was churning less furiously now; the tide seemed to be retreating, but the water still looked ominous and grey, and there was a damp chill to the air.

'I thought this was meant to be the prettiest cave. Blue lights and magic.'

Nick scanned the cave too. 'Yeah, that's what she said. But I think it must be only at certain times. When the light shines in just the right way.'

'So we've ended up trapped in here and we don't even get the full show. Tripadvisor will be hearing of this.'

'And I'll be sending a strongly worded email to the tourist board.'

Wren thought back to her near miss on the chairlift and wondered if he wasn't half right. This holiday had turned into way more of a health hazard than she'd envisioned, even though she'd managed to escape the abseiling and waterskiing that she'd noted – with horror – on Alex's abandoned itinerary. She imagined him in this situation with her and cringed – she could almost hear him ranting and raging. Nothing like this guy, who was trading silly jokes with her. She wondered if Nick was panicking deep down and was doing this for her benefit, or if he was really just the sort of person not to worry.

'So, what do we do now?' she asked, hugging herself and continuing to stare, furrow-browed, at the water.

'I guess we wait. Unless another hero comes crashing through the tunnel.'

'The world's stupidest threesome, that would be.' She flushed again, realising the obvious innuendo too late.

He paused but didn't bite. 'Nope. I think we just have to hang on until the water level drops and we can swim back out. I don't think it'll be too long.' He shivered, and she moved instinctively closer to him. She was just about to ask him again if he was okay when she noticed that the cave had grown quieter. The sound of crashing water had grown faint, and there was a subtle shift in the light.

They watched the water, seeing that the foamy spray that had been spurting into the cave was now growing clearer and less frothy, and after a short while, the mouth to the cave settled into a clear horizon between water and air. Then, bit by bit, the cave began to grow lighter. Sun must have been coming in from somewhere, as the water gradually gathered brightness, glowing as if it was being lit from below. It spread in orbs of turquoise, until the whole surface of the water was phosphorescent with blue light. Wren and Nick looked at each other and gave an incredulous laugh. Without a word they both jumped in.

'Oh my God, this isn't real,' said Wren, beaming like a child, bobbing her hands up and down to make ripples. The water felt warm compared to the chill she'd felt standing dripping wet on that ledge, and she felt the panic of being stuck in here start to lift. Nick looked just as buoyed up and was grinning. He splashed shimmering water at her and she shrieked, splashing back. It was like being in a pool of moonlight.

They trod water, just smiling at each other, and without even trying, Wren somehow drifted closer to Nick. Their feet gently grazed against each other as they cycled underwater, and for some reason, she reached out her hand. He took it, and it seemed quite natural. Maybe she was scared. Maybe *he* was scared. But holding his hand, while they were trapped in their watery prison, felt safer.

They said nothing; the only noise was the lapping of the water on the walls of the cave, and Wren had time to properly look at Nick for the first time. Now that he was no longer sitting behind her on the kayak, or clinging haphazardly to a cave wall, she could really take him in. His sandy hair now looked dark brown, plastered wet against his head, and his hazel-brown eyes were warm and bright. Nice teeth, not too crooked, not too straight, and a comfortable build that looked like he was no slouch but didn't live in the gym. Unlike someone she used to know.

He was looking at her too, and maybe it was the strangeness of the situation but she didn't feel self-conscious. Their eyes met, and she saw a flicker of seriousness through the giddy smile. There was a moment where she felt she should speak, but she didn't and just broke into a wider grin. With the water glowing around them, and the adrenaline of their near drowning starting to fade, the cave seemed to become another world. One where this stranger felt like someone she'd known for a long time.

'You two!' came a shrill voice from the tunnel, and they both jumped as if the water had filled with eels.

A boat sculled underneath the tunnel, which was now passable as the water level had dropped, and at first it appeared empty. Then, as it emerged, Paola and a boatman sat up from where they'd been crouching low to avoid the roof of the tunnel. Paola's eyes reminded Wren of those seen on the mugshots of serial killers.

'Are you fucking kidding me?' she shouted. 'Are you trying to get me shut down? Or arrested?'

Wren bit her lip, feeling chastened. Nick dropped her hand as if they were standing in the headmistress's office, and they trod water guiltily.

Paola glared down at them. 'Well? Get in the damn boat!'

Wren cringed as she swam quickly towards the boat and climbed on with the help of the boatman, who was trying not to laugh. Paola gave him a glacial look.

Nick had scrambled up the other side of the boat, and once they were in, Paola ordered them to lie flat so they could go back through the passage. The oarsman crouched down and steered them through as they stared in cowed silence at the stony roof of the tunnel.

'Um, Paola,' said Nick quietly, 'I'm afraid we let go of our paddles.'

Wren flinched, a bubble of hysteria rising in her chest. Paola, out of her line of vision, made a huffing noise that reminded her of an angry bull. Then, like the explosion of water from the cave mouth, she and Nick dissolved into juvenile giggles, not able to look at each other at all for fear of setting off a fresh bout.

As they lay back on the seat, tears rolling down their cheeks, Wren felt something in her belly that had become unfamiliar lately. It was a sense of being carefree, as buoyant as the boat they were lying on, and having someone beside her who felt the same.

Wren and Nick were dumped unceremoniously on the harbour, where their bags and belongings were waiting for them, having been brought over the island by the tour company. There was no sign of any of their kayak companions, which was both an embarrassment and a relief. She and Nick were the naughty schoolkids kept back after lessons.

Nick went off to return the remains of his ruined wetsuit, and Wren used some nearby loos to get changed. Reunited with her phone and seeing she had half a dozen missed calls, she rang her dad.

Rather than being frantic with worry about where she was, he answered the phone cheerfully. There was a clamour of noise from the other end, people laughing and shouting.

'Dad, sorry if I'm a bit late. I'm not far from the ferry terminal. Are you already there?'

'That's why I was ringing, pet. Lina's introduced me to some pals of hers from the port, and we've had a couple of drinks. They're boating across to a little shindig in Sorrento tonight, and I thought I might...'

Wren broke into a smile. He sounded giddy and a tiny bit inebriated. She didn't think she'd ever heard him like this.

'That's fine, Dad. Will you ring me when you get back to your room after?'

'You're invited to the party, pet. Come along and meet us.'

'No, no. I'll be fine; I'd rather head back now. Bit tired.' The thought of an evening with a bunch of maritime enthusiasts appealed about as much as nights with Alex's gym bros.

'Okay, if you're sure. Text me when you're back in Sorrento.'

'Will do. Have a good night.'

'You an' all, pet.' She heard a cheer and what sounded like the beginnings of an Italian sea shanty in the background, and he rang off.

Nick was walking back over the harbour in his normal clothes, hair half dried and sticking up everywhere. Wren felt something strangely akin to waking up after a one-night stand; the cave had felt immediately intimate, but in the light of day, this Nick had become a stranger again. She folded her arms self-consciously.

'How did it go?' she asked. 'I was expecting you to come back as beaten up as the wetsuit.'

He grinned. 'Paola took it surprisingly well. I think she was just glad to see the back of us.'

'I don't blame her,' said Wren, then an unexpected laugh escaped from her and she shook her head. 'I can't actually believe that just happened. I think I must have brought you bad luck.' She thought back to her disastrous dismount from the chairlift and wondered if she had some kind of klutz-curse on her. She'd been mortifyingly clumsy lately.

He shrugged, an unreadable look on his face. 'I don't know. I think I might be the one bringing the bad fortune at the moment.' His brow furrowed for just a second, then he shook his head. 'Anyway, speaking of bad luck, I've just missed my ferry. And I've had a dozen angry texts and voice notes from my brother.'

Wren winced. 'Nightmare. Um, is he okay?'

'Yeah, he'll be fine. He got on the ferry, hoping he'd find me on there, but now he knows I'm alive, he's calmed down. Nothing an Aperol Spritz won't sort out, and I'll just get on the next one. So, have you got someone anxiously waiting for you too?'

'No, if anything I think my dad's relieved I'm not cramping his style. I'm going to go back to Sorrento and I'll see him tomorrow.'

Nick's eyebrows rose. 'Listen, I don't know about you, but... I still feel a bit shaken up after today. Are you sure you're okay? I can take you back, if you like?'

'Oh, I'm fine! Honestly, don't worry. But now that you mention it, what if I need to look out for you? For all I know, you could be about to succumb to PTSD.'

'Very true. Okay,' he said slowly, looking at his watch. 'How about this? We go and grab a bite to eat. I'm starving. And then once we're both sure the other isn't going to have a breakdown, we'll send each other on their way.'

Wren did feel hungry. And it did feel like the polite thing to do – a bit of a debrief on their cave adventure. So she nodded.

They'd only walked a few paces when she thought to check her own watch.

'Shit,' she said, her hand on her forehead. 'Nick, I'm sorry, but my ferry leaves in about ten minutes. And it's the last one back to Sorrento.'

'Right,' he said, eyes flicking to the harbour, where, sure enough, the ferry was waiting. He paused for a moment. 'Okay, well, tell me to piss off if you want, but I can come over to Sorrento with you, and we can get some food there? Just to make sure you're alright.'

Wren opened her mouth to say again that she was okay, but then he grinned.

'I think I meant to say... to make sure we're both alright.'

Wren smiled. She didn't tell him to piss off, and ten minutes later, she and Nick watched the coast of Capri fade into the distance from the back of the Sorrento ferry.

SIXTEEN

NICK

Nick couldn't be sure, but it seemed like the waiter might have spilled his drink on purpose. He certainly hadn't apologised for it, and the glass of lager had been thumped down unceremoniously.

'Friendly guy,' he murmured.

'He was certainly a *lot* more friendly the last time I was here,' said Wren, grimacing.

'Ah. So he thinks I'm competition,' said Nick, taking a sip of his drink and looking away as he realised that might sound a bit forward. Truth be told, he really did just want to make sure Wren got back safely, and the suggestion of a shared dinner was genuinely out of ravenous hunger, but now he was sitting opposite her, he kept getting flashes of their time in the cave. Floating in the blue water, he was sure there had been a little moment, gone as quickly as it arrived, but it kept coming back to him.

Wren laughed self-consciously, and her hand went to the necklace that lay at her collarbone. She toyed with it, rolling her fingers over a seashell pendant that had pearly stripes. She'd taken her dark hair down from its ponytail, and it hung haphazardly around her face, which was what he thought might be described as heart-shaped. She had round, pink cheeks and blue-green eyes with dark, long lashes.

'I think he might,' she said. 'If only he knew this wasn't actually a date but a post-traumatic therapy session.'

'True. And this spaghetti isn't date food – it's just medicine.' He twirled some pasta around his fork and put it in his mouth, slopping sauce down his chin. 'This is the reason it isn't date food obviously.'

She raised her glass. 'Cheers to that. Let's clink our glasses of tranquilliser and get on with it.'

He tapped his glass against hers and speared some more pasta.

'Most therapy sessions start with a bit of background information, I would imagine,' he said. 'So, Wren, I know you're from the North East, due to the charming accent, but what brings you to Italy? Travel blogger? Mafia connections?'

She smiled. 'You're closer with the first one. Keep guessing.'

'Um. A writer?'

She nodded. 'Well done. How about you? What's your line of work?'

'Uh-uh. I quite like this game. You have to guess as well.'

She bunched up her nose. 'Hmm. Marine biologist?'

'Nope.'

'Graphic designer?'

'You're not even trying. Do these look like the hands of someone who taps on a computer all day, or strokes dolphins or whatever a marine biologist does?' He held up his hands, which were callused and work-worn, and had the odd nick and scar from altercations with Stanley knives and shards of glass.

'A clue. Excellent.' She nodded and stroked her chin like Columbo. 'A blacksmith?'

Nick was mid-drink and almost spat it out as he laughed. 'A blacksmith? Sorry, I hadn't realised I have the air of an extra from *Game of Thrones*.'

'I'm just being imaginative,' she said, shrugging.

'Well, you're a writer. You would be.'

'So, go on, tell me what you do.'

Nick sat back in his chair, nursing his beer glass in both hands. 'No, no, no. I didn't get a free pass on my guess. How about I just tell you when you get it right?'

She chewed some pasta, thinking. 'Or how about this? We have to guess everything about each other, and we can only know the answer when we guess correctly?'

'I like a challenge,' he said, feeling an easy grin spread over his face. She was fun. It had been a long time since he'd bantered back and forth with anyone who wasn't his brother or nanna, which was quite tragic. He was enjoying it.

'Okay, I'll have one more try,' she said. 'Landscape gardener.'

'Not even close.' He dug his fork into a piece of chicken and popped it in his mouth happily. He could do this all night.

They passed a happy half hour exchanging guesses about their identities. Nick successfully guessed that Wren's favourite colour was purple and that she wasn't actually here for her writing work, just a holiday. Wren managed to surmise that Nick was a single dad, but she still hadn't figured out what he did for a job.

She'd just shouted out 'Set designer for a burlesque show!' in frustration when he happened to look at his watch. It was ten o'clock. He winced, both at her guess and the time.

'Wrong again,' he said. 'And we might need to call it a day on the guessing. I'd better be getting back.'

'Oh. Aren't you going to tell me before you go?' she said with a bright smile that didn't quite reach her eyes. Nick was secretly gratified that she looked disappointed.

He shook his head, and perhaps because he was bolstered

by a few beers and a lot of laughs, he found the confidence to say, 'Maybe we could meet up again before we go home? If you like? You can have another go then.'

She hesitated for a moment then nodded. 'Maybe we could.'

He scrolled his phone to see how he could get to Naples from here. No buses or trains were running at this time of night, unsurprisingly. He opened his Uber app, eyes widening at the price, then switched it off. He'd have to brace himself before he confirmed *that* pickup.

'Are you okay? You've gone a bit pale.'

He smiled. 'I'm alright. Just preparing to fund a taxi driver's second home.'

'Oh, shit. Is that the only way to get back?'

'Yeah,' he said, attempting to sound breezy. It wasn't her problem after all. 'To be fair, it is a long way – I should have known. Anyway, I imagine you need to get back too. Can I walk you to your hotel? And I mean that literally – it's not a line! I did say I'd see you back safe.'

'Oh no, honestly. It isn't far from here. Just up the hill.' She pointed to the hillside behind them, and Nick saw the twinkly lights of lit windows above.

'I'm guessing there are some pretty isolated paths up that hill though. Please. I'd never forgive myself if you didn't get back safe. And I owe you one after you tried to save my life today.' He winked.

She thought for a second. 'Well, you had every opportunity to drown me in the privacy of that cave, I suppose. So I can probably trust you. Okay. Thank you.'

They asked for the bill, and Nick listened to Wren's North East accent again. It was a bit more refined than his own, her vowels sounding softer around the edges like a vinyl record compared to his own staccato version, which could cut glass.

'Where exactly are you from then, Wren?' he asked, finishing the last of his drink.

'Well, I suppose you'll have to guess,' she said, leaning forward with her arms crossed on the table. Her eyes twinkled with a challenge.

He grinned. 'The game continues... Okay. What about—?'

Then, just before he could say another word, the surly waiter returned and slapped a little silver tray in between them bearing a folded bill and a couple of dusty-looking mint imperials. He stood over them, waiting.

Wren pinched her lips between her teeth, obviously trying hard not to laugh as they rustled in their pockets for some cash, and they both placed money on the tray. It was whipped away without comment, and the waiter stalked off.

Their laughter escaped like uncorked champagne. 'I don't think we're getting any change,' said Wren, wiping her eyes.

Nick laughed. 'And the offer of mint imperials has been withdrawn. Mind you, it might be for the best. I have a feeling he might have picked out the ones that went off in 2002, just for us.'

The path up the hill was shaded with trees and pitch dark in places. Nick was glad he'd insisted on taking her home. They climbed steadily, swapping jokes about what might have happened if they'd eaten the cursed sweets, until they arrived outside a nice-looking hotel building.

'Here we are,' she said, digging her key out of her bag.

'Here we are.' Nick put his hands in his pockets. If it hadn't been a date they were on, it sure felt like one now. The feeling of standing opposite her stirred memories of doorstep kisses from his past, and he reminded himself he was here as a good deed.

There was a moment where they glanced at each other and looked away.

'I'll be—' He was about to finish with 'off then', but she spoke over him.

'Hang on a minute,' she said, letting her bag fall to her side.

'I have a few more questions for you. Have you ever been to prison?'

'Um, no?'

'Do you have anything illegal on your person? Drugs, knives and so on?'

'Er, I don't *think* so...'

'And did you vote Leave or Remain in Brexit?'

'Remain. Obviously.'

She visibly relaxed. 'Okay. On that basis, do you want to sleep on my sofa? I've got spare blankets. So you're welcome to... if you want?'

'Are you sure? Really, I don't want you to feel like you have to...'

'I'm sure,' she said. 'Don't pay silly money on a taxi. You can sleep here then do the bus or train in the morning.'

Nick nodded. If he slept on the sofa, it would be no different from sleeping in a youth hostel dorm. Nothing dodgy in that. Although he should probably ask her a question too.

'Okay, well I have a question for you. Have you ever seen *Misery*, and have you any aspirations of re-enacting it?'

'Yes, and no.'

'Then thank you very much for your hospitality.'

And with that, they went inside.

After some awkward back and forth to the bathroom, and a quick text to Travis to let him know where he was, Nick tucked his rucksack under the sofa and pulled the blanket Wren had found over himself.

Wren came out of the bathroom dressed in pyjamas, and she scurried to get under the covers, smiling awkwardly. 'Night, then,' she said, switching off the light.

'Night,' he said, still feeling wide awake. He closed his eyes and tried to relax enough to sleep. He was surprised to find that, in the darkness, tiredness stole across him like an energy-sapping thief.

Wren's voice came sleepily across the room. 'One last question,' she murmured. 'Why did you think you'd brought bad luck to me? You looked like you meant it. In Capri.'

Nick opened his eyes and stared into the darkness for a moment. 'Ah, it's nothing. I just had an unlucky day.'

'Did you get trapped on a chairlift too?' Her voice sounded so drowsy, it was almost like she was sleep-talking.

Nick blinked hazily. 'Um, weirdly... yes. Almost. But I'm also looking for someone, and I didn't find them.'

'Uh-huh,' she murmured then paused. 'Is this part of the guessing game?'

He smiled. 'If you like.'

'A friend?'

'No.'

'Your girlfriend?'

'I don't have a girlfriend.' He realised as he said it that he wanted her to know this.

She was quiet for a moment. 'Um... your mam or dad?'

'My dad.'

'I see. Is he lost?'

'Something like that,' he said quietly, feeling his eyes start to close.

He pictured the empty restaurant before he drifted off to sleep.

SEVENTEEN

WREN

Wren woke to the smell of coffee, and when she opened her eyes, there was a cup on her bedside table, steam rising from it in white curls. She shuffled to sit up. Nick was sitting fully clothed on the sofa, sipping his own drink.

'I hope you don't mind me making myself at home,' he said, lifting his cup a little.

Wren took a drink. 'Not at all, especially if you make a coffee as nice as this. Thank you.' She felt a little shy again. 'Did you sleep okay?'

'Like a log. I think yesterday caught up with me.'

'Me too,' she said. She looked at her phone. It was nearly ten o'clock. 'Bloody hell, is that really the time?'

He chuckled. 'I know, I know. I'll be out of your hair once I've finished this brew.'

'I didn't mean—'

'I know. I'm winding you up. But I'd better get back. There's a bus to Naples in twenty minutes.'

'And your brother will be waiting for you, I'd imagine. Tell him I'm sorry for stealing you away.'

'Ha. I think he's quite enjoyed it. Apparently Naples does a roaring trade in knock-down designer gear. Who knew?'

'Oh, right. He's into fashion then?'

'Like you wouldn't believe. Right, I'd best be off then.' He put his cup down and slapped his knees in the universal gesture of leaving someone's house. Standing up, he slung his rucksack onto his shoulder. 'I guess I should say thanks for the adventure?'

Her stomach dropped slightly. This sounded like a proper goodbye, and she realised now she'd been hoping to see him again, like they'd said last night. Should she ask for his number? She opened her mouth to do just that but then snapped it shut again. It was all too confusing. Just last week she'd had a boyfriend, and although Alex had shredded any love she had left for him, he still hovered nearby like an unwelcome ghost. Years of being with him still weighed heavy. Was it wrong to feel like she could move on so quickly? She made a split-second decision.

'Yep. Same to you. Thanks for the memories and all that,' she said, and it came out a little more brittle than she'd intended. It was borne out of feeling awkward, not to mention regretful, but she saw his smile falter.

'Sorry that a fair proportion of them were quite harrowing,' he said, recovering.

'Mentally scarring.' She smiled, the strange tension easing a little.

'And say the same to your dad for me. Apologies for dragging you away yesterday.'

'Quite literally,' said Wren, thinking of her helter-skelter ride through the cave tunnel. Then, on the subject of fathers, she remembered why Nick was here. She hesitated for a moment then asked, 'Will you be looking for your dad again today?'

He seemed unsure for a moment. 'I think I will, yes.'

'I hope you find him.'

'I hope so too. I think I'll go back to Capri. Take another look around.'

'Good! Good plan. I'll keep my fingers crossed for you.'

'Thanks.' He smiled, and Wren wondered if it was a slightly sad smile, or if she was projecting. He headed for the door. 'Bye, Wren,' he said, and he left.

Wren was still in bed, knees pulled up to her chest, holding her mug with two hands. She chewed her lip as she thought. Why did it feel strange suddenly being alone in her room? She'd spent plenty of time alone until yesterday and been quite happy about it. But now Nick had gone, it felt like there was an empty space.

Before Alan answered the door, Wren could smell lemons. When he opened the door, the lemon scent was backed up by the distinctive odour of ethanol. She wrinkled her nose.

'Been having one or two limoncellos, Dad?'

Alan looked like he'd had one or twenty limoncellos. His wild hair was even more unkempt, one side plastered to his head, the other sprayed up like a peacock's tail. He had bags under his eyes that would have required a supplemental payment at check-in.

'Come in, pet,' he said, voice like gravel. He walked slowly to his bed and sat down on the end of it, rubbing his eyes.

Wren resisted the urge to laugh and took a seat on the armchair, setting down some pastries and two cups of takeaway coffee from a nearby cafe. Alan's room was smaller than hers but was still comfortably furnished with a small dressing table, gauzy curtains and Mediterranean prints on the walls.

'So, you had a good night, then.'

He grinned and immediately winced. 'You could say that. Those sailor fellas know how to have a good time. Have you ever played a drinking game, Wren? Because I can't tell if I won or lost.' He took a cup of coffee, sniffed it carefully and took a sip.

Wren laughed. 'Probably both, Dad. Did you enjoy the lighthouse?'

'Oh, Wren, it was smashing. Did you know it was kept by just one man until a few years ago? Only became automated in 2019.'

'Wow,' said Wren, nodding appreciatively but keen to swerve the conversation away from the technicalities of coastal safety measures. 'They were a nice bunch then?'

'Salt of the earth, Wren – proper good lads. And lasses too.'

Wren smirked.

'Nowt like that, you cheeky monkey. We had a good knees-up and put the world to rights. Well, as much as you can when the Italians are trying to decipher your Geordie accent.'

Wren's insides warmed at the thought of her dad in the thick of a lively conversation and remembered the noise that had come down the phone last night. She didn't think Alan had been out for so much as half a pint in the pub for many years.

'So you've got some new pen pals?'

'Better than that.' He smiled contentedly. 'Lina set me up on Facebook and I've joined their group.' He fumbled with his phone and brought up his profile. His badly angled selfie looked like it'd been taken in the reflection of the back of a spoon, but he was grinning from ear to ear.

'Ah, that's lovely, Dad.'

'Yeah, and looka! This one here is my old pal, Neil, from school. He "friended" me. And this one's Charlie from when I used to play snooker.' His eyes misted over a little, and he tapped at his phone screen to turn it off. 'Lost their phone numbers years ago.'

Wren's heart swelled. Maybe this holiday might do more for her dad than just giving him a bit of a tan.

As if he'd read her mind, he touched her hand. 'Thanks for bringing me along, Wren. I didn't realise how much I'd enjoy it. It's been a long time since I've been away.'

'I'm happy you're here, Dad,' she said, realising how sincerely she meant this. Alex seemed a million miles away, and she was glad.

Alan gave a bashful grin. 'You know, it must be nearly forty years since I went abroad.'

Wren hadn't really thought about it, but they'd never been on a holiday outside the UK when she was a child. Bucket-and-spade holidays in Scarborough or Devon, but not once overseas.

'Was that one of your holidays with Mam?'

'Aye. It was,' he said, his eyes misting over a little as he remembered. 'It was before you were born. Cyprus. She loved a bit of sun, your mam. Those were the days before there was all this fuss about sun cream, you know? She used to baste herself in carrot oil so she'd bronze up a bit more.'

Wren laughed, picturing the photos at home where Caron looked as pale as British weather would usually allow. 'What kind of stuff would you do?'

'Oh, this and that. British pubs, a bit of karaoke. Nothing as fancy as this. She would have got a kick out of this; she'd have felt like the lady of the manor. She'd have loved being here with you too, you know. I can picture the pair of you out there by the pool on sun loungers.'

'You can?'

'I can.'

Wren blinked. This had to be the most her dad had said about her mam in a very long time. It was as if a bit of sun and a lot of alcohol had opened a gate that had been tightly locked. Could she ask him again? About Edie and the Kitchen?

Then she saw how comforted he looked by those happy memories, and she couldn't bring herself to say it. Taking the conversation to a place he'd avoided before seemed cruel.

'So, what do you fancy doing today?' she asked instead. 'I think there's only the one lighthouse around here, but I'm sure we could find something else seafaring to do.'

Alan went a little green. 'You know what, pet, I think I might have a bit of a lie-down. Do you mind? I'm still quite... tired.'

Wren bit her lip, trying not to laugh. 'Of course, Dad. I understand.'

'I feel bad. I left you on your own yesterday too. No, no, I'll get myself up, and we'll go and do something.' He stood up abruptly. Maybe too abruptly, as he swayed a bit and clutched his head.

Wren hurried over and gently pressed his shoulders until he sat on the bed again. She went to the bathroom sink and filled the toothbrush mug with some water, then produced some paracetamol from her handbag. 'Here, take these. You have a good rest and we'll meet up later.'

He obeyed and looked up at her, slightly cowed. 'Sorry.'

'Don't say sorry. I'll head out for a wander, and I'll ring you later. We can grab a bite to eat once you're back on your feet.'

He nodded and lay back down on the bed. Wren let herself out, smiling as she closed the door, seeing him retrieve his phone and re-open his new social-media page.

Outside, the late-morning sun was growing steadily hotter. She wondered what to do, now that the day was her own and her dad was taken care of. *Her dad.* This brought to mind Nick again, and she felt grateful that her own dad was safely tucked up in the room behind her, even if currently his blood-alcohol level would set off a breathalyser at a hundred paces. Nick couldn't say the same. Why was his dad missing? Had he run off, or was something else going on? She berated herself for not asking more.

She pictured Nick, and possibly his brother, pounding the pavements of Capri and felt a wave of guilt. She had nothing but time on her hands today and using it to lie on a beach or buy souvenirs suddenly seemed wasteful. Plus, she thought, with a twinge of selfishness, she'd like to see Nick again. But how would she find him? Capri was small, but not that small. She cursed herself for not asking for his number and sighed, heading back to her room to give herself time to think.

She had another cup of coffee, texted Libby and thought about googling Nick. But she didn't know where he lived, what he did for a living, or even his surname. She restlessly washed her coffee cup then went for a wee, almost to pass the time.

Then she spotted something crumpled in the bathroom waste bin. A piece of paper that she didn't remember throwing in herself.

Gingerly, she reached in and plucked it out, unfolding it. On it was a name and address, written in spidery handwriting – *Richard Keyes, Ristorante Giorgio, via San Giovanni, Capri.* Was this his dad? Maybe it had been the dead end he'd alluded to, but the journalist in Wren thought only one thing. A lead was a lead. She grabbed her bag and headed for the coast.

An hour later, she was standing outside Ristorante Giorgio – or rather the pitiful vestiges of it. The dusty forecourt had clumps of litter in the corners, and the windows had that misty look that uninhabited places have. She looked at the crumpled note in her hand and felt a pang of disappointment, mostly for Nick. Where could she go from here?

Wren scouted around for any kind of helpful signage, an owner or proprietor, or a phone number, but there was nothing. She went up to the windows and peered inside. There appeared to be some broken bits of furniture and a few dust sheets but little else. She tried the front door handle then felt silly for doing so. Then she went into the side alley to look at what might have been the staff entrance. There was a grimy little window, and she cupped her hands around her eyes to peer into the gloom. There, on the floor tiles, was a pile of junk mail, and a single letter with a name and address. *Signora Elena Bianchi.* A quick Google search of *Elena Bianchi Capri* immediately served up the proprietor of a brand-new restaurant on the other side of town – *Pastasciutta*. Her heart leaped. What if Nick had seen it too? Could he have tracked his dad down to another place?

It was only a short walk across Capri town, and she found herself standing outside a small, smart-looking but unintimidating restaurant. It was similar to Ristorante Giorgio in that it had an outdoor courtyard with umbrellas, but this place was buzzing with customers, and the smell of garlic and seafood emanated from within. A busy but smiling waitress came to offer her a table.

'Actually, I was looking for someone. Richard Keyes?'

'No, I do not know any Richard Keyes,' said the waitress, shaking her head.

'How about Elena Bianchi?'

'Ah, Elena.' She smiled then called over her shoulder towards the open door in Italian. A stout woman of about fifty came out from the restaurant and walked over to Wren.

'Hi!' said Wren. 'I wonder if you could help me? I'm looking for someone called Richard. Richard Keyes?'

Elena immediately rolled her eyes. 'Not again,' she said sternly.

Wren grinned.

Her smile didn't last for long.

A brief and impatient conversation with Elena revealed that a man of Nick's description had indeed been to ask the very same question that morning and she'd told him that Richard Keyes used to work for her. But she had no idea where he was now. Elena threw suspicious glances at the younger waitress and talked rapidly in Italian, gesticulating with her hands.

She turned back to Wren. 'Why you people come asking about him? He in some kind of trouble?'

'I... I don't *think* so. Well, I don't know.' Wren blinked at the woman, who stood with her hands on her hips, one finger tapping at her skirt.

She looked Wren up and down. 'Like I say to the boy, I don't want to get involved.' And she turned on her heel and went back inside.

The waitress shrugged apologetically and went back to work too.

Wren stood there for a moment, deflated. What could she do now? And why was Elena being so cagey? Again, her journalistic senses were piqued – but what good would it do if she'd told Nick the same thing? He'd probably gone back to Naples feeling infinitely more disappointed than Wren did. Sighing, she realised she had no choice but to give it up as a lost cause and trudged back towards the ferry port.

The sun had almost set as she arrived into Sorrento harbour, covered in fresh sea spray yet again, but the place had been transformed since she'd departed that morning. She'd needed to wait for a ferry ticket in Capri, as they were all booked solid, so she'd passed a few hours nursing espressos and cakes in a little cafe until an evening ticket became available.

On the marina, there had been a smattering of decorations and stalls selling sweets and pastries that morning, but now there were crowds of people packed onto the harbour, and on the water's edge, there was a row of huge floats. The church in the centre of the harbour that she'd seen being festooned with lights was now lit up like a Christmas tree.

She squinted into the distance, trying to make out what was

going on, but couldn't quite see from this angle. It seemed as though each float was some kind of stage with a construction that looked like a theatrical set. She couldn't believe the scale of them – on the nearest one, she could see a few people busying about, and the structure behind them was the size of a house.

She disembarked the ferry and joined the crowd, checking her text messages. There was one from Libby, asking if she could squeeze an Italian waiter into her suitcase, and one from her dad saying that he was meeting up with Lina and the port gang again, giving her the name of a bar where she could come and meet them. The map on her phone gave her its location, which was unfortunately right at the other end of the harbour.

She shouldered through the tight shoals of people, thinking about Nick. She was disappointed not to have found him again, despite her best investigative efforts. And now she was a bit worried about him. What had Elena meant when she said she didn't want to have any part of it? And why did she think there was trouble involved? Her stomach pinched at the thought of Nick out there, somewhere, possibly walking into danger.

She came to a halt; the crowd had stopped moving and had parted, making a path for some people shouting in Italian. Some were dressed in costume, others in normal clothes, and they were carrying what looked like props towards the floats on the harbour.

Wren heard two Americans speaking in English nearby.

'What's going on?' she asked.

The man, who was wearing a baseball cap and vest top, looked at her incredulously. 'You know it's the Saint Anna festival, right? I mean, that's why we're here.' He looked at his female companion with raised eyebrows. 'Isn't that why you're here?'

'Um, not quite. I didn't realise this was going on when we booked. I saw them stringing up the lights, but this is... bigger than I expected,' she said.

'It's a big deal. See those floats? They're all along the theme of sailing – she's the patron saint of sailors, right?'

'And pregnant women,' said his friend.

'So they're going to sail along past the judges over there,' he said, pointing to a raised dais on the harbour front, 'and they do a kind of performance. Cool, huh?'

Wren nodded. It was kind of cool. But she needed to find her dad, so she made her excuses and walked away. The crowd mercifully thinned out a little, and she was able to look at some stalls as she passed through. She bought some little gummy seashells and ate a few as she went, then bought a handkerchief for Libby, as it was supposed to be imbued with a blessing for pregnant ladies. Libby needed all the blessings she could get given her ideas about running the shop with a baby on her hip.

Wren stopped to take a photo of the handkerchief to send to Libby but was distracted by a light thud nearby. A woman who'd been carrying an armful of what looked like colourful hats had dropped one. Wren stuffed her phone and sweets into her pocket and picked up the hat, trailing after the woman.

'Excuse me...' she called. 'Um, *scusi...*?'

The woman couldn't hear her through the crowd, so Wren hurried on to see if she could tap her on the shoulder. She'd almost reached her when they got to the water's edge beside a float bearing a construction of what looked like the Capri grottoes, blue and green light emanating from within. Wren felt a shiver of recognition. She called once more to the woman, but she still didn't hear over the noise of the crowd and walked up a little ramp onto the float.

Wren stopped, and an impatient-looking man with a moustache tried to shepherd her onto the raft too. She shook her head and thrust the hat at the man, but he looked more insistent and took her arm, guiding her up the short gangplank. *Oh, hell*, she thought. *If the hat's that important, I'll just nip onto the float and hand it over.* But as soon as she stepped onto the stage, there was an exchange of Italian voices behind her and a shucking noise as the gangplank was tugged away. With a yelp, she threw the hat over her shoulder and bolted for the harbour edge. The float was very slowly gliding away from the dock, joining the slow procession towards the judging area. Staring open-mouthed at the growing space between the float and the harbour, she went cold. Oh God, she was going to have to take part in the bloody performance if she couldn't get off. Then she heard something that drew her horrified gaze from the retreating land.

'Wren? Wren!'

She looked up sharply, and there he was.

'Nick?' she shouted in disbelief.

He was standing three rows back in the giddy crowd opposite the float. He was staring at her, open-mouthed, and raised his palms in question. 'What are you doing?' he asked, although she could only tell from the movement of his lips.

What am *I doing?* she thought, looking with panic at the growing gap, water glinting darkly below. Then, looking up at Nick again, she took a deep breath, ran a few paces and hurled herself towards the harbour.

Time almost stood still. There was an intake of breath from the people she was jumping towards and an instinctive drawing back from the edge to make space.

As she careered through the air, she thought, *I'm going to make it!* But as her feet just missed the edge of the concrete and she felt air rush beneath them, she realised her mistake. Flailing her arms, she felt the scrape of rough stone and grappled with her hands, somehow managing to hold on, her belly slapping against the harbour wall as she came to an abrupt stop. Voices from above squealed and chattered as many hands reached down to pull her up by the arms.

'Oh, shit! Wren!' came Nick's voice. He'd pushed through and was now visible in snapshots above her as she was hauled up onto the pavement, where she crouched, trying to get her breath. Multiple Italian voices rabbited around her, and several hands patted her down for injuries.

An older Italian lady clucked at her. 'Crazy English lady. You could have been killed!'

Then, in the confusion, she felt a sharp tug at her neck and a scrape of metal on skin. Before she could even register what had happened, she heard Nick shout. 'Oi! Oi! You!'

She stood up shakily to see the crowd pulling away from Nick and another man wearing a tracksuit top and a beanie hat. They were scuffling, Nick trying to grab her seashell necklace from the man's hand.

'Nick, no!' she yelled as the thief tried to headbutt him.

Nick turned his head at the sound of her voice, and as he did, the other man wheeled back his fist and punched Nick in the side of the face near his left eye. Nick staggered, and the man ran off.

'Oh my God,' Wren said, rushing towards him. 'Are you okay?'

He was rubbing at his eye, his face flushed, breathing heavily. To Wren's relief, there was no blood, and his right eye looked reassuringly focused.

He looked down at her and barked a soft laugh. 'Fancy seeing you here.'

EIGHTEEN

NICK

Wren kept touching her neck where the seashell necklace used to be.

'Are you sure you're okay?' Nick asked as they left the thickest part of the crowd and found an area away from the water's edge where there was room to breathe. He led her up a short path where there was a small terrace with a recently vacated bench to sit on. He walked a little faster as a pair of teenagers approached it and cut them off at the pass, guiding Wren to sit down.

He couldn't stop staring at her – how had they managed to find each other again in all that chaos? And also, how had they both managed to risk life and limb again in the process? He touched his eye gingerly and was relieved to feel a little swelling but not the crunch of a broken bone.

'I'm fine,' she said. 'Just a bit of bruised pride, I think.' She rubbed at her neck and frowned. 'I'm more worried about you. He could have knocked you out. You can get killed from a single punch, you know,' she added darkly.

'I could say the same for hurling yourself from a moving raft. I'm made of stronger stuff than that,' he said, smiling. He realised he was trying to impress her, a notion he hadn't encountered with a woman in a long time. His stomach turned over, and he composed himself. 'I'm sorry I didn't get your necklace back. Was it valuable?'

She went to speak and then paused, an unreadable flicker crossing her face. Then she smiled, a little sadly. 'It wasn't worth a lot of money.'

Down at the seafront, the last of the decorated floats glided past the harbour wall. The crowd was still thick with people, and strains of classical music could be heard above the chatter.

'I can't believe you're here,' Wren said. 'I... I came looking for you today. I went to Capri.'

Nick's jaw dropped. 'You did what?'

She blushed. 'I'm not a stalker, I promise. I just wanted to help you find your dad. So... did you?'

He blinked. 'Wow. That's... unbelievably nice of you.' He then felt a wave of guilt. 'Are you telling me you've been roaming around Capri all day, looking for me? I was kicking myself for not giving you my number, and now I feel even worse.' He'd contemplated going back to the hotel that morning but had taken her goodbyes as read. Too many years being out of practice with his feelings. Maybe now he could really believe that he'd misread things.

'Well, that might have helped,' she said with a grin. 'But I wasn't exactly wandering aimlessly – I was a bit more organised than that. I found the note you left in the bathroom bin and I did a bit of detective work. Again – not a stalker, I promise.'

He laughed and nudged her in the ribs. 'It sounds like you've got experience in tracking people down though.'

She laughed too, burying her face in her hands before looking back up at him. 'In a professional capacity, I promise. Writer's research. Definitely not in a "digging three years deep into someone's Instagram" capacity, I swear.'

'So you went to Ristorante Giorgio?'

'I did. And I'm guessing you saw the same letter in the door-way? Elena said you'd been to see her too.'

He nodded. 'That's... quite spooky to think you were just a few paces behind me.' Her smile faltered. 'In a nice way.'

She visibly relaxed. 'So that's where I came to a dead end. Elena said something about not wanting to get involved. What the hell was all that about?'

After the day Nick had had, he now had a fairly good idea. Elena had been slightly more forthcoming when he and Travis had approached her, but he guessed she'd become more suspicious when a second person came sniffing around.

'Well, I'm still trying to figure it out myself. She gave me a name.'

Wren's eyebrows rose. 'You found him?'

'Not quite. She said Richard Keyes had worked for her once, but she didn't know where he was now.'

'Yes, that's what she said to me too. But that's when she clammed up.'

'Right. I suppose she must have been feeling a bit more off her guard when I spoke to her. She told me to speak to a guy in Naples. Sal. Apparently he'd been seen with my— with Richard a little while back.'

'Oh! So... what happened?' Wren sat forward, eager to hear.

Nick grimaced, remembering the afternoon with a mixture of disappointment and unease. 'Elena gave me the name of a bar. So we went to find it, me and my brother. You know how every town, no matter how nice or posh, has a slightly dodgy bit? Well, I found it today.'

He remembered walking beyond the sunlit streets of Naples – people buzzing about, in and out of shops or sitting at pavement cafes – into the shadowy corners of a downtown area. It had felt ominously cooler and darker down those streets.

'We ended up at this bar, Lo Stivale, and it turned out to be some kind of biker bar. Stringy-looking bloke smoking a fag outside, giving me the once-over. I went inside and asked for Sal, and at first they pretended they didn't know who I was talking about. But as soon as I mentioned Richard Keyes, he was suddenly called out from a back room. Turns out he was keen to find Richard as well.'

Wren was listening, rapt. 'So he didn't know where he was either?'

'Not exactly. But he made it quite obvious that if he could get his hands on him, Richard might have something to worry about. God knows what's going on there.'

He paused, remembering how icy the mood had turned when Sal had looked at his mates, and how he'd instinctively felt it better not to ask questions. Travis had practically tripped over his new Italian leather brogues in his haste to drag Nick out of there, and had needed two Negronis and a lie-down to recover. Nick had left him at the hotel with a damp towel over his forehead.

'The only thing he *did* say was that he'd last seen Richard's picture in the paper. Some kind of garden festival last year? He didn't know the exact details, but he was standing in front of a house that opened its gardens to the public, and it had a blue door with a bunch of grapes as a knocker on the photos. It was just in amongst a bunch of other pictures from villages all over the area though, so he had nothing else to go on. And now, neither have I.' He shrugged, trying to look like he'd made his peace with that, but the crushing sense of disappointment still weighed heavy inside him, as well as an uneasy feeling about what kind of things his dad might be mixed up in.

Wren bit her lip and looked out at the coast. Nick found himself staring at her profile in silence, not sure what to say next. He noticed the reflection of the street light on her cheekbone and the upward curve of her top lip. He'd come back to Sorrento tonight after being told about the festivities, thinking it might be a good distraction from his troubled thoughts. But he'd hoped, deep down, that he might see her again.

Her brow creased and she seemed to be thinking deeply. 'I think I might have an idea.'

'Really?'

'Yeah.' She turned to him and smiled. 'Why don't we go to the newspaper office? It's not a huge place, so I can't imagine there's more than one. We could ask if they can find back copies around the time of the garden festival.'

'Do you think they'd do that?'

'Who knows? But it's worth a try.'

He grinned. 'Okay. Does that mean we're teaming up then?'

'If you'll have me? I mean, unless you and your brother want to do it together?' She looked abashed as if she'd overlooked him.

'Half-brother,' Nick clarified. 'Richard isn't his dad. He's here for moral support, and to be fair, he's itching to hit the shops again, I think.'

As he'd left the hotel room, he'd noticed Travis peering out from under his cold compress, looking up the address of another fashion outlet. Nick only hoped he'd arranged international delivery of whatever he'd bought so they didn't have to try cramming it all into his suitcase for the flight home.

'But what about your dad?' Nick asked. 'You can't exactly abandon him.'

Her phone buzzed, and she looked at it. 'Ha. Funny you should mention him. According to this text, he's gone back to his room for an early night. His new pals are taking him on an early-morning fishing expedition. Which I'm invited to. Five a.m. departure.' She tapped a few lines into her phone, shaking her head, then slipped it back into her bag. 'I think not.'

'Well, that sounds like a missed opportunity,' said Nick, a warm feeling spreading into his stomach. 'I mean, who doesn't want to spend the first hours of their day covered in mackerel guts?'

She grinned. 'It's tempting, I know. And while the thought of wresting fish hooks out of the mouths of sea bass is quite alluring, I think I'd rather go to the newspaper office with you.'

She held his gaze for a second, and he felt his breath stick in his throat. Then she looked away, and he cleared his throat. *She just wants to play detective with you. Don't get any ideas.* They sat quietly for a minute, but when he dared to glance back at her, her hand was at her neck again, fluttering over the space where her necklace had been.

'It was my mam's,' she said quietly. 'The necklace.'

The way she spoke was so loaded with meaning that Nick hardly dared to ask the question. 'Is she...?'

'Yes. She died when I was a baby. I've worn the necklace my whole life.' She laughed bitterly but with a wry smile. 'My neck feels weird without it.'

'Wren, I'm so sorry. I should have tried harder to get it back.'

'Don't be daft. You got a thump in the eye just trying.' She looked at him, and her brow creased with concern. 'You're getting a black eye.'

He dabbed at it and winced. But then he noticed as she turned that she had a raw scratch on her neck where that scrote had yanked the necklace away. Without thinking, he reached out to touch it. 'Wren, he's hurt you.'

Their eyes met, but she said nothing, and his hand stayed on the curve of her neck as if it was stuck there. Then a loud explosion cracked above them, and they both jumped as the sky filled with light. His hand dropped away, and they looked up as a huge fireworks display erupted across the bay. They exchanged a brief, amused glance then settled to watch the colourful view over their heads.

After they'd sat there for about a minute, he felt her shift beside him, and he turned to find she was looking at him again. But she wasn't looking him directly in the eye; her gaze was focused on the sore spot underneath. Biting her lip, she reached up and touched it gently. He looked at the graze on her neck too, and he reached for it once more, running his thumb over the reddened skin. Then, as her fingers brushed across his cheekbone, he ran his up under her chin and lifted it slightly. Sparks of light faded from the sky as he kissed her.

NINETEEN

WREN

'Trapeze artist?'

'No.' She could hear the smile in his voice even though she was looking at the path ahead.

'Mercenary?'

'I think I would have handled that mugger a bit better, don't you?'

'True.'

They'd walked slowly up the winding path to Wren's hotel without any discussion about what would happen when they got there. With each step, she wondered if he was escorting her home out of gentlemanly concern, or if he had something else in mind. And she wasn't sure which one she was hoping for. To distract herself from that train of thought, she resumed the guessing game.

'Archaeologist?'

'You can tell by your very active imagination that you're a writer. And no. You can put away your Indiana Jones fantasies right there.'

Their hands brushed together and it felt, to Wren, like she'd grazed a candle – there was a heat there that was both warming and dangerous. What was she doing kissing someone else when she was barely separated from Alex? Despite the fact that she was now single, it felt strange to be in this position with someone new and unfamiliar. But that kiss... It had felt as if Nick's lips were a connection to something she'd never known she was missing.

He held open the gate for her, and they walked up the path to the door of the hotel room.

'So, would I have read anything you've written?' he asked as she unlocked the door.

'Well, that depends on your reading tastes. Are you partial to stories about international crime rings, or do you lean more towards church fetes? And I'm not going to tell you which end of the spectrum I land on.'

'Maybe something in between? I'm just an average Joe.'

No, you aren't, she thought, her pulse quickening as she looked up at him. He was maybe half a foot taller, but his mouth was well within reach, and she wanted to meet it with her own lips. But before she could take a step, he was there.

His lips were soft but prickled slightly with stubble at the edges, and his hands weaved up into her hair so he almost lifted her towards him. She was pulled in to his chest, but it was more than just the intensity of his grip – she was drawn in as if she'd been wrenched into his orbit. Helpless but completely intent.

She reached behind her and found the handle, letting the door swing open, and they went inside, breaking away from each other's lips but not from the eye contact. In the dim light, he looked at her intensely, no longer smiling or laughing or wise-cracking. Once the door closed, and he pulled her towards him again, she wrapped her arms around his neck, and they lost themselves in another kiss.

Ever since she'd met Nick, she'd felt like she'd been riding waves of adrenaline. The Blue Grotto, her ill-timed dive onto the harbour, Nick taking a punch while acting in her defence... This was a different kind of rush, one that made her feel like every cell in her body was tingling; like her head was spinning.

His lips found the tender spot on her neck where her necklace had torn the skin, and he kissed it softly. Then their eyes met for a moment before she reached up and gently pressed her lips to the bruise that was skirting the edge of his cheekbone.

He pushed her slowly backwards, guiding her across the room, until she realised it wasn't just him taking the lead; she was pulling him too. Something flickered inside her. They were like magnets, not just now, but ever since the moment they'd met on the beach. Finding and losing each other but being drawn back together somehow.

His hand moved from her cheek down to her shoulder, then further to the curve of her breast. She breathed in sharply as he stopped there, and it was like lighting a touchpaper. She pulled his T-shirt off at the same time as he flicked the straps of her sundress away from her shoulders and unhooked her bra. Her clothes fell to the floor, and as they pressed their naked chests together, she could feel his heart pounding just like her own.

The guessing game was over – she didn't need to know any more than this. She wanted him more than she'd ever wanted anything.

Her hands worked at the button of his shorts at the same time as he guided her onto the bed, simultaneously tugging her underwear away. His lips worked down her body from her neck, bit by bit, and as they passed below her stomach, she felt as if she'd forgotten how to breathe. The whole time he lingered there she grew more and more lightheaded.

Then she couldn't wait anymore. She sat up and pulled him to her, with a force that he reciprocated, his strong arms almost carrying her further onto the bed. He moved against her urgently, and she did the same until they were one, and the room seemed to fade away. This small universe that contained only them exploded with white heat.

For the rest of the night, Wren realised they weren't just magnetised. It was electric, and the fireworks on the harbour were nothing compared to the sparks that flew between them.

TWENTY

NICK

Light cut through the curtain like an unwelcome alarm clock. Nick blinked sleepily and for a moment forgot where he was. Then he felt the weight on his arm, and the strands of hair on his shoulder, and memories of the night before dropped into place.

His heart spiked, not unpleasantly. Seeing Wren on that float last night, the two of them crashing together again in another chaotic whirlwind. Then the fireworks, the kiss, and... what came after. The little rush of adrenaline he'd felt melted into a warm feeling in his belly, and he smiled up at the ceiling.

Wren stirred next to him and raised one hand to cover her eyes, grinning.

'Morning,' he said.

'Morning,' she replied, half her face still covered. 'Argh. Don't look at me. I've probably got mascara halfway down my cheeks.'

He peeled her hand away. 'No, you're good.' *More than good*, he thought. He'd thought she was pretty since he'd met her, but this morning she looked beautiful. He checked himself as he thought this. It had been a long time since he'd been with anyone, and even then it had been Callie for all those years. He mustn't get any big ideas.

Wren sprang from the bed and wrapped a sheet around herself, hurrying to the bathroom. *Yes, best not get ahead of myself*, he thought. She must have been finding this awkward. He busied himself by pulling on a T-shirt and making two cups of coffee while she was gone.

When she came out of the bathroom, she was dressed in her pyjamas and was fresh-faced. She took the cup gratefully and smiled, sitting cross-legged on the bed across from him. She sipped and looked away self-consciously, fiddling with her hair.

'So...' he said.

'So...' she said – then dissolved into laughter.

'The awkward morning after.'

'Yup.' She gave him a look that was half-smile, half-grimace. He hoped that wasn't performance feedback.

'Not that I'm overfamiliar with an awkward morning after, mind you,' he hastily added.

'No! Me neither,' she said, her face colouring. 'Oh God, this *is* awkward.'

'We've been through worse,' he said. 'I mean, this isn't as disconcerting as getting trapped in a cave or getting punched in the side of the head.'

'How's it feeling today?' she asked, gesturing towards his eye, which he presumed had developed into an impressive shiner. It did hurt quite a bit.

'Can't feel a thing,' he said.

'I still feel terrible. I can't believe I got you thumped.'

'Well, I don't feel too good about making you hurl yourself at the harbour wall either, so I'd say we're even.' He smiled and only winced a tiny bit as his eye crinkled. 'Anyway,' he said, swerving any further discussion, 'since we're both feeling a bit better, maybe we can take one more shot at finding Richard. I'm going to head down to Sorrento after I've finished this coffee. You still want to come?'

'Of course I do. My dad's floating out at sea, probably manhandling a carp, so I'm all yours. I think we're going to get results today.'

'You sound very positive. More positive than I'm feeling. I mean, what are the chances of someone knowing exactly where this door is?'

The chances were surprisingly good. There was only one local newspaper in town, or at least that they could identify, and the guy in the office, who spoke excellent English, knew exactly what they were asking about. It turned out that the garden festival was a beloved annual event that he himself had covered, so he quickly produced a file on his computer with the article in question.

They scanned it and found the picture Sal had described – a house with a blue door and a bunch of brass grapes as a knocker. However, in front of it were about a dozen people, mostly men. It was a candid shot, with some people in profile, some wearing hats, some with sunglasses. There were a few of around the age he might expect, and some a little older, but none of them stood out. Whichever of them was Richard Keyes, he wasn't feeling a cosmic connection to him through this picture.

They asked the journalist where the photo was taken, and he explained the house in question was situated in a small village called Minarolla.

'The most beautiful garden. The place is owned by an English man.'

Wren and Nick took one look at each other, asked for directions and headed off into the hills of Sorrento once again.

Minarolla was a small cluster of terracotta-roofed buildings on the hillside, dotted with green trees and shrubs, and bright pink bougainvillea. They walked past a cafe where old men sat outside drinking espresso and playing chess, and a little school with kids playing in the yard. It was a place for families, Nick thought, which felt mildly reassuring.

Wren stopped in her tracks. 'There it is,' she breathed, pointing to a house on the far side of the cobbled square. It was a large townhouse built of sandy stone, with white-painted windows and hanging baskets on either side of a blue door with a brass knocker in the shape of a bunch of grapes. Nick stood still and looked at it, as if he was trying to see through the walls.

The man at the newspaper office had said it was owned by an Englishman, but now that he thought about it, that didn't necessarily mean it was his dad. His heart sank a little as he considered the possibility that any one of the men in that photograph could have just been passing through. He had so many theories going around in his head, he had no idea what he'd say when he knocked on the door. But the thought that his father could be just behind it suddenly felt overwhelming and he stepped back a pace.

Wren looked at him with concern. 'Are you okay?'

He swallowed dryly. 'I think I just need a minute.'

'Yeah,' said Wren, brow knitted. 'Yeah, of course you do. This is a big moment.'

They went back to the little cafe, and Wren took a table in the sunshine. Nick went inside, finding a shabby but authentic Italian bar with hissing coffee machine behind a Formica counter. Rows of biscotti lay underneath plastic cloches, and there were coffee-themed artworks on every wall. The moustachioed guy behind the counter was also pleasingly traditional, with a cloth thrown over one shoulder. He asked in clipped tones what Nick would like and briskly set to work. The bar was full indoors with people wanting a rest from the sun, and there was a sun-aged old man wearing a fedora sweeping the floor in between the tables and clearing cups. Nick took the coffees and headed back outside.

Wren was sitting with her head back, letting the sun fall on her face. Nick thought again how nice it would be if he was here just to enjoy her company. He glanced at her lips, remembering last night, but any feeling of desire was quelled by his anxieties. He sat down and placed her cup in front of her.

'So... You okay?' she asked, taking the biscotti from the saucer and snapping it in half.

'No. Not really.' He tried to laugh it off, but it came out sounding as brittle as the biscotti.

'I don't blame you. But there's no rush.' She nibbled her biscuit. He remembered what she'd said about her own mother the day before. He was getting an opportunity she'd probably kill for.

He slugged back his tiny coffee and stood up. He set his eyes on the house, feeling determined.

Wren stood up, smoothing down her shorts, and they stepped out onto the street. Nick's heart rate picked up – whether it was from the coffee or the realisation that his moment was here – and he turned and took Wren by the chin. He leaned down and kissed her full on the mouth to the dry cackles and whoops of elderly men outside the cafe.

'I wouldn't be here if it wasn't for you,' he said, pressing his forehead to hers. She smiled up at him then kissed him lightly again.

'I'll be here when you're done,' she said, perching on a low wall and waving him towards the house.

He took a deep breath and marched up to the door, giving the grape knocker a firm rap. He waited for what felt like minutes but was probably only thirty seconds, then the door swung open to reveal a distinguished-looking man in his sixties. He had silver hair, lightly tanned skin and a neatly clipped short beard. He was wearing a blue shirt, open at the collar, and khaki trousers, and looked every inch the Englishman abroad.

'Hello,' said Nick. 'I'm looking for Richard Keyes?'

The man stood staring at him, his face a storm of confusion, brow creased and mouth open. Did he know who Nick was? Did he see a resemblance in him? Nick waited, hoping he would say something... anything.

'*Non capisco, signore...*'

Anything, thought Nick, but that. This wasn't Richard Keyes. For all that he looked like an Englishman, he was quite obviously Italian and appeared to have no clue what he was talking about. But the newspaper had said an Englishman owned the house.

Nick took a step back, feeling his throat tighten. 'Sorry, sorry. Wrong house.' Then he paused. 'Um, hold on, are you the owner? I was told there was an Englishman here. *Inglese?*' He gestured to the house.

The man's eyes lit up. '*Si, si, inglese.*' He gestured to the house too. 'Signor Harrison. *Questa è casa sua.*' He pointed more theatrically to the building. '*Signor Harrison.*'

Nick sighed and tried to plaster a polite smile on his face. Wrong Englishman. And he had no clue who this Italian man was or what further help he could be.

'Sorry to bother you,' he said, disappointment sapping his will to be understood. 'It's Richard Keyes I'm after, not Mr Harrison. Thanks anyway.' He made apologetic gestures then backed away. The man closed the door, looking confused.

Nick walked back to Wren, who watched him approach cautiously.

'No joy?'

He sat on the wall next to her and shook his head, looking down at his shoes.

'I'm sorry. I really am. I was sure this was it.'

'Me too,' he sighed. 'But I think this is the end of the road. I think that guy who answered the door might be some kind of visitor or maybe staff. He said the owner's name is Harrison.' This whole trip had been a wild goose chase, a sun-drenched waste of time. He put his palms on his knees and forced himself to stand up.

'Come on,' he said. 'Let's walk you back.'

She stood up and rubbed his back, then they walked towards the hill path holding hands. They were just about to leave the village when the sound of feet came rushing up behind them. Nick turned to see the man from the house speed-walking across the square.

'Ricky,' he said, pointing to the cafe. '*Ricky!*' He clasped his hands, clearly exasperated he couldn't make himself understood, and Nick gaped at him. But then Wren touched his arm.

'Nick, I think he means a man called Ricky works at the cafe.'

'Richard? Richard Keyes... at the cafe?' he asked, his heart beginning to pound.

'*Si, si! Un signore inglese.*' He pointed at the cafe with even more fervour.

Nick dropped Wren's hand and powered towards it, swinging the door open and stepping inside.

'Richard Keyes?' he asked, looking at the man behind the counter and remembering that he was quite definitely Italian too. He scanned around, wondering who else it could be.

The barista shouted, '*Eh, Ricky!*' and there was clattering from beyond the main part of the cafe, through an opening that was screened off by a beaded curtain. The wizened old man who'd previously been clearing and sweeping nosed through the beads and looked askance at the barista, who waved a dismissive hand at Nick then tapped his watch.

'*Dieci minuti,*' the barista said to the old man and went back to cleaning coffee filters.

The old man regarded Nick, his dark eyes as piercing as a

crow's from underneath his fedora. He looked a little more familiar now that Nick was paying him full attention – he thought he might have been one of the figures in profile wearing sunglasses in the photo in the paper.

'*Cosa vuoi?*' he rasped, his head tilted back, his expression guarded.

Nick's mouth was bone-dry. 'English...' he said, feeling suddenly stupid in his confusion.

Richard, or rather Ricky, narrowed his eyes. 'I said, what do you want?' His accent was southern, maybe with strains of Essex, and his tone was cold and unfriendly. He looked down his long nose at Nick, sizing him up. He was seventy if he was a day, something Nick hadn't been expecting at all, since his mam was only in her fifties.

'Um, if we could go somewhere and talk?'

Ricky stalked towards him, glancing about shiftily. 'Listen, I told them not to send people to my work. He'll get his money when I've bloody got it. Now piss off.'

He started to turn away, but Nick blurted, 'I'm not here for money. I'm Nick. Your son.'

Ricky paused, mouth slightly open but eyes no warmer. He licked his lips nervously. 'Give me a minute,' he said to Nick. 'I'll meet you round the side.'

Nick nodded and obediently walked outside, feeling like a robot in his shock. Ricky could have asked him to lift up his shirt and belly dance and he'd probably have done it, since he seemed to have no control over his own mind. He saw Wren across the square, giving him two thumbs up, which he returned numbly, rounding the edge of the building where there was a bench, sun-bleached and with peeling paint. He sat on it, feeling like he was waiting to go into court or the headteacher's office. After a minute, Ricky emerged from the back door of the cafe, looking over his shoulder. He sat down beside him.

'This is a surprise,' he said, hands on his skinny knees, not looking directly at him. 'It's been a long time since I wrote to your nan. Never heard nothing. Thought that was the end of it.'

Nick took him in – his leathery brown skin, work-hardened hands, rangy build. He tried to find himself in Ricky's features but couldn't see it. His sparse hair was grey with the suggestion of being fair at one time, and maybe there was something about the shape of his mouth, but other than that, he looked as much a stranger as he felt.

'She kept it to herself. For a while. But I came as soon as I found out where you lived.' He laughed nervously. 'Well, roughly anyway. You're not an easy man to find.'

Ricky eyed him sideways, a lopsided grin appearing on his lips. 'That's the way I like it, sunshine. Never let the grass grow under my feet.'

'Right.' Nick resisted the urge to relate this to Ricky's abandonment of him, but it seemed to align well with a shady character like Sal not being able to seek him out. 'So you never thought to come and find me? I mean, if you knew about the Community Kitchen...'

Ricky waved a hand. 'Yeah, yeah. I get you. Let's just say cash flow is sometimes an issue. The flights and whatnot. Out of my budget.'

Nick nodded. Ricky didn't seem to be a man of great means. It kind of made sense.

Ricky looked at him squarely now. 'Well, look at you. Chip off the old block, eh?'

'Do you think?' Ricky's gaze ran over him, like he was cattle at market. There was something steely in his expression. Nick tried to be polite, even in his discomfort. 'I'm not sure I'm seeing it myself.'

'Nah, nah. I can see it. You've got my old dad's eyes.' He nodded, rubbing his bristly chin. 'Yeah, I see it now.'

'Wow.' Nick felt a sudden rush of emotion, realising that he hadn't just found a father but potentially a whole family.

'Sounds weird, but I never really thought about having a grand-father – or grandmother. On your side.'

He cackled. 'Well, don't get too excited – at my age, they're long gone.'

'Of course. Sorry. Do you have any brothers or sisters?' Then a thought struck him. 'Or other children?'

'Nah, just me,' he said, picking at one of his fingernails and looking up into the sun. He reminded Nick of a basking lizard, soaking up the rays. 'And as for sprogs, heh, who knows, eh?'

Nick blinked. 'You don't... know?'

Ricky's eyes glinted. 'Like I said, sunshine, I don't let the grass grow under my feet. Now, tell me a bit more about yourself.'

'Uh, well, I live in Northumberland. Run my own glazing business. I've got a daughter. You... have a granddaughter.'

Ricky's face remained impassive. 'Right. And business going well?'

'Yeah, it's okay, I guess.'

'Uh-huh. But you must have had a good start in life, what with your nan being a high flier and all that. And the family money.' He held Nick's gaze and quickly licked his lips.

'The family money? What family money?'

'Your mum said your nan was well off. Inheritances and whatnot. I thought that's how she started her soup kitchen thing.'

Nick shook his head. 'No. She started it from a trestle table on the street. The rest was donations...'

Ricky's face hardened. 'Right.'

Nick gave a quiet laugh; tried to make light of the mistake. 'Believe me, if there was family money, I'd have an idea about it. Edie's lived in a two-bed bungalow her whole life, and she gets by on a pension now.'

Ricky chewed his lip and stared off into the distance. 'I see.'

The afternoon sun was relentless, baking hot, but the atmosphere around them had turned ice-cold.

'Anyway, I'd best be back to work. Nice to meet you though, Nick.' Ricky stood up and stretched, giving Nick a nod and a smile that now seemed mean around the edges.

'Hold on,' said Nick, jumping up. 'Can I find you later? Catch up a bit more? Where are you living?'

'I'm a bit busy, sunshine. Maybe another time.'

'There is no other time. I'm flying back soon. I mean... I could come back again, fly out—'

Ricky held up a hand. 'Let me stop you there. I'm glad to meet you, but... well, I don't think this is going anywhere.'

'What do you mean? You wrote to Edie, asking about *me*. And I'm here now.'

'I know, and you seem like a nice bloke. But I ain't cut out for fathering. You're barking up the wrong tree.'

Nick opened his mouth to counter him again, but then a sinking feeling dropped into his gut. The family money. Edie being 'high flying'. *Business going well.*

He took a step back, and a bitter laugh escaped from him. 'Right. I think I see what's happened here.'

Ricky didn't even have the shame to disagree. He shrugged and wandered back to the cafe door. 'Careful as you go now,' he said over his shoulder. Then he was gone.

Nick's jaw dropped. This man wasn't his father. Yes, he might have impregnated his poor mother some thirty-three years ago, but there wasn't a shred of paternal feeling in his body. And now it looked like Nick was just one of an unknown number of Ricky's offspring, left behind like rubbish thrown out of a car window. Not enough monetary value to be worth his while. He felt sick, genuinely sick, like he might vomit right there and then where he stood. He swallowed the saliva that had pooled in his mouth and turned around.

Feeling numb, like he'd been plunged into icy water, he

walked away from the cafe as fast as his legs could carry him. The village swam in front of his eyes as he walked over the square, heading for the hill path. He was dimly aware of Wren rushing up to him.

'What happened? Are you okay?' She was breathless with concern.

'I can't,' he managed, turning away. He stumbled towards the hill path then felt a pulse of regret. Wren looked on, her face creased with worry.

'Listen, I'm sorry. I just need some time to get my head together.'

'Of course. Are you sure you're okay?'

'I will be. Are you okay getting back?'

'It's only down the hill – don't worry about it. I need to meet my dad soon anyway.'

She stood there, wrapping her arms around her middle. Nick wavered. This wasn't what he'd expected to be doing after all the help she'd given him, but he was in no fit state for a debrief right now.

He jogged up to her; kissed her lightly on the forehead. 'I'll come and see you. Tonight.'

She nodded, and he walked off down the path.

Nick somehow made it back to Naples after hailing a taxi, the driver rubbing his hands together at the fare he was due to get paid. There was a brief, slightly hallucinatory stop at a cash machine to get the guy his extortionate fare, followed by a drive along the coast that should have had him staring out of the window in awe but he'd seen only in faded snapshots. He felt a momentary pang of guilt at leaving Wren behind in Minarolla that grew fuzzier when mixed with the image of the man he would never call his father sitting hunched meanly on that bench.

He got out of the taxi and walked numbly up to the hotel. Travis was waiting in the doorway and rushed over, his face etched with worry.

'Nick, where have you been? I've been trying to ring.'

'My phone was on silent. My bad.'

Travis's face crumpled, and he reached for Nick's arm. 'Listen, I'm sorry...'

How the hell did Travis know what had happened?

'How did you...?' he started to ask.

Travis's face flashed with confusion, but he shook his head and his expression returned to anguish.

'It's Nanna.'

TWENTY-ONE

WREN

'Wren. Wren, are you in there?'

She came to as if she'd had a dose of smelling salts, blinking fast. 'Sorry, I was in another world.' Almost literally. Now that she was back at her desk at the *Echo*, Italy seemed to be a million miles away. And Nick too.

After he'd walked off down the path from Minarolla she'd, at first, wanted to give him the space that he needed. The urge to chase after him had been so strong, she'd had to remind herself that in spite of the few days they'd spent together, he barely knew her. She could completely understand why he needed to process things alone. But then, after an afternoon of sightseeing with her dad – which was mercifully free of light-houses or shoals of sea bream – she'd waited at the hotel for him to come and see her. He never did. Not that evening, or any of the days that followed before they'd flown home. She berated herself for never getting his number; she couldn't believe she'd felt so coy about asking in the first place, and after everything that had happened, the opportunity had passed them by.

'I didn't think you could get jetlag from a flight from Italy,' said Derek. 'Or did you overdo it on the Prosecco?'

'Ha, something like that,' she said, turning studiously back to her computer screen.

Her desk had become a mountain of trash again, with Post-its surrounding the screen like a lion's mane and several musty coffee cups strewn around. She liked it though. Something about the break-up with Alex had done more than separate her from the man himself. She realised how much she'd been trying to live up to his standards all this time. Just like Alan had hoped, she *had* come home from Italy several pounds heavier, and she still hadn't washed the contents of her suitcase.

Her thoughts drifted back to Italy – and Nick. Why had they played that stupid game of guessing about each other? Cursing that awful waiter, she remembered that she'd missed a chance to find out where he lived too. Without any useful information about him, not even his job, no amount of journalistic research skills were going to help. He was simply... gone.

She hadn't spoken to Libby about him. Even though she was her best friend, and she wasn't particularly prudish, Wren felt weirdly guilty about sleeping with someone so soon after the break-up with Alex. The fact that it was on a holiday she and Alex had booked, not to mention in the bed they would have been sharing, almost made it feel like she'd been cheating. So she'd kept Nick safely in her head, where the two of them couldn't be judged, and where she could remember him in this frustratingly bittersweet way.

Her mind kept flashing back to the night they'd tumbled into her bed, after all the adrenaline of their strange few days together had come to a head. Would she have slept with him if it hadn't been such a wild adventure? If she hadn't felt like she was living in the moment for the first time in ages? She felt her cheeks go pink.

Derek was looking at her with a suspicious expression on his face, but before she could pretend she was just feeling a bit warm, the main door to the office opened.

Erica on the reception desk was looking up at two men in suits, one holding a briefcase, the other with a leather zip folder under his arm. They were smiling placidly down at Erica as she dialled Zara's office line and stared at them with wide eyes. Within seconds of the call connecting, Zara sprang from her office, smoothly extending a hand to the two men and inviting them into her office, closing the door firmly behind them.

'That... does not look good,' said Derek, staring at Zara's closed door.

Gary looked between Derek and Wren with a frown. 'No. It doesn't, does it?' he said.

'It's happening,' said Derek. 'And I was the last in. *And* closest to retirement age.' He loosened his tie and slumped back in his chair.

'That doesn't mean anything. If they're making cuts, then it could be anybody,' said Gary, then he leaned in and lowered his voice. 'I mean, what about Erica? Her sickness record is shocking.'

'Gary, settle down,' hissed Wren. 'The last thing we need is you making a shortlist for the suits. I think we should just stay calm. No news is good news.'

'Wren, for fuck's sake, I don't think you should be using puns like that at a time like this.' Gary crossed his arms, nostrils flaring.

She rolled her eyes then made a show of settling back to her work like any sensible person should do. Setting an example. But her heart was fluttering, and she kept throwing nervous glances at Zara's closed door.

After a session of writing her review of a new brasserie in Corbridge, waxing lyrical about sourdough and avocado while her teeth remained tightly gritted, she glanced around at the general atmosphere of skittishness. Gary was pacing up and down, refilling a cup from the water cooler on repeat. Derek was staring into space. Erica was talking on her mobile, peeking furtively over the top of her cubby. Paranoia really was infectious. She pulled out her phone and started to type in *Journalism jobs*. She'd been scrolling for some time when a shadow passed over her desk and someone coughed. She looked up and dropped her phone.

'What are you doing here?' she spluttered.

'I've come to take you to lunch.'

Wren stirred her cup of tea, wanting something to do with her hands even though the milk was well and truly blended. Alex sat opposite with a plate of superfood salad. Wren had declined to eat – this wasn't the kind of encounter that spurred on her appetite. The cafe was quiet since it was only eleven thirty, far too early for lunch, but here they were.

'You look well,' he said. 'Picked up a bit of a tan in Sorrento.' There was no trace of spite, and he seemed to be trying to keep his tone light.

'Thanks. It was just what I needed. A bit of sun and some time to think. And don't worry, I'll pay you back for your share of the holiday.'

He waved his hand magnanimously. 'Don't worry about it. It's fine.' He then looked her in the eye, seeming more sheepish than usual. Almost meek. 'So you said you'd had time to think.'

'I did...'

'Because I've had time to think too,' he rushed on. 'I want us to talk. About having another go at things. These last weeks, with the arguing and the tension, and then you suddenly being gone, I've realised what I'm missing, and I'm sorry. I'm really sorry, Wren.'

'Sorry for what specifically?' she asked.

'You know. The text and the... checking up on you. I think a lot of how I've been acting is because I'm terrified of losing you.

I've had time to think, and I understand a bit more about where it's coming from. I'm insecure.'

What was happening? Had Alex had some kind of epiphany while she was away or even a full personality transplant? This Alex, who thought humility was for losers? She was still lost for words, but it didn't seem to matter as he was talking enough for two. She stared at him, remembering what Edie had said. Had he stopped trusting her because he hadn't been able to trust himself?

'And I realise I've no right to ask for another chance, but I promise I'll learn from this. Wren, I need you so much.'

Wren deflated, not realising she'd been holding her breath. 'But why? Why would you feel insecure? I've always told you I love you. And showed you, or so I'd thought.'

'I don't know why. But I'm working on myself. And I want to show you that I can be a better man.'

Wren said nothing. What had begun as a seemingly genuine apology, even if it was more than a little overdone, was now sounding so far from the Alex she knew that she could tell he was pulling this crap from some place other than his own brain. It smacked of Instagram quotes. Maybe he'd stumbled across them while posting yet another picture of his abs.

He picked up her hand and went to kiss it, and she flinched, pulling her hand away. He paled and diverted his empty hand to his glass.

Her mind flickered to her most recent kiss, and her cheeks grew hot. A few days ago, she'd been single, her past behind her and a thousand miles away. She'd lain in bed with a man who wasn't Alex, and it had felt like she was another person. It was like her body had woken up. But was that only because she'd felt so deprived? Had this dark time with Alex just made her ache for physical contact from anybody? If Alex had been the drought, then Nick may have just been a drop of rain on the scorched earth of her feelings. As Alex sat opposite her, showing his vulnerable side, she wavered. All the years together hovered around them like clouds, both light and dark. And Nick was gone. He felt as mythical now as the sirens on Capri.

No. With or without Nick, she couldn't look back. It would only be a matter of time before he forgot how sorry he was and went back to his old ways. And now she was sitting across from him, she realised she wasn't sure she cared anymore. It was like seeing someone you used to go to school with, as if that much time had passed. They were the same person but also totally different. And like school friends, they'd outgrown each other.

'Thank you. Thank you for apologising. It means a lot, and it really helps to know that you've given it such a lot of thought. But it's over.'

She stood up. Part of her wanted to reach over and kiss him goodbye, for the familiarity. For the good times. But a new, sterner part of her knew she should follow through with what she'd just said. So she turned and walked out the door.

Back at work, her overriding emotion was relief. The break-up before the holiday had been fraught, angry and sometimes incoherent. They were done back then, but parting in turmoil hadn't felt like closure. What had happened that lunchtime had felt like the proper end they needed. Not that she needed to draw another line under it, but she felt a sense of ceremony when she finished her flapjack and flung the greasy packet onto a pile of papers on her desk without the vaguest intention of tidying it up. She was unpicking years of enforced orderliness, and she was enjoying it.

She rattled through some short pieces about local crime, a person who'd had a decent win on the lottery, and a cats and dogs shelter that was crying out for donations. She pinged them through to Zara, and as soon as she did, Zara's door opened and she leaned her head out.

'Can you pop into the office, Wren?' she asked.

The mood of the room turned funereal. Derek looked at her with open sympathy, while Gary stared with theatrical studiousness at his computer screen, a muscle in his temple twitching. Erica peered up over her reception desk, her jaw hanging slack.

So, here it was. She would be the first to get the chop. She sat down opposite Zara's desk.

'Ah, Wren, darl'.' She steepled her fingers under her chin and gave Wren a bleak look. 'I've got some bad news.'

Wren stiffened. 'Don't worry, Zara. I've... I've been bracing myself. I knew it could happen.'

Her eyes widened a little in surprise. 'Oh. Was she unwell?'

Now it was Wren's turn to look confused. 'Who? Sorry, I'm not following. I thought I was getting laid off.'

'Laid off? No, it's not that. It's Edie Macmillan. I'm sorry, Wren, but she's passed away.'

Wren's mouth fell open. 'Oh my God. When?'

'A few days ago. Her grandson rang to let us know just now.' She looked down at a notepad, having a journalistic habit of scrawling down any information she was given. 'Bloke called Travis. Wanted to make sure you knew before trying to get in touch with her again.'

'I met him,' she murmured. 'Oh, how awful.'

She thought about Travis and the people at the Kitchen, and Edie's other grandson. They must be devastated. And she felt upset herself. She'd only met Edie a handful of times, but she'd been so wrapped up in her story that she'd become more attached than she'd realised.

'There'll be a funeral, of course. He said close friends and family for the crem, as it's only small. But they're having a wake at the Kitchen for anyone else who wants to pay their respects.'

'Right. Well, I'll definitely go along to that then.' She shook her head sadly. 'Poor Edie.'

She got up to leave, feeling deflated. A selfish thought crept in: Edie was gone, and heartbreaking as that was, Wren would never get the chance to ask her again about her mam.

TWENTY-TWO

NICK

Nick wasn't sure what was aching more – his body, his heart or his mind. His muscles were throbbing all over, and he felt cold and shivery, but how much of that was psychosomatic he couldn't tell. His head could be hurting from the mountain of tasks he had to do – calling people who needed to know, making arrangements for the funeral, trying to stay strong for his brother. But it was perhaps his heart that ached the most, for his nanna, who he'd left behind under a dark cloud, thinking that he'd arrive home to let the sun back through again. But she was gone, along with any chance he had to make it right with her.

He looked again at the list he'd made. He'd ticked off all the phone calls on it – from his mam at the top, who was now trying to find a flight back from the cruise's latest stop in Antigua, right down to the newspaper that Edie had been giving interviews to. Travis had handled that one, since he'd met the journo. The last thing they needed was her turning up expecting a cuppa and a chat, although he supposed someone at the Community Kitchen might need to make a statement at some point, what with it being of local interest.

Cards and flowers had come flooding into the Kitchen, some

expensive blooms from donors and local dignitaries, and some frankly heartbreaking hand-picked bunches, possibly gathered without permission from local parks and gardens by some of the Kitchen's current clientele. Edie had lived her life with a long reach, and now that she was gone, people were being drawn back to her as if by elastic. He found comfort in the fact she hadn't been alone. She'd been working in the Kitchen and collapsed suddenly, with Cath and Ailsa both there to catch her as she fell. It had been almost instant, he'd been told. A massive stroke – she was gone before Ailsa and Cath could lie her down.

Travis finished prodding at his phone and sat up abruptly. His grief style had been to sink into his smartphone like an alcoholic sinks into a bottle of whisky. Not that Nick could begrudge him that, after his poor brother had had to pace the hotel lobby waiting to break the news to him.

'I'm going out,' he said. 'Are you okay? Do you need me to do anything?'

'No, I'm good. Where are you off to?'

'Just... meeting someone.' He took one last look at his phone and slipped it in his pocket.

'Oh. An old friend? Or a new friend?' Travis had been spending so much time on his phone, Nick was starting to wonder if he was back in the comfort zone of his dating apps.

Travis rolled his eyes. 'A none-of-your-business friend. Anyway, I'll be back later. You sure you don't mind?'

'Of course not,' Nick said. 'Everything's pretty much sorted anyway.'

Travis left, and Nick sat for a while, twiddling his thumbs, finally pausing in the death admin long enough to remember Wren.

In all the chaos of the horrible news, trying to comfort his distraught brother and hurriedly arranging earlier flights, he hadn't had a minute to go and see Wren before they left. In fact, it was only as he looked out of the plane window at the slowly shrinking island of Capri that the memory of her had dropped into his stomach like a stone.

He felt terrible, and in quiet moments, when he was able to put Edie out of the forefront of his mind, he really missed her. He hadn't meant it to just be a 'holiday thing'. He'd assumed they'd see each other when they were home – she lived in the same county, for God's sake. The same massive, sprawling county, with a population of over three hundred thousand. He was frustrated that he didn't even have her full name or a phone number. He could try to search online for her, he knew, but not just now. He hadn't been there for Nanna when she needed him most, and now, instead of putting his own interests first, the least he could do was focus all his energy on her final journey.

On that note, he decided it might be best to choose what he was going to wear for the funeral.

He went to his room, rifled through the wardrobe for his grey suit – the old one he'd resurrected for the Kitchen anniversary party – some shoes and a black tie. He ran his thumb over the dark silk, dreading putting it on. Then he remembered something that would finish the outfit off – the Omega watch he'd been given by his mam one Christmas. He and Travis had both been given one, Tracey waving away thanks and saying it was to make up for not being around so much. Travis had joked in private about never wearing them together as they'd be too matchy-matchy, so Nick's spent a lot of its time in his top drawer. But when he opened the drawer now, he saw the watch was gone. He rummaged around, but just when he was about to start emptying out his pairs of socks, the doorbell rang. He gave up and closed the drawer.

'Daddy!' said Ruby, flinging herself at him as soon as he opened the door. She crashed against him like a heavy wave and squeezed him around his middle. Behind her, on the doorstep, was Callie, her hands thrust into her jacket pockets.

He was lost for words. Callie never dropped by. They had a

routine that she always rigidly stuck to, and there had never been a casual drop-in since they'd split. He rubbed the top of Ruby's head and blinked into the daylight.

'Um, come in,' he said, finally finding his manners within the confusion.

Ruby walked into the living room and sat on the sofa, fiddling with the tassels on one of Travis's fancy cushions.

Callie sidled in with an awkward smile. 'How are you doing?' she asked.

'I'm okay,' he said. 'Getting there. Have a seat and I'll put the kettle on.'

He returned a few minutes later to find Ruby curled under Callie's arm, both talking quietly. He placed the cups on coasters and sat opposite, prompting Ruby to join him.

She blinked up at him from her spot on his knee. 'Are you sad, Daddy?'

'I am a bit, yes. But it's cheered me up, seeing you.' He mustered a more genuine smile than he'd been capable of for the last few days.

'I'm sad as well,' she said. 'I liked Nanna Edie. She was funny.'

'She was. And she loved you lots, darlin'.'

'She did good cuddles. And I thought you might be missing those, so I've come to cuddle you instead.' She squeezed him around the middle again, and he held her tightly. God, it was hard not to cry, but he wouldn't, not in front of Ruby – or in front of Callie, for that matter.

'What happened to your eye?'

He swallowed, clearing the lump from his throat, and mustered a mischievous grin. 'Well, while Uncle Trav and I were in Italy, there was this sea monster...'

'You're silly,' she said. 'Can I go and look at Uncle Travis's treasures?'

'Of course you can.'

Ruby loved to look through Travis's stock room, with its endless carousel of mad prints, jewellery and bags. She slid down off his knee and disappeared out of the room.

'Don't move things around though, sweetheart,' Callie called after her. Then they were left alone.

Callie took a sip of her coffee and looked around self-consciously. She tucked a strand of ash-blonde hair behind her ear.

'Thank you,' said Nick. 'For bringing her. It's really good of you.'

'That's okay. She loved Edie. And I was pretty fond of her too. No matter what she thought of me.'

'She...' He wanted to say something placatory. *She thought the world of you. She never had a bad word to say about you.* But he knew it would be a lie, and Callie knew it too. Edie had been like a tigress, protecting her grandsons since the day they were born, so she would always take his side. So he settled for, 'She would be glad you came.'

'Remember at our engagement party? When Travis's dad got drunk and his new girlfriend was putting sausage rolls in her handbag, and she got the bartenders to slyly leave the whisky out of his whisky and Coke. She asked the staff to plate up left-overs from the buffet to hand out, so people wouldn't keep staring at his lass, whatever her name was. I can't remember now. But Edie was always great at diplomacy. You're not so bad at it yourself.'

'Ha. Maybe it's hereditary.'

'Maybe it is.'

Nick drank some more coffee then sat with the mug grasped between both hands, shoulders hunched forward. 'Listen, let's let bygones be bygones. I'm over it, Cal. I promise, I barely even think about how things ended between us. Maybe we can move things forward a bit? Talk about Ruby again.'

Callie tensed, putting her cup down and squeezing both

hands between her knees. 'I'm glad you feel that way. But I don't think it's the right time.'

'When's it going to be the right time?' he snapped before he could stop himself.

'Nick, I know you're upset. I don't think we should talk about it right now.'

'Why not? Please don't make this about my nanna. I'm a grown man. It's as good a time as any.'

Her eyes flashed. 'Is it? Do you really want to talk about something that can't be fixed with a click of your fingers?' She shook her head and glanced around the room. 'I didn't come here for this. I wanted you and Ruby to see each other; hoped it would help. But just because you're grieving, I can't pretend that your life is stable enough for sharing custody of her.'

Something lit up inside Nick, like the fuse on a stick of dynamite. He knew he was on borrowed time before he lost his temper. He kept his voice low. 'Do you really think that's why I'm bringing it up? That I would be that calculating? I've felt like this from day one. All I want is to have more time with my daughter, for her to stay with me for weekends instead of being thrown crumbs every now and then.'

Her lips pinched together, and she looked stonily into the middle distance.

'Okay. So when I've got a place of my own, then can we agree that she can spend more time with me?'

She sighed. 'I'm sorry about Edie, Nick, but I didn't come here for a row. We'd best go. Ruby, sweetie, come on,' she called into the other room. 'Time to head off.' She avoided his eye and got up, gathering her handbag.

'Callie, what have I got to do?' he asked, feeling weary, like he'd had a physical fight, not just a verbal one. 'You know I'm not the one who created this situation.'

Ruby skipped into the room before she could answer, and they pasted on smiles. He gave Ruby a cuddle and kissed the top of her head. 'You be good for Mammy, won't you?' Then, over the top of her head, he glared at Callie. 'And Justin.'

Callie crossed her arms, giving him a withering stare.

His jaw tensed, and he shook his head at her. When he looked down, Ruby was staring up at them, looking from one face to the other as if she was watching the world's saddest tennis match. Her lower lip started to wobble. Then Nick's gaze fell upon something on the console table by the door. It was that souvenir penny from the lighthouse, the one that had almost choked him. He'd looked the place up and they were running an event for kids – treasure hunts, colouring sheets, all the usual. He picked the coin up and bent down to her level.

'Hey, hey,' he soothed. 'Listen, I've had an idea about our next little outing. You love the seaside, don't you?' She nodded, her trembling lip growing still. 'How's about we go and see a lighthouse? A big, tall lighthouse where you can see for miles?'

Her face brightened, and although her eyes were damp, she smiled and nodded.

'Come on – off we go,' said Callie, tugging at Ruby's arm and avoiding Nick's eye. 'We'll get some sweets on the way home.'

They left, leaving Nick standing where he was.

He crashed back onto the sofa, throwing the penny on the table and thrusting his hands through his hair. He hadn't meant to punch low. But he hadn't been able to help it. Like a man possessed, he was grafting and saving to get his own place. And yet Callie was so set in her ways about this current arrangement he was scared that even if he did, she might still find some reason to keep Ruby from him. All his patience had been channelled into protecting Ruby from this ongoing row, but now he wondered if he should be pushing harder.

His mind skipped back to that afternoon in Minarolla. His father sitting there, bold as brass, telling him he meant nothing to him. Now that was where he and Richard were completely different. He loved that little girl with all his heart. He could feel the bond with her literally flowing through his bloodstream. But was there something genetic in being absent in his child's life, even if it was against his will?

He leaned forward, resting his elbows on his knees, grinding his palms into the hollows of his eyes. He ached all over. Initially he wondered whether it was grief – some people said that it could cause actual physical pain. But his throat hurt too – it felt like sandpaper – and his chest felt tickly and tight. He was coming down with something. In fact, he'd had a bit of an itchy throat on the flight back from Italy – maybe something he'd picked up there. He thought of Wren. Hopefully she wasn't sick too. It would be just too depressing to know that the only thing still connecting them was a virulent Italian infection.

TWENTY-THREE

WREN

Some people say that being by the sea should be available on prescription, and Wren thought there might be something in that. She was sitting in her dad's back garden on a tired old bench, a blanket over her knees and a cup of tea in hand. Beyond the short fence was the beach, and then the sea, and last of all, the sky. Three constants of fresh air, space and tranquillity. Even the sound was soothing – the rustle of beach grasses and the hiss and thrum of the waves was like a dose of medicine.

She'd been in bed at her dad's house for two days straight, and in case she was still infectious, she hadn't dared go back to Libby's. The last thing her heavily pregnant friend needed was a hefty dose of flu. Wren couldn't quite believe how hard it had hit her, as a usually fit and healthy woman. Well, that was if she didn't count the fact she had a touch of asthma. She'd religiously taken her inhalers up until her teens, but after a few missed doses, and a surprising lack of symptoms, she'd stopped bothering.

It turned out she'd just been lucky to avoid the trigger of a particularly nasty virus for all that time, and whatever she'd been infected with in the last week or so had gone to town on her lungs like an all-you-can-eat buffet. She'd left Libby's and signed off sick from work when she started to feel *really* ill. And then, at her dad's, she'd gone downhill fast. A chest infection that had bordered on pneumonia, by all accounts. She was still cringing about the scolding she'd received from her GP and had reinstated her twice-daily puffs with cowed obedience.

So here she was, back recuperating in her teenage bedroom, taking in the sea air like a convalescent in an old novel. Her dad had been fussing around her like a mother hen, bringing her his culinary specialities of tinned soup and microwave lasagne. The cottage had once again become as cluttered as an overflowing skip since Alan had focused on his nursing duties.

As if on cue, he walked down the garden path with a little tray bearing a fresh cuppa for each of them and a small pile of letters. John was following him closely, wagging his tail.

'Thank you, Carson,' she said, taking the hot cup and swapping it for the almost-empty one she'd been nursing. 'I feel like I'm in *Downton Abbey*, having my post brought to me on a tray.'

'It's my pleasure, m'lady. Mind you, it makes a pleasant change from the *Holby City* drama we've just weathered.' He shook his head.

'You still cross with me?'

'For getting poorly? No. For trying to outwit a diagnosed medical condition? A little bit.'

Wren picked up the reliever inhaler from beside her on the blanket and waved it. 'I'm a reformed character.'

'Good. Because as much as I love having you here, I'd rather you were popping in for a visit with a normal lung capacity next time.'

'Noted.'

John jumped up, putting his front paws on Alan's lap, sniffing eagerly at the tray between them.

'Hey, buggerlugs, them's letters not biscuits.' He shooed John down and patted his head. 'These came for you.'

Wren considered the pile. She'd been expecting them – she'd asked for her post to be forwarded on to her from work. She wanted to do some work on her laptop now she was feeling back in the land of the living.

She reached for the top letter, saw it was just a circular from a recruitment agency and put it back down again. It felt like a portent of doom – one she had no intention of exploring at that moment.

Alan sighed easily. 'Eeh, just think. It wasn't that long ago we were sunning ourselves in Italy, riding chairlifts and whatnot – now look at us.'

Wren smiled. Her dad was still high on the holiday. He seemed to have had the time of his life and hadn't stopped reminiscing, especially about the friends he'd made from the lighthouse. Wren, meanwhile, had kept her own holiday friendship to herself.

'Lina texted me this morning, asking after you. I told her you're on the mend. And Carlo sent me this, looka.'

He produced his phone and gleefully showed her a meme about seagulls, which Wren didn't get. But she laughed appreciatively anyway. Seeing her dad being enthused about new friendships was such an unexpected bonus of the trip. He'd even started making murmurs about seeing some of his mates from 'back in the day' that had been in touch via his new Facebook account.

'Now, I'm going to have to go in to work the morra. It's the kiddies' open day, remember?' he said, giving her an appraising look. 'Do you think you'll be alright?'

'Well, as it happens, that's meant to be my first day back at work. Zara's asked me to go to St Nicholas Lighthouse and do a piece for the paper since I'm in the area and I've got a man on the inside. Easing me back in gently.'

'Oh well, that's smashing! You'll get to see the old man in action.' He looked very pleased with himself.

'And I'll be out from under your feet in a couple of days. I'm going to stay at Libby's again so I'm closer to work.'

'You can't stay there forever though, Wren. Not when the babby comes along.'

'I know. I'm going to look for a flat this week too.'

'There's no rush. I know it's not ideal for work, staying here. But you know you've always got a place with me.'

'I know,' she said, smiling. But she also knew that even if she wasn't here, she wouldn't have to worry about him so much anymore. The house might still be a mess, and John might still be her dad's closest friend, but she could see a change in him since their holiday. A new-found confidence with other people that he must have lost while being a single parent to her for all those years.

Her hand reached for her missing necklace again, as it did several times a day. Each time it landed on bare skin, it was like it had been ripped away afresh. Alan noticed her doing it and gave her a rueful smile and a pat on the shoulder. He'd tried to cover his disappointment at the loss of such a special tie to her mam, clearly for Wren's benefit, but she could see he still felt upset.

He leaned back, sipping his tea and looking out at the sea, so she picked up her pile of post again and thumbed through it. More circulars. An invitation to the AGM of one of her professional subscriptions. And then, in amongst the dull-looking window-envelopes, there was a handwritten one in spidery letters. *Serenity Rowbottom* – and the address of the newspaper office. Her heart spiked.

She opened it and stared down at a greetings card which bore a photograph of a field of blue flowers. Inside was a short note.

Dear Serenity,

I hope you don't mind me calling you that; I've thought of you with that name ever since you told me. It's a pretty name, and a memorable one, and it's a shame for it to be hidden away.

I'm writing, first of all, to thank you for the lovely present. What a lovely surprise seeing the Kitchen back in the old days – such a thoughtful gift that I will treasure.

I read your note, pet. When you're back from your holidays, I'd like to talk to you again about your mam. We did meet, and I remembered her the moment you told me your real name, but I was frightened that I was doing the wrong thing by saying so. And when you showed me that lovely photo, I still didn't dare. I was thinking of your dad – it seemed like he hadn't told you the whole truth. I'm sorry I did that, but now I realise, you're a grown woman, and if you have questions, then I should really answer them.

Can you pop in and see me, and I can tell you all about it?

All the best, Edie

The paper fluttered from her hands, and her dad caught it before it was picked up by the breeze. She stared into the distance, her fingers tingling as though the card had been hot. It was literally a letter from beyond the grave. One that was taunting her with an answer that was almost in her grasp. But it was cruelly out of reach. Edie was gone, and so was what she'd wanted to say.

She was dimly aware of her dad next to her and that he was reading the note. He folded the card neatly and placed it on top of the pile. Neither of them spoke for a while.

'I think we need to have a chat,' he said eventually.

The next day, Wren stood on the narrow cliff edge beneath the lighthouse, thinking. She'd finished taking photographs and notes on the children's event inside. Dozens of little people were darting from one activity to the next, sometimes under people's legs, and the noise was deafening. She had a headache that persisted from her bout of flu, or maybe from the cacophony of thoughts in her mind, and she needed some fresh air and a bit of quiet. There was still so much to process.

Caron Rowbottom hadn't died of cancer, like she'd been led to believe. She'd died of a drug overdose while living rough in Newcastle when Wren was too young to know her. Her dad had cried when he'd told Wren the truth.

'Oh, she was wild when I met her,' he'd said in the garden, over cups of tea that had gone cold. 'I was sheltered really, never got up to much more than sneaking a cheeky ciggie out of your granda's pocket. But she used to take me along to parties, where all sorts of things went on.'

Wren's eyes must have popped.

'That stuff wasn't for me, pet. But *she* was. And when we got married and we came out to the cottage, I felt like my life was beginning. The trouble was, she thought her life was over. She started drinking, you know... secretly.'

'Dad...' She'd reached for his hand.

'But you came along, sweetheart, and she stopped all that. For a time. She got depressed, then I started finding the bottles again, then bits of... What do you call it...? Paraphernalia.'

Hearing her dad talking about it had been like an out-of-body experience. The idea of him in that world, even at its edges, was bizarre. His voice had trembled as he'd carried on.

'Eventually she started disappearing for days at a time. It was just you and me, pacing the floor. When I begged her to stay, or begged her to leave, she chose the latter. Then I found out she was homeless, and I tracked her down to the Community Kitchen. She wasn't happy to see me, so Edie said she'd have a word. But the next I heard, she'd died.'

'Dad, I... I can't believe you've kept this to yourself this whole time,' she'd said, breathless.

'I'm sorry, Wren. I'm so sorry for not telling you sooner and for pretending it was me that Edie was talking about. I just didn't want you to remember her as anything but perfect. And she was, except for this one thing.'

'No, I mean, I can't believe you've coped with this on your own.' She'd hugged him tightly for a long time.

Now, she'd left her dad in the lighthouse, holding court with a tour group gathered around him, flamboyantly waving his arms as he told stories of near disasters off the Northumberland coast. He was always in his element talking about the history of the lighthouse, but he seemed to have an extra spark about him today. It was as if telling Wren the truth about her mam had lifted a heavy burden she never knew he'd been carrying. And now that he was gathering new friends like clams on a rock as well as catching up with old ones, he seemed to be finding a new version of himself. Or, more likely, resurrecting an old version of himself that Wren had never seen, that had existed before caring for his troubled wife and becoming a single dad.

The summer wind was surprisingly chilly and was fairly strong this high up on the cliff. She pushed her hands into her pockets and walked closer to the edge, peering down at the sea below. She thought of the Bay of Naples and the bright turquoise waves compared to the steely grey-blue of the North Sea and wished she was back there. With Nick.

Up above, at the top of the lighthouse, she could hear the voices and shrieks of lots of children. The outdoor platform had been opened up for a stream of visitors to climb up and have a look out from the highest point. She smiled at the thought of how busy the day had become – her dad would be so proud of the open day's success.

Then, out of the corner of her eye, she saw something arc through the air to her left and land a few inches from the cliff edge. She looked over to see what appeared to be an orange plush toy in the shape of a lobster. She glanced up at the platform, hearing loud sobs, and through the railings could just make out someone crouched with their back to her, comforting a small child. They must have dropped it over the edge.

The wind blew, and the lobster rolled a little closer to the precipice.

Looking up again, she tried to signal that she would retrieve it for them, but they'd stepped out of sight. Never mind; she would take it up and wave it around until she found them.

Walking across the grass, she could see the lobster teetering on the edge. It was past the stakes in the cliff edge that warned against crossing beyond, but she stepped just a shade over so she could reach. And as she closed her hand over the soft toy, the ground under her right foot shifted. And then it crumbled. Screaming, she felt her foot slide away from her and wheeled her arms, trying desperately to fall backwards rather than forward. The horizon in front of her came in and out of focus, then she felt a strong grip on the back of her jacket.

A hand wrenched her backwards, and she heard a familiar voice.

'Whoa there. I've got you.'

TWENTY-FOUR

NICK

The funeral notice had stated 'close family and friends only' for the crematorium service, but the place was still packed to the rafters. Nick shifted in his seat, uncomfortable in his suit, rubbing his bare wrist. He'd looked high and low for his watch, but it still hadn't turned up. Looking across the pew, he saw Travis's matching watch glinting in the low light.

Travis leaned in. 'If this is just the nearest and dearest, then I hope Cath's laid on plenty of vol-au-vents for the wake.'

'I know,' said Nick, craning his head towards the ram-packed pews behind them. 'Nanna would be mortified at the fuss.'

He turned back, rubbing at his sore neck. It was still aching a little from the vicious bout of flu that had seen him in bed for two days, but now it throbbed afresh. He and Travis, along with two of Edie's friends from the Kitchen, had borne her coffin up the aisle. The physical weight was insignificant really – she'd been a tiny, waif-thin woman – so he wondered if the ache in his neck and shoulders was psychosomatic. An imprint of his last contact with his nanna lying heavily on his shoulders.

Her coffin was now on a plinth, surrounded by flowers, and

Nick felt a rush of sorrow rising from somewhere in his belly, coursing up through his lungs and closing his throat. He hadn't realised he'd made a sound until he felt his mam's hand slide over his. He squeezed his eyes tightly shut, clenched his jaw and coughed away his emotions.

The errant Tracey LaGrande – a stage name that had now become the only name she was known by – had sashayed into the arrivals lounge at Newcastle Airport early that morning, pulling a small suitcase behind her, along with a duty-free carrier bag loaded with Benson & Hedges. She'd hugged her sons, enveloping them in a cloud of nicotine, Chanel No. 5 and overdue affection. They'd had little time to talk before heading to the funeral service, so Nick felt like he was sitting next to an unopened book. He'd had the blurb from Richard Keyes in Italy, and now, when the time was right, he'd want the full story from her.

But first she had a eulogy to deliver. She gave his hand a quick squeeze and stood up, smoothing down her black bodycon dress that only Travis had deemed appropriate for the occasion. She stood at the lectern, laid out a crumpled piece of paper and slipped on some reading glasses. Her voice rang out in the chapel, a mix of Bonnie Tyler and Jimmy Nail, her accent unsoftened by many years at sea, away from the North East, and Nick tried his best not to judge the warmth and familiarity with which she spoke. Over the last few years, his mam had barely seen Edie, but as daughter she took precedence over her grandsons, and she was never one to miss an opportunity to shine.

'Is she quoting power ballads?' whispered Travis, after Tracey slipped in 'if I could turn back time', followed soon after by a reference to Edie's good heart burning like 'an eternal flame'. At 'She really was the wind beneath my wings,' Nick let his eyes go unfocused and tuned out.

A hand snaked into his from the other side of Travis, then

Ruby squeezed with her little palm. She'd faced the funeral with the wide-eyed curiosity of a kid her age. The death part was sad, but the fascination with all these people dressed smartly in black, the flowers and the ceremony was enough to distract her from the grim reality. Beyond, Callie gave him a pinched, dutiful smile, as did Laura, who'd also come along to pay her respects. In the row opposite sat Ailsa and Cath, both dabbing at their eyes and, to Nick's surprise, Liam, sitting next to his grandmother. He gave Nick an awkward, sympathetic smile.

Then came the macabre final moment when the coffin slid behind a curtain, and it was over. Nick filed out with everyone else as Tracey took the lead with shaking hands, and in the throng of people he found himself separated from Ruby, Callie and Laura. Even Travis was nowhere to be seen. He took the opportunity to go outside and get some fresh air.

He went around the corner of the building and leaned against the wall, resting against the cool brick, taking restorative breaths. A few of the congregation wandered past, talking about how lovely the flowers were and how there hadn't been a dry eye in the house. Then he heard a voice, a one-sided conversation, and Liam came around the corner with his mobile phone against his ear. He was wearing a black sports jacket with a Newcastle United logo on the breast and some black jeans, and hadn't noticed Nick.

'Yeah, yeah, I can meet you there,' he said. 'Is that the industrial estate out the back of Hangforth? Yeah, I know it.' There was a pause while he listened. 'Yep, we'll talk about the money then.' And he hung up.

Nick drew back. What was that all about? But before he could wonder any further, he saw the sun reflecting off Liam's wrist. Was that...? Nick's stomach plummeted as he remembered the empty place where his watch had been in his drawer.

Heart pounding, he walked over to Liam, pasting a smile on

his face. 'Hiya. I just wanted to say thanks for coming.' Nick's eyes flicked down to Liam's wrist. The watch was exactly the same as the one that was missing. But how could he be sure?

'Nee bother,' said Liam. 'Your nanna was always nice to me,'

'Uh-huh,' Nick murmured, glancing at Liam's wrist again. Liam shifted uncomfortably. What could Nick say? He could hardly ask outright, but now, with the strange and possibly dodgy phone conversation he'd just overhead, he couldn't help but feel suspicious. He took a deep breath but found himself saying, 'The wake is at the Kitchen. I'll see you there, shall I?'

'Aye,' said Liam, walking off.

Nick watched him go. He had to believe that Travis was right to trust him, but he made a regretful note to double- and triple-check the flat when he got back. He hoped for Travis's sake that it turned up; that he would find it in a jacket pocket or a travel bag, and then he could just chalk it up to an unfortunate coincidence.

Ruby appeared around the side of the building. She grabbed his hand. 'Mammy says it's time to go to the party,' she said.

Nick gritted his teeth, staring after the retreating figure of Liam, heading towards the gates. It wasn't the right time to dwell on it. For now, he had to attend the most depressing 'party' of his life.

The congregation entered the Community Kitchen through the main doors, which were festooned on either side by floral tributes, notes and trinkets from well-wishers. There were sealed letters, scrappy handwritten notes, flowers picked and tied with string, inexpensive petrol-station bouquets and some personal items ranging from scarves to sobriety tokens. Nick felt a lump in his throat seeing these meagre items – the people that she'd

helped, or was still helping, had given some of their few possessions in tribute to his nanna.

Inside, the Kitchen was heaving with people. The staff had
laid out trays of buffet fare, giving him flashbacks to the prawn-
sandwich incident and the ensuing conversation with Edie at
his hospital bed, which he hadn't known would be one of their
last. He cursed his father for something else – taking him on a
fruitless wild goose chase that had robbed him of the last few
days of his grandmother's life. He shouldered his way through
the crowd, stopping now and then to shake hands with people
who knew he was Edie's grandson.

He eventually made it to the back of the room and scanned
around for Travis, of whom there was no sign. He needed to
speak to him about Liam, and how he should be more careful
about who he trusted, not just because of the missing watch but
also due to the shady-sounding phone conversation he'd overheard. Who was he meeting on an industrial estate, and what
kind of money were they going to talk about? Travis needed to
stay well away from this lad.

He opened the door to the education suite, wondering if he
could find him in there, but it was almost as busy as the main
dining room. Laura was by the careers display with a glass of
wine in hand, and she waved.

'Thanks for coming,' he said. He hadn't had the chance to
speak to her in the chapel. 'It's good of you.'

'Oh, I wouldn't have missed it. Your nanna was always
lovely to me, and I liked her a lot. How are you bearing up?'

'I'm alright, Laur. Thanks.' He could sense she wanted to
dig deeper into his feelings, so he scoured his memory for a
distraction. 'Ruby's still buzzing about the lighthouse.'

'I'm not surprised. That tour guide had her wishing to be
the next Grace Darling by the time he was finished.'

'Tell me about it,' said Nick, thinking back to a few days ago
when he'd had a brief reprieve from funeral preparations.

Laura had come with them to the lighthouse – Nick had invited her along as she was at a loose end and was dropping Ruby off again anyway. For the whole car ride, Ruby chattered away about how excited she was and how much Ian the Lobster was going to enjoy it too. She held him up to look out of the window as they approached St Nicholas Lighthouse and parked up. She practically ran inside, with Laura and Nick following behind, and when he pointed her in the direction of the colouring sheets that had been laid out in the lobby, she simply pointed upwards.

'You want to go to the top?'

She nodded.

'Come on then, darlin'. Let's go and see how many steps you can count.'

One hundred and thirty-seven steps later, they stood on the platform of the lighthouse gazing out at the sea. Ruby was trans-fixed, looking through the bars of the railings.

'Anyway, how are you?' Nick asked Laura while they rested their elbows on the ledge. 'You still seeing that new fella?'

Her face lit up. 'Yeah, I am.'

'Funnily enough, I saw you both a while back, the day we took Ruby to the beach. In the bistro – you looked well loved up.'

'Ha! Well, you might have witnessed a momentous step in our relationship.' She grinned then took a deep breath. 'He's asked me to move in with him.'

'Oh, really?'

She scrunched up her face. 'Yeah. But you know me. Captain Cautious. I've asked him to give me a bit more time.'

'Are you not sure then?'

'I'm this close,' she said, holding up her finger and thumb, millimetres apart. 'He's come out of a long-term relationship and I think their finances need unpicking. I don't want to get in the middle of all that, but if he loves me, he'll wait.'

'Too bloody right. If he's the right one, then he won't go anywhere.'

He looked out at the sea and was reminded of Wren, she and him bobbing on the waves in their kayak. In the pit of his stomach, he felt a squeeze at what he'd just said to Laura. *Maybe sometimes the right one does get away.*

He shivered then. It was colder up there than he'd expected.

'Can you watch Ruby for a minute?' he asked Laura. 'I've left my jacket in the car.'

'Yeah, no problem.'

He left the two of them, Ruby holding Ian out through the railings to give him a better look, and wove down the spiral steps towards the car park. As he passed through, he spotted a familiar face – the man who walked his dog on the beach was giving a talk to some visitors. *Small world*, he thought and noted that the guy had picked up a bit of a tan since he'd last seen him. Nick went to the car, shrugged on his jacket and wandered back into the lighthouse, only to find that all hell had broken loose.

Laura and Ruby were down in the lobby, the latter crying her eyes out.

'What's happened?' he asked, rushing forward to hold her by the shoulders.

'She's okay,' Laura reassured him, stroking Ruby's hair.

'It's Ian!' Ruby sobbed. 'He fell down.'

'Ah, no. Where is he now?'

Please don't be in the sea, he thought.

'Thankfully not,' Laura said. 'A woman picked him up. *She nearly slipped off the cliff edge*,' she said under her breath, to avoid upsetting Ruby further. 'I was just going to find her and see if she's okay, and get Ian back. I think they took her to the staff area.'

'Right. It's okay, I'll go and find her.' He kissed Ruby on the top of the head. 'Don't worry, darlin'. I'll go and fetch him for you.'

He scanned the lobby for a staff-only sign and headed for it, Ruby hiccupping and sniffing behind him as he went. He tentatively popped his head round the door into a separate short corridor, not wanting to just barge his way in.

'Hello?' he called.

A man came out of a side room. He was tall with salt-and-pepper hair and wore a badge on his fleece gilet that read 'Cliff'. Nick bit his lip, trying not to smile at it.

'What can I do for you?' he asked congenially.

'Um, I'm looking for my daughter's toy lobster? I hear he went on a bit of an adventure.'

'Ah, yes. He certainly did. So did his rescuer – would have toppled off the cliff if I hadn't grabbed her quick enough.'

'I'm so sorry. Is she here? I'd like to say thanks, if I can?'

'Hold on – I'll just go and see.'

He walked into the side room and returned thirty seconds later with Ian, handing him over with a regretful smile. 'She says it's no bother, no need to say thanks. *Still calming down,*' he whispered, nodding towards the closed door. 'She's just glad your little girl's got her friend back.'

'Right. Well, we're very grateful. Hope she's okay. And thanks again.' He waved the lobster and headed back to the lobby, wondering why drama seemed to follow him everywhere he went lately. After some cuddles and the promise of an ice cream, Ruby had settled down too, and they'd enjoyed the rest of the day without further incident.

The noise in the Community Kitchen had turned up a notch as it continued to fill with people, and he was just about to raise his voice to ask Laura how the story of Ian the Lobster's skydive had gone down with Callie when he felt a rough tug on his shoulder.

He turned to see Callie herself, her face pale and her eyes wild.

'Nick. I can't find Ruby. Anywhere.'

All thoughts of lighthouses and lobsters disappeared as he pushed his way through into the main dining hall.

'You check outside again,' he yelled at Callie over his shoulder as he dove into the crowd. Laura had rushed off to check the other side rooms, shouting Ruby's name. It was drowned out by the 'One, two, three...' of a local band that had ex-Kitchen attendees in its line-up, and Nick could barely hear himself think as they began a loud rendition of 'I'll Be There for You' by The Rembrandts.

'Ruby!' he called, pushing through to the entrance hall, checking the store cupboard that branched off it and even behind the heavily stacked coat pegs. Nothing. Where could she be? The seeds of panic started to take root in his belly. Ruby barely went anywhere without an adult's hand to hold, and now she was somewhere within this mass of people, or worse, somewhere outside. Callie was screaming her name out in the street, so he plunged back into the dining room.

He grabbed his phone from his pocket and tried to call Travis, just in case she was with him, but there was no answer.

He looked down at the floor and, ludicrously, up to the ceiling. He scoured beyond shoulders and elbows and tops of heads. He searched down by waists, knees, feet. Eventually, he emerged behind the food service counter, where he threw open cupboard doors, even the warming oven, just in case. Nothing.

He pushed through the doors to the back rooms, where there was nobody around, and checked the bathrooms, which were unoccupied. Then he went into the main kitchen, which was also empty, barring the aftermath of food preparation. Cake crumbs littered the surfaces, and he absurdly thought that Edie wouldn't have tolerated this kind of mess. Running his hands through his hair, he tried desperately to think of what he could do next. And then he saw a wrapper on the floor – a paper wrapper from a choc ice, an old-fashioned brand that was familiar to him, even from his own childhood. He remembered being given them as a treat out of the cavernous walk-in freezer. And he remembered Edie giving them to Ruby too.

His heart in his mouth, he raced from the kitchen into the hall, where the door to the freezer room was closed tightly.

'Ruby,' he bellowed, hammering on the door. 'Are you in there?'

'Daddy!' came a voice faintly from inside. 'I can't get out.'

He yanked at the handle, which he thought he'd fixed up a treat last time, but it was stuck rigidly and wouldn't move.

'Ruby darlin', can you give the handle a turn for me? Have a try.'

There was a faint wobble as she tried from the other side.

'I can't, Daddy. It's stuck.'

'Okay, don't worry. Daddy's going to get you out.'

He raced to the store cupboard down the corridor, throwing his phone onto the shelf as he rummaged around, and grabbed a screwdriver from the toolkit. In a growing panic, with shaking hands, he worried away at the handle, slipping every now and then, murmuring reassurances to Ruby inside. The damn thing was rattling; there must have been something loose inside the workings.

When it finally popped open, the cold air rushed out as fast as the adrenaline coursing through him. He hurried inside, still holding the screwdriver, and wrapped his arms around Ruby, who was freezing cold, clutching Ian, and had a mouth covered in chocolate. On the floor were several empty choc-ice wrappers.

'I wanted one of Nanna Edie's treats. To remember her by,'

she said, blinking up at him with eyes that were both innocent and guilty, depending on the context.

'You dafty,' he said, rubbing the top of her head. 'You gave me and Mammy a bit of a scare. Come on – let's get you out of here and warmed up.'

He stood up and took her hand, ready to head out to the warmth and chaos of the main hall, where he could return Ruby to her worried mother's arms. But just as they turned to walk out the door, the strains of 'Lean on Me' coming from the dining room were sharply extinguished by the thud of the freezer door being pushed closed, followed by the metallic clank of the interior handle falling off onto the floor.

TWENTY-FIVE

WREN

Wren stood in front of the Community Kitchen, steeling herself to go inside. The building was the same, but since the last time she was here, almost everything she felt about it had changed. Only a few weeks ago, the Kitchen had inspired her work, leaving her fascinated by the sense of community and the incredible women that kept it all going. She'd been writing a love story to the place. Now it felt like a tragedy. Edie was gone, and the story about her own mam had seemingly died with her, until her dad had finally told her the truth. So now the Kitchen was like hallowed ground in a way. It held the ghosts of both Edie and her mother.

She stood up straighter and walked inside. It was packed with people – the request that anyone other than close friends and family come to the wake rather than the funeral service seemed to have been a very good plan. She could see nothing but the heads and shoulders of people around her. The mood was a mix of sombre and celebratory; people were dressed appropriately in black, grey and navy, but there was a band tuning up on the raised platform she'd last seen at the anniversary party.

Wren filtered through the crowd saying hello to the odd person she was familiar with, nodding and smiling politely to those she wasn't. She reminded herself she was partly here for work and tapped a few notes into her phone about the atmosphere. Zara was expecting a nice little article about Edie's legacy, although how Wren could summarise that, she had no idea.

She came across Cath and Ailsa, who looked drawn and tired but were still raising a smile for everyone. A skill they'd honed over the years, no doubt, always putting others first. Wren wondered what would happen to the Kitchen now that Edie was gone – who would be in charge? Obviously, it was the wrong time to ask, so she settled for platitudes and kind words instead.

Finally, she found herself at the photo wall, where she'd once scoured the pictures for an image of her mam and come up with nothing. It was quiet there, so she stood looking at the wall, dangling her glass of warm wine in her hand. So many people. It was no wonder her mam had blended into the crowd.

So now she knew. Her mam hadn't been a volunteer here or a friend of Edie's. She'd been one of the people Edie had tried, and failed, to help. One of her sad stories that she didn't like to talk about. The back of Wren's throat felt hot, and the photographs swam in front of her eyes as she thought about how close she'd been to hearing it from Edie herself. Maybe Edie hadn't known what to say or had been bound by some code of confidentiality, but that letter she'd received, saying Edie was ready to talk, had come just a little too late. At least it had spurred her dad on to tell her the truth though, and she supposed she had Edie to thank for that.

She reached into her handbag and pulled out the snow globe she'd bought for Edie in Italy. Snow was falling on the little lighthouse and miniature grottoes inside. The cave mouths reminded her of Nick, another person who was gone from her life. She wasn't sure why she'd brought it with her. She'd considered leaving it here, since it was meant for Edie anyway. But who would be bothered about a random trinket brought back from Wren's holiday? Now that Edie was gone, it was meaningless. She shook the snowflakes into a vortex one more time and slipped it back into her bag.

Wiping her eyes, she coughed away the tight feeling in her throat. Again, she reminded herself she had a job to do and forced herself to nudge through the assembled crowd, asking people to give her quotes about Edie. It grew progressively harder, as she was hemmed in on all sides, speaking to people almost nose to nose, and then the band struck up the first few chords of 'I'll Be There for You' by The Rembrandts. She soldiered on, undeterred by the commotion of someone yelling a name over the music. *Rudy? Ruby?* It was verging on chaos in there.

She was just typing some notes into her phone when the screen lit brighter and vibrated in her hand. A call from Libby. She answered it.

'Wren! My waters have broken all over the shop floor. What shall I do?'

Wren's chest spiked with adrenaline as she heard the muffled tones of Jenson in the background, complaining about the mess. This was followed by the slightly less muffled tones of Libby telling him to 'Grow the fuck up – it's only amniotic fluid.'

'Lib, stay where you are,' Wren barked down the phone. 'I'll be right there, and I'll drive you to hospital.'

'Thanks, Wren,' she said, laughing nervously. 'I don't fancy getting a backer on Jenson's penny-farthing if the contractions start.'

Wren stuffed her phone into her bag and started to shove through the crowd to the main door, but there was a group of young lads, half-cut, half-tearful, swaying arm in arm to the band. Groaning, she changed course then remembered she could try going out the back way, past the kitchen and staff toilets. That route was clearer, and before long she emerged into the cooler air of the corridor, blinking in the dim light. A door was open, half-blocking the thoroughfare, so she bustled past it, slamming it closed. A few moments later, she was in her car and driving as fast as she dared back to Cravenwick.

Wren arrived to the sight of a whey-faced Jenson, pulling hard on a menthol cigarette against the shop window. He looked like he would forever be haunted by the harrowing things he'd just witnessed. She rushed through the door to find Libby sitting on a pile of paper carrier bags on the shop sofa. She looked up bleakly, holding the edges of the sofa cushions with white knuckles.

'I never thought I'd see the day I wanted plastic carrier bags baaaaack...' she wailed as a wave of pain rolled over her, squeezing her eyes shut and segueing into a long moan.

'Contractions started then?'

Libby nodded, lips pressed together, until it passed. Then, as night turns to day, her face relaxed, and she and Wren locked eyes. They both burst into nervous laughter.

'There's going to be an actual baby coming out of me very soon,' snorted Libby.

'You can't keep the bump forever, no matter how much it suits you. But isn't it a bit early?'

'Two weeks.'

Wren swallowed. Was that something to worry about?

'It's fine. I think.' Libby had read her mind. 'But I'd rather do this with a smidgeon of medical assistance...'

Wren snapped to attention. 'God. Yes. So let's get in the car.'

'Can you get the hospital bag?' Libby asked as her face started to contort again.

As Wren ran up the stairs, Libby yelled in pain. In the bedroom was a zipped-up travel bag with some medical notes on top – surprisingly organised for her. Wren snatched it up then ran back downstairs. Libby staggered to the car and eased herself into the passenger seat.

'Come on then – let's go,' said Wren with a smile. She was starting to feel a little excited about the impending birth. Auntie Wren. It had a ring to it. She turned the key in the ignition.

Nothing. Not even a splutter, or a whirr. She tried again. Complete silence.

Wren turned slowly to face Libby, who, despite the pain she was in, managed to look wryly amused.

'Well, isn't that awkward timing?' she said before being consumed by another searing contraction.

Wren bolted from the car. 'Fuck,' she whispered, pulling her phone from her pocket. Were you allowed to ring an ambulance for this? Or a taxi? Did they charge extra for a clean-up fee? Jenson looked on unhelpfully. Wren made a snap decision and started scrolling for taxi numbers, and was just about to dial a number when a car pulled up to the kerb.

'You okay, Wren?' Alex asked, climbing out of the driver's seat of his Audi.

Wren froze. What the hell was he doing here? But then, in her state of mild panic, she remembered the time and realised he was on his way home from an early shift. She nodded to the car, and he looked inside. Libby gave a stoic wave.

'She's in labour?' he said, his eyes widening.

'Yep. And my sodding car won't start.'

'Right. Well, I can take you to the hospital. Come on – let's switch her over.'

Wren hesitated. She didn't want to get tangled up with Alex again, not right now. But taking one look at Libby's contorted face in her useless car, she realised it was the best option she had. A taxi could take a while to come, and an ambulance might be overkill. So she nodded and helped hoist Libby from one car to the other.

Alex took one look at the sodden paper bags that Libby tried to put on his rear passenger seat and produced a massive Sports Direct bag for life instead. Always resourceful, not to mention very protective of his fancy car, Wren thought as she slid into the other side. But she was also grateful that he'd happened to show up at just the right time.

As they sped out of Cravenwick towards Hexham General Hospital, she thought that fate was a funny thing. Alex turning up out of the blue reminded her of how Nick had been there, standing on the marina just when she'd needed him. She realised that although she needed Alex right now, it was purely practical, a favour accepted. But Nick had felt like he was written in her stars.

TWENTY-SIX

NICK

Nick's throat was raw from yelling so loudly, but the music was still thumping away, and the passage wasn't the busiest of thoroughfares, not when there was so much going on in the main hall. His first instinct had been to reach for his phone to call Travis, but his pockets were empty – he'd left his damn phone in the store cupboard while he was rummaging for tools. His hands felt sore from hammering on the door, which, due to the handle falling off, was locked tight. With trembling, freezing fingers, he'd tried to screw the handle back on, but it wouldn't stay – in his panic to remove it in the first place, he must have damaged some of the workings.

They'd been in there for more than ten minutes now, and Ruby's lips had a tinge of blue about them that Nick didn't like at all. He'd bundled her into his suit jacket, cursing that it wasn't the season for a warmer coat, and poured out the contents of some large boxes, feeling ludicrous as he packed the cardboard around her. Anything to try to keep her warm.

What the hell had possessed somebody to shut the door on them? To be fair, nobody would have expected a man and his little daughter to be hanging out in a walk-in freezer, but couldn't they have had a cursory glance? When the door had clanged shut, he'd leaped immediately to bang on the door to alert them, but they must have been in a hurry, as they hadn't seemed to have heard.

'Ruby darlin', we'll be out in just a minute,' he said with way more confidence than he felt. Her eyes were shiny, and she nodded just once, her little face framed by cardboard.

'I know, Daddy. It's alright.' Her voice was tiny and shook a little, maybe from the cold or from the fear she was trying to hide.

It set off a bolt of fury at his helplessness, and he looked around for the twentieth time to see if there was anything, anything at all, that he could use to get them out of there. There was nothing but boxes upon boxes of frozen food, and feeling slightly insane, he wondered how effective a big bit of frozen meat might be at battering the door down. But then he realised he could try something else with the screwdriver. He'd been the one who'd built those storage shelves, a few years ago, and he'd wager that as long as the screws weren't too rusty, they'd come apart easily enough.

Quickly, he cleared a set of shelves of boxes and set to work dismantling the rectangular metal struts that held the horizontal shelves together. Wielding one, with the fierceness of a character from *The Walking Dead* facing an approaching zombie, he went to the door and began wedging it into the frame with all his might.

It wasn't budging, but then he heard Ruby start to whimper behind him, and he pushed even harder. He would get them out of there even if it killed him.

He heaved and thrust at the metal, levering it back and forth until he felt the slender edge slip in between the junction of the door and frame. It stuck there, and he stood back a few paces then raised his leg, booting it as hard as he could, hearing the satisfying crack of the door frame giving way. He was so elated by the rush of warm air that he felt almost nothing as the metal pushed up his trouser leg and gouged a long, deep cut along his inner calf.

He turned to Ruby and picked her up, carrying her out of the frigid cavern to find Callie and Laura running into the corridor.

'Oh my God, Ruby!' Callie screamed, grabbing her from Nick's arms, allowing him to stagger on his wounded leg. He bent down, completely out of breath, and braced his hands on his knees, wheezing. 'What the hell happened?' she asked, patting Ruby down for injuries and stroking her hair.

'She got locked in the freezer,' panted Nick. 'Then I did too...'

'Where's that blood coming from?' Laura asked, pointing to the drips and splatters on the corridor floor.

'Me. I think,' said Nick as the walls of the corridor started to tilt, and he fell to his knees.

The nurse in A&E gave Nick a strange look as she stitched and bandaged his injured leg. 'Have I seen you here before?' she asked.

She had, indeed, seen Nick here before, when he'd been here with the seafood allergy, but he was too mortified to admit it. 'I must just have one of those faces,' he said, wondering how after years of generally good health, he'd managed to end up in A&E for the second time in just a few weeks.

Almost as mortifying was the journey here, after which he and Ruby had been hurried off to separate cubicles, leaving him alone to reflect on it. He'd barely hit the deck when Justin had wandered into the corridor, jingling his car keys. He'd been there to collect Callie, Ruby and Laura, and his eyes had grown wide at the chaotic sight of them all.

It had been the sight of, rather than the actually fairly

minimal loss of blood that had given Nick a bit of a turn, but as soon as he'd seen Justin, he'd scrambled to get up. Justin had hooked his elbow and tried to help, asking, 'You alright, mate?'

Nick had flinched at the overfamiliarity but had been forced, without Travis or his mother in sight, to accept a lift in Justin's car, while Ruby was sandwiched in the back, having been divested of her cardboard packaging but still wearing Nick's suit jacket. There had been silence, except for Callie murmuring soothingly to Ruby and the occasional click of the indicator switch.

Nick's jacket made a reappearance through the cubicle curtains, on the arm of Callie.

'Knock, knock,' she said quietly, shouldering meekly through and placing his jacket on the back of a nearby chair. 'How are you feeling?'

'I'm fine. More importantly, how's Ruby?'

'She's absolutely fine. All warmed up, no harm done, and already getting excited about telling her friends about her adventure.'

'Well, that's a relief.'

'Thanks to you.'

Nick winced. 'If I'd been quicker to get her out before someone closed the door...'

'You got her out anyway, didn't you? And mangled your leg in the process. You must have been like a wild animal.'

Nick didn't feel like a wild animal right then. A wounded animal with a sore leg maybe, but all the fight had gone out of him, so he just nodded.

Callie's face was hard to read. It looked as if she was finding *herself* hard to read, if anything.

'You love her. I never doubted that, you know,' she said softly. He went to reply, but she held up a hand. 'Let me finish. I know I've been protective of her...'

He listened, not daring to speak.

'... but today has reminded me that she's just as much yours as she is mine. If it had been me in there, the mothering instinct would have come out like a tiger too. I'd have beat my hands bloody on that door. So I can see now that it runs just as deep for you, and I... I haven't considered that enough. I'm not saying... I don't know what I'm saying. But maybe, when I've calmed down a bit, we need to have a talk.'

Nick's eyes flickered up to hers, and he saw that through the fatigue, there was the tiniest bit of warmth.

'Okay,' he said. 'I'd like that.'

She nodded, her lips a straight line. 'Okay then. I have to go. But one more thing. It was Justin who helped me make sense of today. He told me how hard it would have been to smash open that lock. Real "lifting a car to save someone's life" stuff. And it was him who told me to tell you so.' And she slipped out between the curtains.

Not long after, Ruby popped in to say goodbye and give him a hug, and Travis texted to say he was coming to collect him. He was just pulling his blood-stained trousers up his tender leg when Travis appeared in the A&E corridor, tie rakishly undone.

'I feel like I should get a parking pass for this hospital, big brother,' he said. 'Are there going to be any events at the Kitchen that you *don't* get blue-lighted out of?'

'Very funny,' said Nick, getting up to test his leg. It was sore to stand on, but he wouldn't be in need of crutches. 'I'm fine, by the way – thanks for asking.'

'Good. Now can we get back home? Our mother's already started on the gin and Dubonnets, and I'm worried she'll drink enough to break my no-smoking policy. I don't want customers returning clothes that smell like they've been rubbed around an ashtray.'

Nick sighed. All he needed was a shower with a bin bag

over his stitches, and bed, but he now remembered he'd need to catch up with his mam. He wasn't sure he had the energy for chit-chat, never mind the looming conversation about Richard Keyes. He followed Travis out of the A&E department and into the main lobby of the hospital, wincing as he went.

Travis turned back and saw that Nick's pace had slowed. 'Look, stay here, and I'll bring the van over. I've parked miles away.'

Nick gratefully accepted, feeling a deeper throb setting in, and wandered over to near the lifts, looking at the various posters about incontinence, counselling and how to wash your hands. He turned around and someone caught his eye. A man walking from the lifts, looking at his phone, dressed in trendy sportswear. Nick recognised him – it was the guy Laura had been with in the bistro in Newcastle: her new boyfriend.

He was blandly scrolling, then he glanced up and around, as if he was waiting for someone. Had he come to pick up Laura? Their eyes met, and Nick held his gaze, remembering just as the guy gave him a funny look that he would have no clue who he was.

'Alright, mate?' Nick said, feeling obliged to explain himself. 'Sorry, you don't know me. We just have a mutual friend. Your girlfriend actually.'

The man looked him up and down. 'Right. I don't think we've met. Have we?'

'No. We haven't. God, sorry, this is coming across weird. I know your face – I saw you two out in Newcastle – so I put two and two together.'

'Yeah. I'm Alex.'

He held out his hand, narrowing his eyes, and Nick wished he hadn't said anything and just walked past. This guy didn't seem the friendliest, but Nick took his hand anyway. 'I'm Nick.'

There followed a very firm handshake, and at the same

time, the lift doors pinged behind them. The doors opened, and Nick stared in disbelief.

Wren walked towards them, her mouth hanging open in surprise. 'Nick?' she breathed. 'What are you...?'

'*Wren?* I can't believe...'

Laura's boyfriend's eyes flitted between them, his brow furrowed. 'So how do you two know each other?'

'Sorry, mate,' started Nick, although Wren had opened her mouth to reply too. 'Weird coincidence. This is Wren – we met on holiday in Italy, just last week. Wren, this is Alex.'

Alex and Wren's mouths snapped shut.

Nobody spoke for a second, and Nick felt the uncomfortable urge to fill the awkward silence. 'I mean, Wren... wow. I can't believe it. What are the chances?'

Alex glared at him. 'Is this what you meant then, pal? That you're *friends* with my girlfriend?'

Nick blinked. What was he going on about? 'Um, I was talking about Laura...' And almost as the last syllable left his mouth, the penny dropped. Wren and this Alex were standing surprisingly close together for strangers, and the look of horror on both their faces said volumes.

Wren wheeled around to face Alex, her face turning from thunder to rainclouds. Nick just stood there mutely, in shock.

'You fucking bastard,' she said to Alex, her voice like ice. And then she turned away and walked off without looking back.

'Nice one, you daft prick,' said Alex to Nick, following after her.

TWENTY-SEVEN

WREN

Alex answered the door straight away, looking dishevelled and hollow-eyed. He didn't look filled with panic though, so she assumed *Laura* wasn't in the building.

'Come in,' he said, and she did.

The kitchen was less tidy than usual, which was odd considering how much of a neat freak Alex usually was – there were piles of papers and correspondence on the breakfast counter, and some half-eaten plates of food. Plates of healthy, plant-based food, of course, but half-eaten all the same.

She got straight to the point. 'I want us to decide what we're doing with the house,' she said.

As soon as she'd left the hospital, she'd gone straight to a letting agency and furiously signed a contract for the first furnished flat they had available.

His face grew pained. 'Wren, please, we haven't even... we haven't even spoken about *us*.'

'What *us*?' she barked, incredulous. 'There is no us. There's you and Laura. And then me. Who now needs to pay for somewhere else to live, so we need to come to some arrangement.'

His tortured expression turned rapidly into a sneer. 'Just

you? What about that guy in the hospital: your *friend* from *our* holiday? Speaking of which, we need to talk about how you're going to pay me back for my share.'

She gaped at him. 'Your share? So much for saying I needn't worry about it. Well, I suppose you can take it out of whatever you owe me to buy me out of the house. And as for Nick, I can't believe you've got the nerve to say anything about him, considering you've already settled down with someone new.'

She flushed at even the mention of Nick's name. She still couldn't believe he had been standing right there in the hospital lobby. Of all the times she'd wished to see him again, the fates had manifested him at the worst possible moment.

His nostrils flared. 'I begged you to come back to me – you know I wanted to make us work.'

'But *why*? You've clearly got feelings for your new girlfriend. Why the hell would you try negotiating with me? I'd have thought us breaking up would be exactly what you wanted.'

He mashed his hands against his eyes. 'It's not that simple. Wren, we've been together for so long, we've got the house, friends, a life. We're practically married in all but the paperwork. I couldn't just...' He ran out of steam and looked at her pleadingly.

What the hell was he trying to achieve with all this agonising? Which of his 'girlfriends' did he actually want? Not that it would have made any difference to her because, after all, she'd fallen for Nick. And now, standing here, she realised it was the first time she'd given her feelings a name. She'd fallen for Nick, and she'd lost him all over again when she'd walked out of the hospital. All because of this piece of work. Her heart was of two halves – aching for Nick and rock solid in the face of Alex.

'It's over, Alex. Get your head around it.' She pushed her shoulders back and breathed deeply. 'I just want us to agree how we're going to deal with the house, then we can get on with our lives.'

'I'm not selling,' he said abruptly. 'This is my home. I'm not moving out.'

'Alex,' she said, trying to keep her tone the gentle side of exasperated. 'You can't afford this house on your salary. Neither could I. It's a joint income kind of figure. So I'm sorry, but unless you can buy me out and find a way to continue the monthly payments, then it's our only option.' And hopefully a quick one, she thought, knowing that the small amount of savings she'd put aside wouldn't cover many months of rent on her new place.

He folded his arms over his chest and glared at the floor, jaw clenched. It irritated Wren to see how obstinate he was being, but then he'd always been like this – just now, she could look at him objectively and see how unreasonable and childish he could be.

The piles of papers caught her eye and she realised they were mortgage documents and letters. Despite his petty reluctance to talk to her about it, he'd clearly been thinking along the same lines.

She picked up a sheaf of paper. 'Alex, please. I can see that you've thought about it, and you know the numbers don't add up.' She waved the papers then thumbed through them. Statements, circulars, all kinds of communication from the mortgage lender were in there. But one in particular caught her eye.

Dear Mr Black,

Further to your enquiry about the process for transfer of equity and the addition of a new borrower to your current mortgage product, please find attached...

The date was more than six weeks ago. When they'd still

been together. Getting on and in love – or so she'd thought. The papers fell from her hands, and the one she'd read fluttered to Alex's feet. His eyes widened.

She let out a harsh breath of laughter. 'My God. I thought you were an arsehole this afternoon. But I was wrong. You're the fucking Antichrist!'

He avoided her eyes, a flush spreading over his chiselled cheekbones.

'You've been seeing her for ages, haven't you? And you've been making your little plans to move her in, to make sure you covered yourself financially before you dared give me the boot. Got all your ducks in a row. I mean... how fucking cold-blooded is that?'

Edie had been right about trust. All the times Alex had questioned her faithfulness, he'd been applying his own shitty moral compass to her.

'It was just for information,' he blustered. 'I could tell you were thinking of leaving, and I wanted to know all of my options. Just in case.'

'Sure, Alex. Well, now I'm out of the picture, you can crack on.'

His mouth pinched. 'She... she hasn't agreed to move in. Yet.'

Wren picked up her bag and hooked it over her shoulder. 'You'd best start working your charm then. I know now why you wanted me to stay so much. Not because you love me, but because I make the books balance if she won't sign on the dotted line. Well, it's time you got yourself a new investor.'

And with that, she walked out of Alex's house and out of his life forever.

She'd barely reached the bus stop at the bottom of the road when she sat down heavily on a low garden wall. It was all too overwhelming. There was simply too much for her head to process. Libby and the baby. Poor Edie dying. Her mam and the truth she hadn't had time to properly digest. Her fresh start away from Alex. And Nick. Lovely Nick, who'd come into her life like a dream, far away in another country, so that it seemed almost unreal. And then he'd been there, just today, as solid and real as any man, and she'd just walked away. The amount of things swirling around her mind almost made her dizzy. She didn't think she could take any more. And then her phone rang.

'Wren,' came the soothing tones of Zara's voice down the line. 'I'm afraid I've got some more bad news.'

TWENTY-EIGHT

NICK

They set grimly to work as soon as they got inside, opening Edie's bureau drawers and sifting through the many bits of paper inside. Nick went through to the kitchen to make them some tea. It struck him that he'd never picked the kettle up and found it stone cold before. His nanna had loved a brew so much that it had always been at least lukewarm, whatever time of day he was visiting. He clicked the switch then stood with his hand pressed hard to his mouth, his eyes wet.

'Ah, come here, pet,' said Tracey, coming into the kitchen with her arms outstretched. She squeezed him tightly like he was a little boy, but he felt the trickle of one of her tears on his neck.

They each took deep breaths and stood apart, putting matching hands on hips. The physical distance between them over the years was an uncomfortable bedfellow with sentimentality. So he clapped his hands and cleared his throat. 'Come on then. Let's get started.'

They sorted through Edie's bits and pieces, loading trinkets of no clear purpose or nostalgia into the black bags. In went half-consumed rolls of Polos, takeaway menus and confusing gadgets from the JML catalogue. Tracey found a set of coasters from the 1970s, clutched them to her chest and nestled them into her handbag. Nick found a Christmas decoration he'd made at primary school – an angel made from a toilet-roll tube and cotton wool – and put it on the coffee table until he could decide if it would be weird to keep it for himself.

They'd worked in silence for a while, when Tracey said, 'Do you want to talk about Richard then?'

When Nick had got home the previous night, worn out from his stint at A&E and his run-in with Wren, any urge he'd had to bring it up had dissipated. He'd almost been too weary to search the flat for his missing watch, but he'd tried his best. He'd been frustrated to find no sign of it, although he would look again when he could think straight. The alternative was too grim to contemplate. And even if he'd had the energy, Tracey had been three gins along and unstoppable in her recollections of Edie, ranging from bittersweet to plain maudlin. It wouldn't have been right to interrupt her last night, but now it seemed the time had come.

'You got my messages then.'

'I did. But not until I heard about your nanna. So there's been that to contend with.'

'Right.'

They busied their hands with the contents of the drawers and didn't look at each other.

'So did you find him?'

'I did.'

Her shoulders lifted a little, and she sighed. 'Christ alive,' she said. 'There's a receipt here from a toaster she bought in 1985. The woman wouldn't part with anything.' She flung it on the discard pile.

Nick leafed through some old postcards. 'What possessed you to get involved with him, Mam?'

'I was young and stupid.'

Nick said nothing, waiting for her to carry on, and finally she did.

'It was 1989. Me and the girls had gone on holiday to Butlins, for a bit of a laugh. You know, Malibu and Cokes, sitting round the pool, then dancing all night in the disco. We all had awful jobs, working for awful men in offices and shops, so we wanted to let our hair down a bit. And then I met him. Your father.'

'Tell me he wasn't a red coat?'

She smiled, clearly picturing the resort's troupe of entertainers. 'No. He wasn't a red coat, I didn't fulfil that cliché. But I certainly ticked the boxes for a few others. I first saw him in the disco with his friends. He was good-looking, though he seemed to be very aware of it. But he was confident, older, and he made me feel like I was the most gorgeous woman in the place. Feeding me all these lines... Looking back now, I should have realised he was far too smooth to be genuine, but I was naive. We went back to his chalet, and I won't embarrass you with the details of that bit.'

'Appreciated,' said Nick, squirming.

'So we spent the rest of the week together, and his friends were constantly making little jokes about us, asking when he was going to put a ring on my finger and when I'd be going home to meet his family. I thought it was funny at the time, that they were ribbing him so much. I kind of assumed he hadn't been the romantic type until he met me. What a fool I was.' She gave a bitter laugh and looked off into the distance.

'On the last night, one of his friends pulled me to one side and explained what all the jokes were about. When they wound him up about putting a ring on my finger, they were referring to the one that matched the ring he'd hid in a drawer in their chalet. And when they joked about meeting his family, they really meant his wife, who was at home, oblivious.'

Her shoulders slumped and she shook her head. 'I was

devastated. I was young, stupid and quick to lose my heart, and even in those few days, I'd started to fall for him. I looked for him everywhere, but someone must have given him the heads-up that I'd been told the truth, and the bastard hid himself away until they all disappeared back home the next day.

'One of my pals had cosied up with one of Richard's friends, so when I found out later that I was pregnant, I got in touch with him. He must have felt sorry for me, because he gave me Richard's number. I had to hang up twice when his wife answered; I felt sick to my stomach and couldn't work up the courage to call again.' She paused, looking crushed by the memory. 'But then, when you were born, I gave it one more try. He answered this time – I told him he had a son called Nicholas – and he hung up. I never saw or heard from him again. Until, it seems, he saw me on the Community Kitchen documentary and started joining some potentially lucrative dots.'

Nick nodded, and they said nothing for a while, silently placing items in little piles or in bin bags.

'If it's any consolation, he doesn't seem to have changed his ways. He lives alone in Italy, sweeping floors, and seems to have rubbed a lot of people up the wrong way. You had a lucky escape.'

'I was lucky in more ways than one, son. I got you,' said Tracey gruffly. 'So judging by what you've told me, you won't be keeping in touch?'

Nick laughed quietly. 'No. Although if he hears that Nanna left me and Travis the house, then he might come sniffing about again. And I'll tell him where to go. He seemed to be of the opinion that our family was loaded.'

Tracey blushed. 'Well, I was young and keen to impress. I might have sold him a story about being a bit more flash than I actually was.'

Nick shook his head and smiled. Tracey had always been a

woman of smoke and mirrors, putting on the razzle-dazzle for all to see.

Edie had always said she was going to leave the house to the boys – she'd been open about it for years – and her solicitor had confirmed it a few days ago. She'd left Tracey a generous nest egg, since she had no need of property with her rootless life-style, and the boys had been left the house. They could keep it, sell it, whatever they wanted to do, but they were to share the proceeds and set themselves up for the future. He wanted his nanna back more than life itself, but this gift she'd left meant he had a chance of building the home he'd been needing for himself. And, with any luck, Ruby.

Tracey sniffed. 'Well, you do right, son. You don't need him. You're living proof that you don't need a dad as long as you've got a few strong women in your life.'

He thought of Ruby, being mostly without her dad too, and his stomach clenched.

'I don't want that for Ruby,' he blurted. 'She's got a dad. I'm right here, but she must think I'm a million miles away sometimes.'

'This is going to work itself out, son. You might have the DNA of that waster out in Italy, but you've been brought up with the morals of a local patron bloody saint! And I'm not talking about me.' She winked, then her face grew serious.

'Oh, pet. I know I'm your mam. But I can admit I was just a bairn myself when you were born, and your nanna raised the both of us. You're Edie's bairn, through and through – responsi-bility definitely skipped a generation. Now Travis – he's more like me. He's not one for settling down, that lad. But you're a family man. So stop being so hard on yourself. You're a great dad. Just have a look at those stitches on your leg and give your head a wobble.'

She slapped her knees and got up. 'Right. I'm making another brew.' And she walked off. Sentimentality over.

He sat for a minute, trying to shake off the weird feeling of being mothered, then went back to the task of tidying, getting up to stretch his legs and tackle another part of the room for a while.

Walking over to the mantelpiece, he saw a photograph propped up, with an old, yellowed envelope tucked behind it. He picked it up.

It was a picture from the Community Kitchen, an old one, maybe from the eighties or nineties. It was a shot of Edie and a woman he didn't recognise, most likely a regular to the Kitchen. She had black curly hair and a smile that didn't reach the eyes, and had Edie's arm around her shoulders. She wore a thin jacket, zipped halfway up her chest, and in between the fabric, around her neck, was a necklace. Nick blinked.

He held the photo closer to his face. He'd seen this necklace before. It was a chain bearing an ornate seashell. Gold with pearly stripes. And the last time he'd seen it was when it had been yanked from Wren's neck in Italy. His mind raced. He remembered Wren saying that it was her mam's and that she'd died. Could it be her…?

He turned it over. On the back was written: *Edie and Caron Rowbottom, 1991.*

He'd wished so hard that he might see Wren again. But then, seeing her with her boyfriend, and the confusion that had ensued, that feeling had disappeared as fast as Wren's coat-tails as she'd vanished through the automatic doors. He'd felt glued to the floor by uncertainty and had just let her go, feeling like he had no right to follow them. And if he was honest, he'd felt crushed by the discovery that she wasn't, after all, single. She must have been glad to leave Nick, her little secret, behind in Italy, until he'd inconveniently reappeared. But, boyfriend or not, she deserved to see this picture of her mother, even if she had no interest in seeing Nick himself.

'Mam,' he shouted through to the kitchen, 'I'm just popping out.'

He pulled up to the Community Kitchen and climbed out of the van, limping a little on his sore leg. He'd managed to strain the stitches a bit, running out of Edie's house. He went straight inside and found Cath, who was just undoing her apron at the end of her shift.

'Cath,' he said, not stopping for pleasantries. 'Do you know who this is?' he asked, thrusting the photo under her nose.

She smiled and cocked her head to one side. 'Ah, look at her,' she said. 'This must have been years ago.'

'I know, how time flies and everything. But do you recognise the woman with my nanna? The woman wearing the necklace?'

Cath took the photo and squinted at it. 'Oh, love. I don't really know. There's been that many come through here, it could be anyone.'

Nick sighed, his shoulders slumping. It had been too much to hope for, he supposed. Cath was right – over the years, the Kitchen had looked after thousands of people. It had hardly been likely that she would remember this one particular woman out of all of them.

'Are you okay?' she asked, her brow creasing with concern. 'Is it important?'

'Kind of. But don't worry. I'm fine.'

He reached for the photo just as she turned it over, and she pulled it back again, frowning. '*Rowbottom*. Caron Rowbottom. Now I *do* know that name. Not the commonest name in the world. I'm sure that journalist was called something Rowbottom.'

Nick's eyebrows rose. 'The journalist?'

'Yeah. The one from the *Echo*. She was interviewing your nanna.'

'*That* journalist? What...?'

'Yes, that's right. She had a funny first name... some kind of bird.'

Nick stared at her, something inside him starting to vibrate, as if he was a bottle of lemonade that had just been shaken. He could barely catch his breath. 'Wren?'

'Yes, that's the one,' she said, beaming. 'Wren Rowbottom. Lovely girl.'

'She is,' he said, his heart pounding as he snatched back the photo, making Cath jump. He grabbed her by the shoulders and planted a kiss on her cheek. 'Thanks, Cath.'

And he raced back to the van, not even noticing the throb in his calf.

It was late in the day, but he was glad to find the doors of the *Northumberland Echo* still open when he arrived. His bloodstream was flooded with adrenaline and the realisation that he needed to see Wren so badly it hurt. And the fact that Wren, *his* Wren, was the journalist that Edie had been talking about made the adrenaline surges feel like rocket fuel.

He paused in the lobby, hesitating now. *His* Wren. That was how he thought of her, even after everything. He considered the devastation he'd caused with her boyfriend, the messy, awful fallout, and wondered again if he was doing the right thing. Alex seemed to have been cheating on her, and in Italy she'd been cheating on Alex. And Nick was in the middle of it all, wishing that it could all be as simple as things had been back then, when he and Wren were in another world. But as complicated as this situation was, she deserved to have this photograph.

He entered the office to find what could only be described as chaos. There were piles of paper everywhere, and a woman in a crumpled suit was standing in the middle of all of it.

She looked wearily at Nick. 'I'm sorry, but we're closed.'

'Oh. Sorry, the door was unlocked, so... I'm not here on official business if that makes a difference?'

'It might. How can I help?'

'Um, I'm looking for Wren. Wren Rowbottom? I'm told she works here.'

The woman's face spread into a genuine smile, but it faltered. 'Ah, Wren. It wasn't my favourite day at work, telling her she was out of a job.'

Nick's eyes widened.

'We're closing down,' she said. 'It's a sign of the times, unfortunately. But she'll be snapped up elsewhere, I'm sure of it. She's a very talented writer. Can I ask why you're looking for her?'

Nick swallowed. The first thing he wanted to say, to his surprise, was, 'I think I might have fallen in love with her on holiday.' He couldn't say that. And he didn't want to say too much about Wren's mam and her personal life, in case this woman, who seemed to be her ex-boss, wasn't to know such details. So he said, 'I'm Edie Macmillan's grandson. From the Community Kitchen? I've a message from her.'

Her face softened. 'My condolences. Your grandmother was a tremendous woman. But I'm sorry, Wren is moving to a new place and hasn't left me a forwarding address yet, and even if she did, I wouldn't be allowed to give it to you.'

Nick's shoulders sagged. 'Of course. I understand.'

The woman eyed him. 'I can pass on a message for you when I speak to her next? Or you can try the bookshop?'

'The bookshop?' Nick looked at her, confused.

'Yes. Cravenwick Pages. It's closed now, but it'll be open again in the morning. It's run by Wren's friend, so she might be able to help?' She shook her head, realising something. 'Ah. On second thoughts, Libby won't be there. She's just had a baby, and she's still in the hospital. But Wren is there a lot of the time.'

The bookshop? The place where he'd installed those new windows and been scared half to death by the pregnant owner? Nick reeled. How many different ways had Wren been in his life without him even being aware?

'Thanks,' he said, turning to go, stupefied with surprise. 'I'll try there.' He walked towards the staircase, shaking his head slowly.

'And if you do find her there,' the woman said behind his back, 'tell her to ring me with her new address, once she's stopped sofa surfing.'

'Will do,' said Nick, and he went down the stairs and out onto the pavement.

So Wren was sofa surfing and changing address. It didn't sound like the movements of someone in a relationship. A little flame of hope lit inside him. Like Wren's boss said, the bookshop would be closed, but he wanted to go and look at it, still in disbelief that Wren didn't just have a link to that place but was friends with Libby herself. He rounded the corner, realising that must have been the reason she was at the hospital yesterday.

The bookshop was there, further down the street with a light on in the upstairs window. *What if...?* If Wren had been between addresses and staying with friends, and Libby wasn't home due to being in hospital... His eyes locked on the warm, orange glow from the window. What if Wren was up there now? His pace quickened. He could knock on the door. What's the worst that could happen?

He came to a stop directly outside and looked up at the very window he'd replaced a little while back. She could be just on the other side. Then he noticed that the light inside was flickering. The shapes and shadows that it cast on the glass looked weird, like the lamplight was flaring and moving around. And then he noticed the wisp of black smoke from the window frame.

'Fuck,' he whispered, running over to rap on the door. He rapped, then he hammered, then he bodily thumped the wooden door until it shook.

'Wren!' he yelled up at the window. '*Wren!*'

He'd drawn the attention of a group of boozed-up teens over the road, and they wandered over to see what was going on.

'Call the fire brigade,' he yelled over his shoulder as he continued to bang his fists against the wood. But there was no response from above.

Adrenaline surged through him like fire itself, and thoughts swarmed inside his mind. Was she even in there?

He screamed up at the window again... Nothing. She might be out. But she might not be. He had to do something – right now.

The bookshop hadn't been in the best repair when he'd worked there, and he held that thought as he took a few paces back and focused on the door. Then he ran at it full tilt, shoulder down, and prayed that the lock and hinges were as flimsy as everything else in the building.

The door didn't budge.

He backed up again, a few steps further this time, and threw his whole weight at the door. This time it gave.

He crashed through into the shop and saw smoke drifting down through the door to the flat. He covered his mouth with his shirt and ran towards it.

TWENTY-NINE

WREN

The weight of the new baby in Wren's arms helped her feel the most grounded she'd been in days. Life may have been thrown into the air like shrapnel from a grenade, but while she sat by Libby's hospital bed with little Margaret, she could pretend it didn't matter where the pieces landed.

'So, which Margaret is she named for? The princess or the prime minister?' she asked Libby, not taking her eyes from the baby's sleepy gaze.

'The writer,' said Libby, laughing. 'You know I love a bit of Atwood. I'm earmarking this child as a future feminist warrior.'

Wren bounced Margaret a little in her arms and put on a sugary voice. 'Baby's going to smash the patriarchy, isn't she?' she crooned.

Margaret started to wriggle and fret, so Wren hastily passed her back to her mother.

Her mother. Libby soothed and hushed the baby, her face glowing through the tiredness. It had been so hard to picture it, when Margaret was still inside Libby, but now they looked picture perfect. A lump grew in Wren's throat.

'I've got the flat ready for you two,' Wren said, coughing

away the wobble in her voice. 'For when you're back from your mam's.'

Libby's mother had arrived like a whirlwind, shooing Wren and Alex away to take on her duties as birthing partner, and had insisted Libby would be staying with her for a few days after she left the hospital.

'Oh, you're a pet. Thank you.' She reached over and squeezed Wren's hand. 'It might not be too long. She's already driving me mad with advice. Apparently I need to get Margaret into a routine. That would be fine, if I'd ever had one myself.'

Wren laughed. 'That's true. I've never known anyone better prepared for chaos. But it's all good to go, and I move into my new flat in a few days, so I'll be out from under your feet. Unless you need me – any time, any day.'

Libby winced. 'I'm sorry about your job, Wren. But you'll find something new, I'm sure.'

'I hope so. And I was just congratulating myself on getting a flat so close to work too.' She rolled her eyes. 'Best made plans and all that. I just feel so guilty about the piece about the Community Kitchen. It was going to be a tribute to Edie, and now it's for the shredder.'

'I know, but it's not your fault. Don't beat yourself up about it. And you never know, you might still be able to use it.'

Wren tried to smile. 'Thanks, Lib. But I think a local-interest piece won't have as good a home as the local paper. And listen to you, being all motherly and reassuring. And so it begins, eh?'

Libby set about getting Margaret settled for a feed with the help of a friendly midwife. It made Wren think of her own mother, holding her in a hospital bed in her brief respite from addiction. She still felt there were questions unanswered now that Edie was gone. What had she planned to tell her? Maybe it had been nothing more than her dad had already explained, but it was as unknowable as the current location of her stolen necklace – ripped abruptly away and gone forever.

'Anyway, I'll leave you to it. I'm going to head up to the Community Kitchen and break the news that the piece isn't happening. I'll come back tomorrow though.'

She leaned down and kissed Libby on the cheek then headed out of the ward, down the stairs and into the car park. She was just heading for her newly repaired car when she saw Max, the author from the book launch at Cravenwick Pages, putting coins into the parking machine. He was holding a bunch of flowers and a balloon saying 'It's a Girl!'

Wren smiled to herself. It could be a coincidence. God knew, she'd witnessed one hell of a coincidence when Nick had appeared here at this very hospital. But judging by the way Max seemed to be giving himself a little pep talk, it didn't look like it. It looked very much to Wren like there was a plan for Libby, and Max had been written into it. As she pulled away, she wondered when her own plan might start to come together.

It was late in the day when she got to the Community Kitchen and they were just wrapping up the evening service. There were a few diners sitting drinking cups of tea or coffee, maybe postponing the time before they needed to head back out to the streets or hostels, or wherever they may be spending the night. Her heart ached at the thought of her mam sitting here years ago, maybe with a bag full of the things she needed. Except for Wren. She hadn't needed Wren enough to stay around for her.

She straightened her back and reminded herself she was here in a professional capacity, and went to find a familiar face. She found Ailsa in the education suite, tidying up the leaflets and displays.

'Hello there, pet,' she said, her face creasing into a tired smile. 'It's lovely to see you.'

'Lovely to see you too,' said Wren, allowing herself to be wrapped in an embrace. 'How are you all doing?'

'Oh, so-so. It's still so strange without her around. I keep expecting to hear that snazzy designer cane clicking up behind me, but...' Ailsa shrugged. 'She has left quite the legacy though.'

'She has,' said Wren. 'How will it be run now she's gone?'

'Well, we've had a sort of informal "board" of long-standing staff for a while. So, on we go.'

'That's good. Listen, Ailsa, I came to tell you... the piece for the paper. It won't be happening anymore. The paper's being closed down.'

'Oh, Wren,' she said, her face crumpling. She reached out and rubbed Wren's arm. 'You poor thing. What will you do?'

'Don't worry about me,' Wren said, trying to smile. 'I'm just so sorry the story isn't going anywhere, especially since it would be such a fitting tribute to Edie.'

'It's a shame,' said Ailsa, 'but you know Edie would only be worried that you're okay. She wouldn't have minded one bit. You know what she was like, fending off the attention.'

'Thanks for being so understanding. I'd like to come and volunteer sometime. If you'll have me.'

Ailsa's face lit up. 'Of course we'd have you! Any time. You're an old hand now anyway.'

Wren nodded. The idea of serving out food to those in need brought the image of her mother swimming back into her mind. It was never far away. Maybe Ailsa might know something.

'Ailsa? Can I ask you a question?'

'Yes, pet, what is it?'

Then the door to the education suite clattered open, and in walked Cath. She saw Wren and blinked. 'Well, how's that for a coincidence?'

'Huh?' said Wren.

'I've not long had Nick in here, looking for you. Well, he

was looking for a woman in a photo, to be precise, but when I mentioned your name, he went tearing off.'

'Nick...?' Wren felt like she was falling backwards down a tunnel. *My* Nick? What could he be doing looking for her here? Her expression must have showed her utter confusion.

'Sorry, you might not have met. Nick is Edie's grandson. He had a picture of a lady called Caron Rowbottom, and I told him you've got the same last name.'

What was happening? Wren's head felt light with all this information. Nick, here at the Kitchen. And he was Edie's *grandson*, Travis's brother? The world seemed to expand and contract, bringing Capri closer and pushing Northumberland further away, until they collided in her mind. And now her mother's name had been thrown into the mix.

'I... I don't understand.'

'Are you okay?' asked Ailsa, touching her shoulder and giving Cath a worried glance. 'You've gone very pale.'

'Um, yeah. I'm okay. I think. So... Nick is Edie's grandson?'

They nodded.

'And he came here with a picture of my mother?'

'So *that's* who it was,' said Cath. 'I didn't know who she was, my darling, but when I told him about you, he took off. I told him you worked at the paper. He hasn't been gone too long.'

Wren stood, open-mouthed, for a moment, staring at the two women, who peered back as if she might need psychiatric intervention.

'Um, I think I need to go.'

She drove towards Cravenwick, her fingers drumming the steering wheel, her lips clamped between her teeth. *The Echo.* The idea that he could be there right now and had been right at the tip of her fingers all this time rocked her. Her heart fluttered as she pulled into the high street. She headed for her normal parking spot opposite Cravenwick Pages and got out of the car shakily. Locking the car, she glanced up at the shop.

As she got closer, she frowned. The lights were on upstairs. No. *That isn't lights.* She broke into a run as she saw smoke wisping from the window and rolls of dark clouds billowing from the open door. A cluster of teenagers hovered outside, one of them on the phone, speaking excitedly to the emergency services.

'Oh God,' she moaned, her hands in her hair, looking up at the building. 'Oh God, what's happened?'

'It's on fire.' A sallow-faced teen girl wearing a hoodie over a skater dress looked at her as if she was a moron.

Wren stared at her, unable to form a reply – then she heard her name being called.

'Wren!' It was muffled and distant, and she looked around to see where it was coming from. 'Wren!'

'Some man just went in there. Thinks there's a woman inside,' said the teen blandly, looking up at the glowing window.

Her name emanated from within again, and with a rush of horror, she recognised the voice. The same one that had echoed through a cave in Capri, in another world. Without even a pause, she ran into the building, the teens shouting after her to stop.

'Nick! Nick! I'm here!'

She could see nothing through the smoke and coughed painfully. Covering her mouth, she went deeper inside, towards the door to the upstairs.

'*Wren?* Wren, I can hear you – where are you? I can't get to you,' came a voice from above.

She stood at the bottom of the stairs, clinging to the doorway. 'I'm here, Nick – I'm down here! Come down – we need to get out!'

There was a series of dull thuds, then a pair of hands

reached for her through the dark. She took hold of them and pulled him towards the door. Seconds later, they emerged into the street, grabbing at each other, making sure they were whole. She looked up at his smoke-stained face, and he gazed back, blinking and panting.

'You're okay,' he said, putting his hands on her face, as if checking she was real.

She touched his face too, staring up at a man who would dive into a fire for her. She'd dived into a fire for him too. She was dimly aware of sirens.

Then, just as they stood there staring at each other, there was an immense roaring, whooshing sound, and the window above burst open, the heat and pressure within causing it to explode. Tiny cubes of glass rained down on top of them, landing on their hair and clothes, scattering around their feet like a halo. Wren felt a flicker of recognition, one she was too disoriented to process, then felt a tug on her elbow. It was only when the firefighters pulled them away from each other that she allowed herself to let go.

THIRTY

NICK

They sat, soot-stained, against the bonnet of Wren's car, each with their arms wrapped around their chests. The fire was out, and the last of the smoke drifted from the shattered window in dusty tendrils against the darkening sky. The firefighters and paramedics had packed up and gone, leaving the window boarded up. The fire officer who'd pulled them apart had later explained that the likely source of the fire had been the washer-dryer – or more accurately, the shonky electrical socket that powered it. Nick wished he'd been surprised.

'I did not have any of this on my bingo card for today,' murmured Wren beside him.

'Me neither,' he agreed. 'Although I don't know what's more of a shock – nearly being consumed by fire or finding you, yet again.'

Wren smiled wearily. 'Definitely the latter. I mean... I don't think I've got the energy for this right now, but how the hell did we randomly meet up in Italy when I knew your nanna all along?' She faltered. 'I'm so sorry, Nick. I'm sorry you lost her.'

'Thanks,' he said, swallowing the instant lump in his throat. 'She was a good 'un.'

'She was. I came to the wake. I can't believe I didn't see you there.'

'That's... weird.'

'I've been to the Kitchen so many times. I've met your brother—' She stopped and gasped. 'I've seen a picture of you dressed up as Buzz Lightyear when you were little!' She burst out laughing then clapped a hand over her mouth, her eyes flickering between amusement and distress.

She looked up at the bookshop, and her face darkened. 'I shouldn't be laughing. My friend is going to be devastated. She owns this place – I've been staying here since Alex and I broke up.' She paused and then her cheeks reddened. 'You do realise that we broke up a while ago, don't you? We weren't together when I went to Italy, and we...'

Nick felt a somersault in his chest. The whole story of Alex and Laura still seemed shady, but for now he was just very glad Alex and Wren were no longer together, and that what had happened in Italy was free of any kind of scandal. His nanna would now wholeheartedly approve.

'This is all my fault, you know. I thought I was being helpful, doing some loads of washing before she got back,' Wren said, putting her hand to her forehead.

'From having the baby,' said Nick.

She shot him a look, eyebrows raised. 'How did you know that?'

'I know who Libby is – I've done a bit of work for her in the past. And however scary she might be, I can't imagine she would blame you at all. She could probably blame her dodgy electrics though.'

He edged a little closer to her so their arms were just touching. 'Are you okay, Wren?' he asked quietly.

'According to the paramedics, yes. Otherwise, I'm not sure.' She gave a short rueful laugh. 'Is it weird that I feel better having you here though?'

'Maybe,' he said. 'We haven't known each other long, and I wasn't sure I'd ever see you again. But we haven't half packed in some escapades in that short time. I feel like I'm getting used to handling the aftermath of things together.'

'I know what you mean. I can't believe I'm going to say this again, but maybe we need another dose of post-traumatic food and drink.'

Nick laughed. 'It seems to do the trick. Near drownings, muggings, fires...' He glanced down at himself, his sooty clothes giving off the strong aroma of an ashtray. Wren looked and smelled much the same. 'Listen, I think Libby's kitchen and shower facilities might be out of order. Do you want to come back to mine? I can offer you a shower, a takeaway and there may just be a bottle or two of beer in the fridge. Not quite the same as the Italian wine, but it might be close enough?'

Wren sniffed at herself and wrinkled her nose. 'Are you sure? I might need to borrow some clothes.'

'Don't worry – my brother's got your back there.'

She pressed her palms against her eyes. 'Ugh. I'm not sure how I'm going to break the news to Libby. She's got a brand-new baby and no home to bring her to. You know, she only just had this place fixed up a month or two ago.'

'I know,' said Nick, looking up at the boarded-up first-floor window. 'It was me that fitted the windows.'

Wren slowly turned back to face him. She stared at him, saying nothing, her mouth hanging slightly open.

'What?' he asked.

When they got back to the flat, Wren went straight in the shower, so Nick raided Travis's stock room for the least garish ensemble he could find. He settled on some jogging bottoms with a subtle grey zebra print and a T-shirt that surprised him by just being plain black. He laid them on the bed then went to the kitchen to open two bottles of beer, hearing the shower turn off. He respectfully stayed away from the hallway as she scampered from bathroom to bedroom, and he gave her about twenty minutes before knocking gently on the door. There was no answer, so he edged open the door to find her fast asleep on the bed, her wet hair wrapped up in a towel. The back of the T-shirt, which he'd neglected to check, had the word *Hellraiser* printed in purple lettering. The irony of this wasn't lost on him. She looked so peaceful he didn't have the heart to wake her, so he took a shower himself, grabbed some clean clothes from the laundry pile and went back to the living room.

He took a sip of his beer and looked at the note his mother had left on the coffee table. It explained, briefly, that she had to catch an earlier flight back to work or she might lose her spot to some 'upstart fresh out of drama school' and that she'd call soon. There was a trail of kisses on the page that doubled the character count.

'She always did like to overcompensate for her absence,' came a voice from behind him. Travis sat down next to him on the sofa, wrapping his velvet dressing gown tighter around his middle and resting his legs on the coffee table.

Nick sighed. 'If the singing jobs ever dry up, at least she'll always be able to get a job as a magician's assistant.'

'Trouble is, you never know when she'll pop up again after she's disappeared. Adds a layer of extra suspense to the show.'

Nick smiled and shook his head. Their mother would never change. She wasn't a woman to be tied down, by geography, family or even simple good manners.

'So...?' said Travis, raising his eyebrow.

'So?'

'So, who do you have in your room? You've opened two beers, and unless you had two showers, then you must have company.'

Nick reached down and picked up the other bottle, passing it to Travis. 'She's asleep. And it's a long story.'

Travis took a drink. 'Well, I've got time. Mine's asleep too.' He winked and settled back into the cushions.

'Who...?'

'Never you mind; tell me about you. I never thought I'd see this day. I thought you'd sworn off women.'

'It's not like that. It's... weird.'

Travis's eyebrows shot up, and he almost spat out his mouthful of beer. 'Please tell me you've not gone from Benedictine monk to the subject of a Louis Theroux documentary in one fell swoop.'

'Not that kind of weird. It's a weird situation. Do you remember that journalist that interviewed Nanna? You met her at the Kitchen.'

Travis nodded eagerly.

'And do you remember that girl I talked about from Italy? The one from the kayak trip, who helped me find my... sperm donor.'

Travis's head cocked to one side. 'Wait, wait. There's *two* of them in there? Seriously, Nick, Louis is assembling a camera crew as we speak.'

Nick laughed. 'Give over. No. They're the same person. I've just met her again, after her friend's bookshop caught fire. Which also happens to be the one I replaced the windows in a while back. One of which almost flattened her.'

Travis's jaw dropped, and he placed a palm to his chest. 'That was *her*? That *is* weird. Hold on – I met her.' His face broke into a knowing grin. 'She's pretty.'

'She is. But she's just here to sleep – no funny business. She's been having a rough time.'

'So have you. Maybe you have some common ground there.'

'To be fair, a lack of common ground isn't the issue here. It's actually spooky how much we've crossed paths without even realising. And I don't want to rush things. But I haven't been able to stop thinking about her, and now she's *here*.'

'Maybe it's fate.'

'It's a funny sort of fate then. Every time we've met, there's been some kind of disaster. Getting stuck in a cave in Capri, getting mugged, nearly getting burned to death. I can't work out if the universe wants us to be together or if we're destined to kill each other.'

'Okay, you'll have to fill in some of *those* blanks for me later. But maybe you're destined to be together and die of old age in each other's arms. Like *The Notebook*.'

Nick steepled his fingers together and smiled, despite his exhaustion. 'I'm not sure what notebook you're on about. But it would be nice if you're right.'

They sat and drank in silence for a while.

'Listen, bro,' said Travis, 'you know you're welcome to stay here as long as you like. But now that Nanna's house is sitting empty...'

Nick turned to look at him. 'Yeah? Well, that might be an idea. Until we sell it.'

'There's no rush. The money's not an issue. But if you lived there, you'd instantly have a room for Ruby.'

In all the chaos of late, Nick had barely had time to think of practicalities. But Travis was right. If he moved in there, he could do up the spare room within days. Ready for his girl. If Callie and he could reach an agreement, of course. And she *had* said she was willing to talk.

'I could do that. And even if Callie says no, then at least I'd be out from under your feet.'

'Why are you assuming she'll say no? And also, you're Ruby's parent too. It's a two-way conversation you should be having, not waiting to be handed down a judgment.'

Nick laughed sadly. 'I know. But it's complicated.'

'Listen, Nick, Callie cheated on you. But she's also a good

mother, and otherwise a nice person. Deep down she has a good heart.' He tapped Nick's chest. 'And so do you.'

Nick smiled in spite of himself. 'You know, with this new-found wisdom, you're starting to remind me of our nanna.'

'Now, steady on...'

A door clicked down the corridor, and they heard the whoosh of the shower being turned on. Nick looked at Travis, then his eyes fell on a black sports jacket by the table that he hadn't noticed before. It had a very familiar Newcastle United logo on the front. 'Is that Liam?' he asked under his breath.

Travis nodded, clamping his lips between his teeth to suppress a smile.

'Trav, we need to talk.' He looked towards the bathroom again and groaned. 'I wish I didn't have to bring this up – but I don't want you to get hurt.'

'What do you mean?' said Travis.

Nick swallowed. 'Listen, I know you've become good friends, but... my watch went missing after we were in Italy. And I think I saw it on Liam's wrist at the funeral. I sincerely hoped I was wrong, and I've turned the flat upside down just in case, but... it seems possible.'

'Do you mean this watch?' said Travis, peeling back his dressing-gown sleeve to reveal an Omega on his wrist.

'Yes, the one that matches yours,' said Nick, nodding at it.

'Nick, this *is* yours. I borrowed it from your drawer.'

'Why the... why would you do that?'

'Because I gave mine to Liam.'

Nick blinked, lost for words. Of all the possible scenarios he'd considered, this one had never entered his head.

'I... I'm serious about him, Nick. We've spent a lot of time together over the last few weeks, and... oh God, I can't believe I'm saying this, but I think I'm falling in love with him. I know those are words you never thought would come from my mouth.'

Nick thought he'd had enough surprises for one day, but at this, his jaw dropped. Travis sat back in his seat, looking uncharacteristically coy.

Then, with a sinking feeling, Nick remembered the shady-sounding phone conversation he'd overheard – something about meeting at an industrial estate and exchanging money. If Travis was falling for this lad, he needed to be sure his brother was fully informed, even if it felt like Nick was bursting his bubble.

'There's something else that made me worry,' said Nick reluctantly.

'Okay, what?' asked Travis.

Nick repeated what he'd heard after the funeral.

Travis burst out laughing. 'Oh my God, Nick, I'm cringing for you. Liam got an apprenticeship with a carpenter. He went down there the other day to have a look around the workshop and talk about his wages.'

'Shit,' said Nick, and he sat there in silence while Travis hooted with laughter.

'You know, for a long time, I thought I was genetically incapable of settling down. Of falling in love, having a one and only. God knows, Tracey couldn't be held down, and my dad is the North East's answer to Hugh Hefner. I thought that bit of me didn't exist. But it does.' He got up and smoothed down his dressing gown. 'And if I can admit that my Grindr days are over, then you have to agree that anything is possible, big brother. Nothing is inevitable. Talk to Callie, Nick – things can change. And on that *sage* note, I'm going back to my room to wait for my boyfriend.' And he walked away.

Nick sat for a while, pondering. Being given a life lesson from his little brother was a strange and unsettling event, to say the least. And the point he'd made might take a while to sink in. *Nothing is inevitable.* It was a day of contradictions. Talking to Travis had made him realise that his story wasn't already written for him, but the woman lying in his bed suggested otherwise. She felt as inevitable to him as the sun coming up in the morning and setting at night. He got up and went to her.

The lamp light was on as he lay down next to her on the bed, and she opened her eyes sleepily. 'You're here,' she said, barely awake.

'I'm here,' he said, sliding an arm underneath her so her head rested on his shoulder. 'You can go back to sleep. I'll still be here in the morning. And the morning after that.'

She nestled closer into the crook of his arm, her weight pleasingly heavy against him.

'That sounds nice,' she murmured thickly. 'But no fires. And no smashed windows.'

'I can't promise,' he said, smiling against her hair. 'We have form.'

Her arm wrapped over his chest, pulling him close. 'It's strange. We keep trying to kill each other. But I've never felt so safe.'

THIRTY-ONE

WREN

'Well, if it was a steak, I'd send it back,' said Libby, staring up at the charred remains of the first floor of the bookshop from the street below. She was holding a sleeping Margaret on her shoulder, the baby blissfully unaware that her childhood home had gone up in smoke before she'd even entered the building.

'Yes, I prefer my home a little less well done too,' agreed Wren, daring a look at Libby, who seemed to be taking things a little too well, considering. 'Seriously though – I'm so sorry.'

Libby nudged her with her hip. 'Stop saying sorry. You can't be held responsible for faulty wiring. And I can't say I wasn't warned. Your new boyfriend read me the riot act when he did the windows.'

Wren smiled and found herself shuffling her feet shyly. In amongst breaking the bad news about the bookshop, she'd managed to explain to Libby the almost unexplainable presence of Nick in her life. 'He's not my boyfriend. He's just... a nice man that I can't seem to shake off.'

Libby smirked. 'I don't see you doing a lot of shaking. Didn't I see him helping you carry boxes up to the new flat?'

She *had* seen Nick do just that. But in the chaos of the fire, the loss of his nanna and her newly ended relationship, their meetings had been practical and comforting, except for a few stolen kisses. He seemed nervous to push her, and she felt the same. They were treating one another like an expensive ornament being packed into storage – delicately, respectfully, but knowing that it couldn't be left behind or given away. Despite this, they couldn't stay away from each other, and she feared for the universe's response if they did. Its determination to drive them together might lead to an earthquake or a meteor shower if they weren't careful.

She turned her attention back to Libby. 'What did they say about the books?'

'Surprisingly, other than a section that was smoke-damaged, they were largely unscathed. I can't quite believe it. Cravenwick Pages might live to see another day.'

'It will. I'll help you with everything, Lib. Down to the last insurance paper, the last lick of paint. I'll be there.'

'I know you will,' she said, stroking Margaret's back. 'But what about you? Any news on a new job? Because I've got a vacancy when we re-open. Jenson quit, even though I offered to pay him while we're closed. Apparently I have a "chaotic aura".'

'You do. I love that about you. Jenson is an idiot.'

Libby shrugged. 'Anyway, the offer is there. Just to tide you over until someone inevitably snaps you up.'

'Thanks, Lib. Although you might be sick of the sight of me after living in my flat until then. You're free to change your mind at any time.'

In the few days since Wren had moved in, she'd filled the flat with all the possessions she'd taken from her old house. It was smaller, so it was crowded and stacked with piles of books, reams of clothes and mismatched furniture. It was a happy mess, instantly cosy and felt like an extension of her own personality. Alex would have hated it.

'Don't be daft. I'll owe you one after putting up with me and a newborn baby.'

Wren shook her head, despite the previous night with the two of them alternating pacing the floor with a screaming Margaret. Wren was finding her new role as Margaret's de facto stepmother quite challenging, which reminded her of seeing Max in the hospital car park, looking every bit the person to take the mantle.

'Anyway, speaking of new boyfriends...' she said, a slow smirk edging across her lips.

Now it was Libby's turn to look awkward. 'I don't know who you could be referring to.'

'Hmm. Okay. Well, I may have seen a certain debut author outside the hospital, trying to look his very best self for a certain bookseller. With gifts in hand.'

Libby lifted her nose, blustering, 'He's been very kind.'

'Kind of into you, you mean?'

Libby's face broke into a reluctant smile. 'Maybe. But we'll see. For now it's just me and Margaret against the world, or at least against a wrecked flat and a singed bookshop. After that – maybe.'

'Correction. It's you, Margaret and *me* versus the crispy bookshop.'

Libby's face crumpled, a mixture of exhaustion, overwhelm and gratitude, and she enveloped Wren in a one-armed hug, Margaret gently sandwiched between them.

'Thanks, Wren,' she said. 'Although life's kind of busy for you too.'

Wren squeezed her. 'I'll never be too busy for you.'

'Maybe you will, and you have my blessing. Look behind you.'

Wren broke away from the hug and turned around. Nick was getting out of his van with a large bag for life and a tray of takeaway coffees.

'I thought I might find you here,' he said, holding out the coffees to Wren and the bag to Libby.

'What's this?' asked Libby.

'Just a few bits for the baby. I know everything must have been lost in the fire.'

Libby welled up again. 'Nick, you shouldn't have.'

He waved a hand. 'Don't get too excited. There's a package in there from the Kitchen that they do for mothers and babies – wipes and nappy bags and what have you – and Travis put a few things in from his kids' collection.'

Libby reached into the bag and lifted out a Babygro with the Chanel logo on it, a pair of tiny snakeskin-print trainers and a marabou feather headband.

'Just the essentials,' he said with a wry grin.

Libby gave a low squeal of gratitude and hugged him. 'Thank you. And I promise, I will listen the next time you give me home maintenance advice.'

'Make sure you do,' he said good-naturedly then nodded at the smoke-stained shopfront. 'And you know who to call when you need that window replacing. Again.'

'And I'll make sure I'm wearing a crash helmet,' said Wren.

'Ha ha,' he said, deadpan. 'Anyway, I was hoping I could borrow you for a bit?'

Wren looked at Libby, who was biting her lip with her eyebrows raised, mischievously gleeful. 'Go on. I'm going up to your place anyway to do a mini fashion show with Marge.' She glanced into the bag. 'I, for one, can't wait to see her in the mermaid-shimmer leggings.'

'I'm not sure I want to miss that,' said Wren.

'Don't worry, I'll take plenty of photos,' said Libby over her shoulder as she walked away. 'I'll see you when you're back, whenever that might be...'

Wren turned back to Nick, who was now holding open the van door like a chauffeur.

'Come on – I've got something I want to show you.'

Wren crossed her arms, pretending to think. 'If it's a kayak, I'd rather not, thank you very much.'

'It's not a kayak, and I promise I'll take very good care of you.'

'In that case, I'll get in. But I'm doing my seat belt up tightly.'

Edie's house looked different in many ways but still so familiar. The neat, well-maintained front garden was unchanged, and Wren now realised that it must have been Nick who was keeping on top of it for her. Inside, the furniture was the same, but the place had been streamlined, cleared of the clutter and trinkets, and there was a scattering of male accoutrements here and there. Jackets hung on the coat pegs, trainers by the door, a Wickes catalogue on the coffee table. She stood in the hallway, one hand on the living-room door, taking it in.

'You're living here now?' she asked.

'Just for a while,' he said.

Wren looked again at the slightly spartan front room. Then she remembered something she still had in her bag.

'Well, this calls for a house-warming present,' she said, producing the snow globe and giving it to Nick. 'It was meant for Edie. But I think you should have it.'

He shook it, and a smile spread over his face. 'This brings back memories.'

'Doesn't it just?' she said with a grin.

He placed it on the windowsill underneath the front window, and they both looked at it for a moment as the snowflakes settled around the lighthouse and caves.

'You know, I've been thinking,' she said. 'About the lighthouse and the sirens in the grottoes.' Nick turned with interest. 'One of them lures people into danger, and the other warns people away and saves their lives. It reminds me of us. Every time we've got close it's like the sirens have called us into some dangerous situation. But then you coming into my life feels like I'm out of harm's way.'

'Like I'm the lighthouse?'

Wren gave a quiet laugh. 'It's silly, I know.'

Nick said softly, 'I think it's very apt. And just so you know, I feel like you're my lighthouse too.'

They looked at each other for a moment then broke away, smiling to themselves.

'Anyway,' said Nick, 'I'll show you why I'm living here, and why I need a bit more space than I had at Travis's.' He pointed through the corridor towards the spare-room door.

Wren walked over and looked inside. Gone were the double bed and the bookcases loaded with books, and in their place was the bedroom of a little girl's dreams. There was a cabin bed with ladders up to the sleeping area, and underneath was a small desk surrounded by fairy lights. Gauzy curtains hung at the windows, and a plush baby-blue rug covered a large part of the floor, which had been stripped to reveal honey-coloured floorboards, freshly sanded and polished. A box of toys stood in the corner, waiting to be played with.

'For your daughter?'

Nick nodded, a contented smile on his face. 'She's going to be staying every Friday night from now on.'

'She's going to love it,' said Wren. 'Is this what you wanted to show me?'

Nick shook his head. 'No. But I couldn't resist giving you a look. I've barely been able to tear myself away from looking at it myself.' He paused, giving the room a last once-over, then closed the door. 'What I want to show you is in here.' He nodded towards the kitchen, and she followed him.

On the kitchen table there was a book, and on top of the book was a photograph. Even from the doorway Wren could recognise the face of her mother alongside a younger version of Edie. She rushed forward and picked it up, tears pricking at her eyes.

'When I came to the bookshop to find you, the night of the fire, I was coming to show you this.' Nick's voice was gentle, and he stood back, letting her absorb what she was seeing.

Wren couldn't reply. Her finger traced the outline of her mother's face. Caron's face was thin and weary, but there was colour there, and she was smiling. A snapshot of contentment, a feeling Wren was sure couldn't have been a constant for her mother, but it was evidence that light had occasionally glimmered through the cracks in her life. Sunshine that Edie and the Community Kitchen had shone on her for a short while.

'She wrote to me. Your nanna,' Wren whispered. 'She was going to tell me about my mam, but then she—' Her throat felt thick and ached so much she had to stop. Her eyes swam at the image of the two women, both gone now.

'That explains why I found this picture on her mantelpiece. She must have had it ready to show you. When I saw the necklace in the photo...'

Wren touched her bare neck instinctively. It was both gone and returned to her.

'I just... I didn't think it was the right time, after the fire. But when I came back here and sorted through some more of Edie's stuff, I found that photo album too.'

On the table was a burgundy book, its edges embossed with faded gold. She flipped it open to find a piece of paper, yellowed with age and a heavy crease mark through the middle from what looked like years of being folded away. It lay on top of pages of photographs slotted into plastic sleeves, two per page, front and back.

'I found it in one of the photo pockets. I think it must have been slipped in with the photo of your mam.'

She felt Nick's hand on her shoulder.

'I'm just popping out front to water the plants.'

His hand disappeared, and Wren glanced up at the kitchen window, still beaded with the morning's rainfall. She opened the letter.

Dear Edie,

Thank you for the loan of the jacket – I'm going home tomorrow so I won't need it now. I thought about what you said when we talked, and I'm going to give it another shot. I'm going to try really hard this time. Like you said, she deserves it, even if I still think she deserves better. Maybe I can be better.

You know what, I listened to everything you said, and you were right. But what really made me think was seeing your Tracey with her little lad. Watching her playing with him, singing with him, it brought it home to me what I'm missing. And she's doing it on her own as well. If I can sort things out with Alan, then Serenity could have the both of us.

Do you know why I called her Serenity? It means peaceful, and that's what she is to me. When I was carrying her, I felt a calm like nothing else, like she was keeping me anchored. Then once she was born I felt untethered again, and now here we are. But maybe, if I can just beat this once more, I can be an anchor for her. We'll see.

Anyway, thank you, Edie. Not just for the jacket. For everything. And when I'm sorted, I'll bring Serenity in to see you.

Love, Caron

Wren sat holding the letter for some time.

Nick was sitting on the garden wall when she went outside, the late-afternoon sun making his sandy hair look tipped with gold.

He was facing the street, away from her, and his T-shirt stretched across his broad back. She walked to him and pressed herself to it, wrapping her arms around his front and resting her cheek on his shoulder. He flickered momentarily with surprise, but then she felt his muscles ease into her, fitting like a hand into a glove.

'Thank you,' she murmured.

He said nothing, just squeezed her forearm. The emotion she felt from holding her mother's handwritten letter in her hand detoured into a strange realisation that made her laugh out loud.

'I thought it was weird bumping into you in Italy, but it turns out we go back way longer than I realised.'

'I know,' he said, giving a tiny shake of his head. 'It's... mad.'

'And you were the reason my mam was coming back to me.'

'*You* were the reason your mam was coming back to you,' he said, pulling her arms tighter around him. Then he spoke so quietly, it was almost a whisper. 'I'm so sorry she didn't make it.'

Wren's throat tightened. It had been so close. The letter was dated the day before Caron died. Who knows what had happened between writing it and her death. A last hurrah with her habit? It had to be. Now that she'd read her words, she knew her mother wouldn't have simply changed her mind.

Caron Rowbottom had been through some terrible times that had pulled her out of the orbit of her own family, out of the life she was meant to have. But she'd been drawn back in by love, even if she never quite managed to make it home. Life was chaos, and love was the seam of peace that ran through it. You just had to keep trying to come back.

Maybe all the things that had happened recently had been for a reason, to put Wren on the path she was meant to be on. Alex was meant to cheat, so she could see him for who he really was. The paper was meant to close, so she could find something new and exciting to do, even if that hadn't materialised yet. And even Nick, right here in front of her, had appeared in her life in a cloud of shattered glass. Peace masquerading as mayhem. She certainly felt her heart rate slowing and a warmth in her chest while she was near him.

He loosened himself from her grip and turned around on the wall to face her, opening his legs so she could stand between them. She did – and wrapped her arms around his neck. In this position, she was slightly taller than him, and she lowered her forehead to rest against his.

'Are you okay?' he asked.

She smiled. 'I'm better than okay. You've given me the missing piece of my puzzle. Well, you and your nanna between you.'

'It was all her – I just stumbled across it. And thanks to her and that photo, I was able to find you again. And in a way, that's thanks to your mam too.'

'I bet she never imagined that little boy in the kitchen would grow up to be the man that almost flattened me with a windowpane,' said Wren.

Nick chuckled. 'Or that you and that man would go on a hair-raising, white-knuckle trip around the Amalfi Coast. Hang on. Speaking of being flattened, I never did get round to telling you off about the bookcase.'

Wren squinted at him. 'What bookcase?'

He shook his head, grinning. 'Never mind. Just something that came back to me.'

He stood up, keeping his arms around her, and she watched his expression turn more serious. 'Wren, I know things are messy at the moment. For both of us. But all I want to do right now is kiss you.'

She didn't reply and just pressed her lips to his, kissing him deeply and for so long she began to feel dizzy. When she let go, he held her face in his hands, looking searchingly into her eyes.

'Are you sure this isn't a bad time?' he asked.

'I don't know. Maybe a better time than being mugged?' she murmured.

'Or being trapped in a cave?' His face drew closer.

'Or being burned alive?'

Their lips met again, and his hands delved into her hair.

'We seem to be quite good at getting into scrapes,' he breathed.

'Or getting each other out of them,' she said, sliding her hands up the back of his neck to hold his head close.

A cloud moved overhead, letting a brighter beam of evening sun shine down onto the garden. Just inside the living-room window, the snow globe caught the rays, and light glowed from the tiny grotto caves.

'So are we good for each other or bad?' he whispered against her lips.

'I don't know,' she said, pausing to kiss him again. 'But I'm prepared to take the risk.'

THIRTY-TWO

GRAND REOPENING OF CRAVENWICK PAGES AFTER HORROR BLAZE

By Derek Hutchins, *Evening Gazette*

Beloved Northumberland bookshop Cravenwick Pages has reopened its familiar doors to the public following its shock closure three months ago after a fire in the upstairs living quarters. A blaze stemming from an electrical fault in a household appliance meant that the popular shop had been closed for renovations, much to the disappointment of its loyal customers.

However, there was much to celebrate as the shop threw a reopening party as a thank you to those who had helped with the restoration project, as well as welcoming customers to come and view the revamped store.

Owner Libby Lang said, 'I am so thrilled to share the refurbished bookshop with our regular customers, as well as any new visitors. I have to stress that this wouldn't have been possible without the help of so many wonderful volunteers and local tradespeople – glaziers, electricians – we even had the

services of a very talented stylist who helped with the updated
decor, although we had to hold him back from the leopard
print!'

Ms Lang, who gave birth to her daughter Margaret around
the time of the fire, went on to praise the efforts of volunteers
from Newcastle's Community Kitchen, whose charitable
endeavours clearly extend beyond the great work they do
providing meals for the homeless. She explained that the staff
and some of their patrons came regularly to help with
labouring or even making refreshments for those working on
the repairs.

Ailsa Poole from the Community Kitchen said, 'When we
heard that Libby had ended up effectively homeless after the
fire, we did what we do best.'

Cath Hall, also from the Community Kitchen, agreed. 'We
were delighted to help, and it was a real pleasure to see the
community coming together. My grandson is a carpenter, and
he and his boss came on evenings and weekends to get the job
done. The response from the local area was really quite overwhelming.'

Community appeared to be the theme of the event – even
the entertainment was laid on free of charge by Northumberland band Men On A Mission, fronted by local civil servant
Justin Peters, who said, 'It's all for a great cause.' Employees
from St Nicholas Lighthouse, Alan Rowbottom and Cliff
Shearwater, were on hand to man the barbecue.

The link between Cravenwick Pages and the Community
Kitchen can be further explained by the presence of local free-
lance journalist and bookshop employee Wren Rowbottom,
who attended the bash with partner Nick Macmillan, grandson
of the late Edie Macmillan, who founded the charitable
venture.

He said, 'My grandmother was a great reader – she had
quite the collection of books herself – so she'd be delighted to

see everyone turning out to lend a hand restoring Libby's shop.'

Even Mr Macmillan's daughter Ruby, aged six, made a contribution to festivities, with a batch of cupcakes bearing a book motif, baked with the help of her mother.

'Both Cravenwick Pages and the Community Kitchen are close to my heart,' said Ms Rowbottom. 'Libby is a dear friend of mine, and I'll be working alongside her now that the bookshop is back open. It's just lovely to see everyone helping out. That's truly in the spirit of everything Edie Macmillan's legacy stands for.'

Ms Rowbottom has penned a history of the Community Kitchen, with stories of the staff and patrons through the years, as a tribute to the late Mrs Macmillan, which is set to be published next year. 'I know where I'm planning to host the book launch,' she quipped.

A LETTER FROM LILY JOSEPH

Dear reader,

Thank you so much for reading *The Near Miss*. I hope you enjoyed diving (or kayaking) into the world of Wren and Nick as much as I enjoyed writing it. If you'd like to be the first to know about my latest releases, you can sign up at the following link. Your email address will never be shared, and you can unsubscribe at any time.

www.bookouture.com/lily-joseph

You might be interested to know that *The Near Miss* was inspired by a real near-death experience... that happened to me! I was the woman covered in safety glass, wondering what would have happened if I'd been a few feet closer, and thankfully I lived to tell this tale. But it did make me think – if you're only a few seconds from meeting your maker, then what if you're just as close to meeting the man of your dreams? And that was where Wren and Nick came in. I hope you were rooting for them to find each other through all the bumps, bruises and minor burns.

Another inspiration for this story was the People's Kitchen (www.peopleskitchen.co.uk) in Newcastle-upon-Tyne, on which the Community Kitchen is very loosely based. They serve more than 250 meals a day, 365 days a year, and are staffed entirely by volunteers. It's been a pleasure and privilege to base a small part of this story on such kind and generous people.

Thank you again for reading, and if you enjoyed it, I'd be extremely grateful if you could write a review. I'd love to hear what you think, and it might help others to find and enjoy it too! And please keep an eye out for my next book, which I'm working on right now and will be released later in 2024. I love hearing from readers, so in the meantime, you can find me on social media or my website.

Love from Lily

www.lilyjosephauthor.com

 facebook.com/lilyjosephauthor

x.com/LilyJoWriter

instagram.com/lilyjosephwriter

ACKNOWLEDGEMENTS

How to begin? Since books have a beginning, middle and end, then that might be the best way to start thanking everyone that's helped me get here.

I first learned a love of books through my parents, Caroline and Ken, who are avid readers and always kept our bookcases well stocked. I can't thank you enough for putting the Storyteller books in front of me and some earphones on my ears to hear them read aloud. Since then, I've rarely been seen without a book in my hand, and this is thanks to you as well as my grandparents, who inspired you too. Special mention to the grandparents who inspired my author name! I'd also like to thank Jeff and Chris, who have shown unwavering support for my writing.

Next (though she'll probably never see this) I'd like to mention a very special primary school teacher, Mrs Arnott, who wrote me a letter when she left to live in the Netherlands. You told me you would one day see my name on the cover of a book, and you were right. It took over thirty years, but I still remember how you believed in me.

I joined the Romantic Novelists' Association in 2021 as part of their New Writers Scheme, and I truly couldn't have done this without them. The resources and encouragement you give to writers of romantic fiction changes lives, and I would especially like to thank the three readers who gave invaluable advice during that time.

Clare Coombes, my agent at Liverpool Literary Agency, has been incredible throughout. Your razor-sharp insight and constructive feedback has helped bring this idea to life, and you've been the absolute best support. Thank you also for championing Northern writers!

Huge thanks to Nina Winters, my amazing editor. This book has evolved through your enthusiasm, brilliant advice and attention to detail. The end result is all I could have hoped for in my debut novel, and for that I'm truly grateful to you! I'd also like to say heartfelt thanks to the Bookouture team for nurturing a newborn novelist and for your incredible support from day one. You've made this such an enjoyable experience, and I feel very lucky to be welcomed into the Bookouture family.

I'd like to give a shout-out to friends and family who looked at me in complete surprise when I outed myself as a secret author and have since gone on to be wonderful cheerleaders. Jill, Simon, Penny, Luke, Paige and Tyler – thank you for everything. And also Ade, who I know would've got a real kick out of all this.

My children, George and Freya, who make me laugh every day and often come out with some incredible one-liners which will probably feature in a book one day. You make me so proud, and I love being your mum, even when I hiss at you for hovering around my desk asking when tea will be ready.

Finally, to Chris, aka quiet coffee-bringer, expert plot-hole finder, and my biggest and best supporter. Thank you for not blinking an eye when I decided to go *even more* part-time to follow my dreams, and for being there for me every step of the way. It isn't hard to write a romcom when you're lucky enough to live in one every day.

PUBLISHING TEAM

Turning a manuscript into a book requires the efforts of many people. The publishing team at Bookouture would like to acknowledge everyone who contributed to this publication.

Commercial
Lauren Morrissette
Jil Thielen
Imogen Allport

Cover design
Beth Free

Data and analysis
Mark Alder
Mohamed Bussuri

Editorial
Nina Winters
Ria Clare

Copyeditor
Laura Kincaid

Proofreader
Emily Boyce

Marketing
Alex Crow
Melanie Price
Occy Carr
Cíara Rosney
Martyna Młynarska

Operations and distribution
Marina Valles
Stephanie Straub

Production
Hannah Snetsinger
Mandy Kullar
Jen Shannon

Publicity
Kim Nash
Noelle Holten
Jess Readett
Sarah Hardy

Rights and contracts
Peta Nightingale
Richard King
Saidah Graham

Printed in Great Britain
by Amazon

44411289R00169